ISBN-13: 978-1-58023-005-6
ISBN-10: 1-58023-005-9

Jewish science fiction and fantasy? *Yes!*

"This classic collection of science fiction and fantasy stories with Jewish characters and themes contains gems that are both charming and provocative . . . and the writing is first-rate."
—*Bloomsbury Review*

"If fabulous authors and intriguing issues aren't enough of a reason for you to read this anthology, I have an even better reason for you. These stories are funny! Whether the issues are assimilation or possession, humor is definitely a strong part of these stories."
—Barnes & Noble *Explorations*

"A delightful collection of stories that shows just how universal themes of intermarriage, assimilation and other hot Jewish topics are.... Science fiction fans will like it, plain old fiction lovers will love it."
—*Baltimore Jewish Times*

"[It] is a thought-provoking commentary on the current state of Judaism in the world as well as an extraordinary collection of writings."
—*The Rhode Island Jewish Herald*

"Through the lens of Science Fiction, these thirteen tales grapple with issues of Jewish identity using the palette of SF to tell truths that are universal to us all, regardless of religious affiliation."
—*Science Fiction Age Magazine*

"Whether a fan of science fiction or not, this is a book you will laugh and cry through. It will have a permanent spot on your bookshelf."
—*Being Jewish*

"A showpiece of Jewish wit, culture, and lore . . . [it] is *the* premier collection of science fiction and fantasy in a uniquely Jewish vein."
—*The Midwest Book Review*

More Wandering Stars

An Anthology of Outstanding Stories of Jewish Fantasy and Science Fiction

Edited by Jack Dann
Introduction by Isaac Asimov

A book for Jew and gentile, male and female, human and not-so-human, it will intrigue and delight everyone who picks it up.

6 x 9, 192 pp, Quality PB
ISBN-13: 978-1-58023-063-6; ISBN-10: 1-58023-063-6

Mystery Midrash

An Anthology of Jewish Mystery & Detective Fiction

Edited by Lawrence W. Raphael
Preface by Joel Siegel

An award-winning mystery-filled collection of thirteen short stories.

6 x 9, 304 pp, Quality PB Original
ISBN-13: 978-1-58023-055-1; ISBN-10: 1-58023-055-5

Criminal Kabbalah

An Intriguing Anthology of Jewish Mystery & Detective Fiction

Edited by Lawrence W. Raphael
Foreword by Laurie R. King

All-new mysteries that will tantalize and captivate mystery lovers and Jewish fiction enthusiasts alike.

6 x 9, 256 pp, Quality PB Original
ISBN-13: 978-1-58023-109-1; ISBN-10: 1-58023-109-8

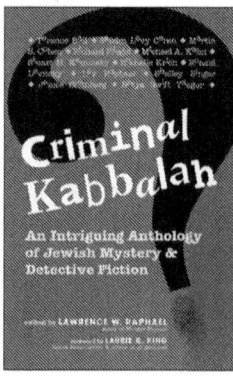

Wandering Stars

AN ANTHOLOGY OF JEWISH FANTASY & SCIENCE FICTION

Edited by Jack Dann

For People of All Faiths, All Backgrounds
JEWISH LIGHTS Publishing

Wandering Stars:
An Anthology of Jewish Fantasy & Science Fiction

Library of Congress Cataloging-in-Publication Data

Wandering stars : an anthology of Jewish fantasy & science fiction / edited by Jack Dann ; with an introduction by Isaac Asimov.
      p.   cm.
Originally published: New York : Harper & Row, 1974.
Contents: On Venus, have we got a rabbi / William Tenn — The golem / Avram Davidson — Unto the fourth generation / Isaac Asimov — Look, you think you've got troubles / Carol Carr — Goslin Day / Avram Davidson — The dybbuk of mazel tov IV / Robert Silverberg — Trouble with water / Horace L. Gold —Gather blue roses / Pamela Sargent — The jewbird / Bernard Malamud —Paradise last / Geo. Alec Effinger — Street of dreams, feet of clay / Robert Sheckley — Jachid and Jechidah / Isaac Bashevis Singer — I'm looking for Kadak / Harlan Ellison
      1. Fantastic fiction, American—Jewish authors. 2. Science fiction,

American—Jewish authors. 3. Jews—Fiction. I. Dann, Jack.
PS648.F3W36   1998
813'.0876088924—dc21   98-10588
                                                          CIP

ISBN-13: 978-1-58023-005-6 (pbk.)
ISBN-13: 978-1-68336-477-1 (hc)

Manufactured in the United States of America

Cover art: *Genesis: Fourth Day* (© 1996) was created by Michael Bogdanow, an artist, lawyer, and musician living with his wife and children in Lexington, Massachusetts. *Genesis: Fourth Day* is part of his "Visions of Torah" series of contemporary, spiritual works of art based on Torah and other Judaic texts.

Cover design: Maria O'DonNell

For People of All Faiths, All Backgrounds
Published by Jewish Lights Publishing
www.jewishlights.com

To my mother Edith N. Dann, who still makes the best chicken soup.

Contents

The editor would like to thank the following people for their help and ideas:

Rabbi David S. Boros
George Zebrowski
Gardner Dozois
Joe W. Haldeman
Harry Altshuler
and, of course, Victoria Schochet.

Why Me?

Isaac Asimov

When I was asked to do the introduction to this collection, that was the question I asked.

"Why me?"

One answer is that I am suspected of being Jewish. At least, my mother is Jewish and my father's mother was Jewish, and that makes both my father and myself Jewish by definition.

I don't do anything about it, you understand. I attend no services and follow no ritual and have never even undergone that curious puberty rite, the bar mitzvah. It doesn't matter. I am Jewish.

How can that be? Oh, well, even without the kosher stamp of religion, I bear the cultural stigmata (you should excuse the expression). I was born in a Russian shtetl, and I was brought up in Brooklyn in the very last decade in which you could still find pushcarts lining the streets and candy stores on every corner. In fact, I worked for thirteen years in my father's candy store. What's more I can tell jokes in a Yiddish dialect like a master, and I can speak Yiddish itself quite fluently. I like music in the minor, and turn faint when my favorite person places butter on her corned-beef sandwich. "Mustard," I whisper. *"Mustard!"*

"Why me?"

Well, I write science fiction and fantasy.

There was a time, you know, when you didn't associate Jews with science fiction and fantasy. To write great novels—yes, that was permitted Jewish boys, along with playing violins (not saxophones or guitars), playing chess (not poker or pool) and becoming a doctor or a lawyer (or, in an emergency, a dentist or an optometrist—but not a ballplayer).

The result is that a great many novels written in America deal with Jewish themes. After all, what else are all those great Jewish novelists going to write about? Methodists?

But science fiction and fantasy (in cheap magazines yet—feh) was different. In the days when I was an avid groper for those cheap magazines, the stories dealt entirely with Americans of northwest-European extraction who fought Homeric battles with space pirates, outer-world monsters, and evil wizards (to say nothing of Martian princesses *in brassieres*). What kind of a place was that for Jewish boys?

I do not say, mind you, that there were no Jews among the scribblers who filled the pulp magazines. There must have been, for despite her best efforts, an occasional Jewish mother lost control. Think of all the Jewish boys who went on the burlesque stage (bums!) and became millionaires (geniuses!).

Many of the Jewish pulp writers, however, used pen names as a matter of sound business sense. A story entitled "War-Gods of the Oyster-Men of Deneb" didn't carry conviction if it was written by someone named Chaim Itzkowitz.

To give an actual case, that excellent writer Horace L. Gold, whose marvelously funny story "Trouble with Water" is included in this collection, and who is as Jewish as stuffed kishke, wrote outstanding science fiction for years under the name of Clyde Crane Campbell, you should again pardon the expression.

Jewish names which sounded German were, of course, permitted, for after all they might really *be* German, and Germans were northwest Europeans, who (though they were not quite as superior as *they* thought they were) were *pretty* superior, for people who didn't speak English.

As far as I know, though, I was the first science fiction writer of note who used his own name, where that name was a mixture of a Biblical Isaac and a Slavic Asimov.

Why? Because I didn't know any better, that's why. To me, the name Isaac Asimov had a swing to it. For some reason (possibly superior genes) I was happy with it. I never longed for anything more glamorous. Had someone offered me the name Leslie Fotheringay-Phipps and begged me with tears in his eyes to take it, I would have refused.

In fact, I adopted so proprietary an attitude toward my name that for a long time I felt annoyed at my brother for sharing my last name and at I. Bashevis Singer for sharing my first name. However, my brother is a nice guy, and I. B. S. is a good writer, as you can see from his story in this collection—so I'll permit it for a while longer anyway.

Then, too, one of my major reasons for wanting to write was to see my name in print. *My* name, not some stranger's.

Take William Tenn, who also has a story in this collection. His name isn't William Tenn. Who, in his whole life, ever heard of a name like William Tenn? What William Tenn's name *really* is, is Philip Klass. Now whenever Phil claims to be William Tenn, he is met with profound disbelief. Words like "hallucinatory megalomania" and *in gantzen ah meshugener* are heard.

This, at least, I was never troubled with. My pen name and my real name are identical and both are as Jewish as I am.

Only I didn't write on Jewish themes. I didn't think of Jews, particularly, in connection with robots, wrecked spaceships, strange worlds with six suns, and Galactic Empires. The subject didn't come up in my mind.

And yet sometimes it popped up. My first science fiction novel, *Pebble in the Sky*, dealt with a stiff-necked group of Earth people facing a Galactic Empire that felt contempt for them. Some people thought they saw a resemblance to Judea and the Roman Empire of the first century there and, who knows, maybe they were right. And one of my chief characters was named Joseph Schwartz. I didn't come right out and say he was Jewish, but I've never found anyone who thought he wasn't.

Sometimes, too, it was necessary for me to have a character whom, for nefarious purposes of my own, I wanted the reader to underestimate. The easiest trick was to give him a substandard version of English, for then he would be dismissed as a comic character with at most a certain limited folk wisdom. Since the only substandard version of English I can handle faultlessly is the Yiddish dialect, some of the characters in *The Foundation Trilogy* speak it.

But times changed. After World War II, with the vanishing of the Nazi menace and the rise of the United Nations, racism became unrespectable. At once, all kinds of ethnic consciousnesses became popular and, to my own personal amazement, science fiction and fantasy, dealing with Jewish themes, turned out to be possible—so that a superb collection such as this one could be put together eventually.

Indeed, caught up in the new spirit, even I wrote a fantasy that was deliberately and entirely based on a Jewish theme. It was "Unto the Fourth Generation" and it is included in this collection.

That is still another answer to the question "Why me?"—because I have a story in this collection.

Anyway, what with one thing and another, even without the bar mitzvah and the ritual, I feel I'm doing my bit and I grow impatient with those who take up a Jewisher-than-thou attitude.

Which reminds me of a phone conversation I once had with a gentleman whose real name I won't use (because I have forgotten it) but to whom I will give, at the proper time, a fictional name of equivalent aura.

It came about because the *Boston Globe* gave a bookfair at which I was asked to speak and at which I did speak. As it happened, the fair fell upon Rosh Hashanah, something I didn't realize, because unless someone tells me, I never know when it comes. That is not an excuse, just a statement, because if I had known it was Rosh Hashanah, I would have delivered my speech anyway.

The next day, however, I received a phone call from a stranger, who said he was Jewish, and who demanded to know why I had consented to talk on Rosh Hashanah. I explained, politely, that I didn't keep the holidays and that seemed to infuriate him. At once, he flung himself into a self-righteous lecture in which he descanted on my duties as a Jew, and ended by accusing me of trying to conceal my Jewishness.

Breathing a short prayer to the God of Aristotle, of Newton and of Einstein, I said, quite calmly, "You have the advantage of me, sir. You know my name. I don't know yours. To whom am I speaking?"

And the Lord God of Science proved to be on the job, for the man on the phone answered, "My name is Jackson Davenport."

I said, "Really? Well, my name, as you know, is Isaac Asimov, and if I were trying to conceal my Jewishness, the very first move I would make would be to change my name to Jackson Davenport."

Somehow that ended the conversation.

But to Jackson Davenport (not his real name, remember), wherever he is, I have this further word: The reason I am writing this introduction is that, despite all my infidel ways and beliefs, I am Jewish *enough*.

WILLIAM TENN

On Venus, Have We Got a Rabbi

What is a Jew? Is "Jewishness" a mystical experience, a system of laws, a sense of kinship, a religion, or a myth? Is there a Jewish ethic, a Jewish character, a Jewish mystique? If the Jew can be identified, can he be as easily defined—or is he, as Franz Rosenzweig claimed, an indefinable essence?

There is a story from the Talmud that suggests the character of the Jew and the "essence" of his religion. A proselyte came to the great sage Hillel and said, "Teach me the whole Torah while I stand on one foot." Without losing his temper Hillel replied, "What is hateful to you, do not do to others. This is the whole Torah, the rest is commentary. Go and study it." As Hayim Donin says, "It is, however, still essential to 'go and study' the rest."

In William Tenn's story of the future, the Jews are still studying, still suffering, making jokes, myth, religion, and still being Jewish. If that "indefinable essence" cannot be defined, it can certainly be described. Can a creature that looks like a pillow growing a short gray tentacle be a Jew? To answer that question Tenn keeps asking, What is a Jew?

Mark Twain has written, "If the statistics are right, the Jews constitute but one percent of the human race. It suggests a nebulous dim puff of star dust lost in the blaze of the Milky Way. Properly the Jew ought hardly to be heard of; but he is heard of, has always been heard of . . . He has made a marvelous fight in this world, in all the ages; and he has done it with his hands tied behind him."

On Tenn's Venus the Jews are still fighting with their hands tied. In the best tradition of Twain and, of course, Sholom Alei-chem, Milchik, the TV repairman who speaks for all the Jews in the universe and the entire human race, tells his story.

EDITOR'S NOTE: *This is an original story written expressly for this volume and cause for celebration, since it is the first story that William Tenn has written in seven years. That is a long time to keep your readers waiting. The editor hopes this is the beginning of a William Tenn renaissance. Welcome home.*

*

SO YOU'RE LOOKING AT ME, Mr. Big-Shot Journalist, as if you're surprised to see a little, gray-haired, gray-bearded man. He meets you at the spaceport and he's driving a piece of machinery that on Earth you wouldn't even give to a dog's grandmother, she should take it with her to the cemetery and be buried in it. This is the man —you're saying to yourself—this nobody, this piece of nothing, who's supposed to tell you about the biggest, strangest development in Judaism since Johannan Ben Zakkai sat down with the Sanhedrin in Jabne and said, "The meeting will please come to order."

Are you talking to the wrong man, you want to know? Did you come across space, fifty, sixty, I don't know, maybe seventy million miles just to see a schlemiel in a cracked helmet with a second-hand oxygen canister on his back? The answer is this: you are not talking to the wrong man. Poor as he is, shabby as he is, unlucky as he is, you are talking to the one man who can tell you all you want to know about those trouble-makers from the fourth planet of the star Rigel. You are talking to Milchik, the TV repairman. Himself. In person.

All we do is put your belongings in the back of the module and then we get in the front. You have to slam the door—a little harder, please—and then, if this is still working and that is still working, and the poor old module feels like making another trip, we'll be off. Luxury it definitely is not, a spaceport limousine you certainly could not call it, but—module, shmodule—it gets you there.

You like dust storms? That's a dust storm. If you don't like dust storms, you shouldn't come to Venus. It's all we got in the way of scenery. The beach at Tel Aviv we don't got. Grossinger's, from ancient times in the Catskills, we don't got. Dust storms we got.

But you're saying to yourself, I didn't come for dust storms, I didn't come for conversation. I came to find out what happened to the Jews of the galaxy when they all gathered on Venus. Why should this schmendrik, this Milchik the TV man, have anything special to tell me about such a big event? Is he a special wise man, is he a scholar, is he a prophet among his people?

So I'll tell you. No, I'm not a wise man, I'm not a scholar, I'm certainly not a prophet. A living I barely make, going from level to level in the Darjeeling Burrow with a tool box on my back, repairing the cheapest kind of closed-circuit sets. A scholar I'm not, but a human being I am. And that's the first thing you ought to know. Listen, I say to Sylvia, my wife, don't our Sages say that he who murders one man murders the entire human race? So doesn't it follow then that he who listens to one man listens to the whole human race? And that he who listens to one Jew on Venus is listening to all the Jews on Venus, all the Jews in the universe, even, from one end to the other.

But Sylvia—go talk to a woman!—says, "Enough already with your Sages! We have three sons to marry. Who's going to pay for their brides' transportation to Venus? You think for nothing a nice Jewish girl will come here, from another planetary system maybe —she'll come to this gehenna of a planet and go live in a hole in the ground, she'll raise children, they won't see the sun, they won't see the stars, they'll only see plastic walls and elevators and drunken cadmium miners coming in to spend their pay and have a *goyische* good time. You think just because a girl likes the stereo transcript of one of our sons and is willing to come here and marry him, we don't have to pay her fare and maybe something a little extra she should enjoy herself on the way? Where do the Sages say the money comes from? Do they say maybe we should nail up a new collection box in the *shul:* 'Help the Milchik boys find brides —their father is too busy with philosophy'?"

I don't have to remind you—you're a journalist, you're an educated man—what Solomon says in Proverbs about women: a good one, he says, has got to cost you a lot more in the end than pearls. And still, someone in the family has to think about money and the boys getting brides. That's the second point. The first point is that I'm a human being and a Jew, two different things maybe, and I've got the right to speak for all human beings and for all Jews.

On top of that, I'm a Jewish father with three full-grown sons here on Venus, and if you want to do an injury to your worst enemy, you say to him, "Listen. You're Jewish? You got three sons? Go to Venus."

And that's the third point. Why I, Milchik the TV man, am telling you this, and why you come all the way from Earth just to listen to me. Because I'm not only a Jewish father, but I'm also— Listen. Could I ask you a question? You won't be offended? You sure you won't be offended?

You're not Jewish, by any chance? I mean, do you have any Jewish ancestors, a grandfather, a great-grandmother maybe? Are you sure? Well, that's what I mean. Maybe one of your ancestors changed his name back in 2533—2533 by *your* calendar, of course. It's not exactly that you *look* Jewish or anything like that, it's just that you're such an intelligent man and you ask such intelligent questions. I couldn't help wondering—

You like Jewish food? In twenty, twenty-five minutes my poor old tired module will pull us out of this orange dust and into the Darjeeling air lock. Then you'll sit down to a Jewish meal, believe me, you'll kiss every one of your fingers. We get almost all of our Jewish food shipped here from Earth, special packaging and special arrangement. And, naturally, special cost. My wife Sylvia makes a dish, they come from all over our level just to taste: chopped reconstituted herring. It's an appetizer and we like appetizers in our family. So what I've been telling you, after all, is only an appetizer. I have to get you in exactly the right mood for the main dish, the big story you came for.

Sylvia makes all the food we eat in the *shul*—our synagogue.

You know, the hamantashen, all that. She even prepares the formal Saturday morning breakfast, the bagels and lox and cream cheese that all the men must eat before they say their Sabbath prayers. We're all orthodox here and we practice the Levittown rite. Our rabbi, Joseph Smallman, is superorthodox Levittown: he wears a yarmulka, and on top of the yarmulka a black homburg which has been passed down from father to son in his family for I don't know how many centuries.

Oh, look how you're smiling! You know I've moved from the appetizer to the main dish. Rabbi Joseph Smallman. It's only Venus, and it's maybe the seventh or eighth Darjeeling burrow listed on the map, but have we got ourselves a rabbi! To us he's an Akiba, a Rambam.

More than that. You know what we call him when we're alone, among ourselves? We call him the Great Rabbi of Venus.

Now you're laughing out loud. No, don't apologize: I heard a chuckle come out of you, like a belch, you should excuse the expression, after a big dinner.

This Milchik the TV man, you're saying to yourself, he and his neighbors in the burrow they come to maybe seventy or eighty Jewish families, they're making a living, with God's help, out of the holes in each other's pockets—and *their* rabbi is the Great Rabbi of Venus? The littlest hole in the ground claims the biggest fire?

It's impossible, maybe? Is anything impossible to the Most High, blessed be His Name? After all, as the Sages tell us, "The last shall be first." Just don't ask me, please, which Sages.

Why is he the Great Rabbi? Well, first of all, why shouldn't Rabbi Smallman be a Great Rabbi? He needs a certificate from the Great Rabbi Licensing Bureau? You have to graduate from the Great Rabbi Special Yeshiva to become a Great Rabbi? That's first of all: you're a Great Rabbi because you *act* like a Great Rabbi, you're *recognized* like a Great Rabbi, you make *decisions* like a Great Rabbi. And you must have heard something of how he acted and how he decided when all the Jews in the universe held a congress right here on Venus. If you hadn't heard, you wouldn't have come all the way from Earth for this interview.

Other people had heard, too. They'd heard of his piety, learning, and wisdom—of his modesty, of course, I say nothing—long before the First Interstellar Neozionist Conference on Venus. People heard and people talked, and they came from as far away as the Gus Grissom Burrow to ask him for rabbinical decisions.

You've got the time to listen to just one example? Sure you've got the time: you're driving through a heavy dust storm in a module that's coughing its guts out, a module that knows Milchik the TV man gives it the best of everything—charged-up power cells, a brand-new fan belt—even if it means that he can't afford to put food on his own table. For Milchik, the module will keep going no matter what, when by itself it would ask for nothing better than to lie down and die in comfort. And the module also likes to listen to Milchik expounding *Halacha,* the holy rules and laws.

About five years ago, something terrible happened on the eve of the Passover. There was an explosion aboard a cargo ship on its way to Venus. No one was hurt, but the cargo was damaged and the ship arrived very late, just a couple of hours before the first seder was to begin. Now on this ship was all the special Passover food that had been ordered from Earth by the twenty-four Jewish families of the Altoona Burrow, and the special food was in cans and airtight packages. When the delivery was made, the Altoona people noticed that the cans had been banged about and dented —but, worse than that, most of the cans had tiny holes all over them. Disaster! According to the Rabbinical Council of 2135 on Space Travel Kashruth, food which is in a punctured can is automatically unclean, unclean for daily use, unclean for Passover use. And here it is almost the seder and what can they do?

These are not rich people: they don't have reserves, they don't have alternatives, they don't even have their own rabbi. If it's a matter of life and death, all right, anything goes; but it isn't life and death, all it means is that they'll have to eat *humetz,* non-Passover food, they won't be able to celebrate the seder. And a Jew who can't celebrate the Deliverance from Egypt with matzo, with bitter herb, with charoseth, with Passover wine, such a Jew is like a bride without a wedding canopy, like a synagogue without a Torah scroll.

The Altoona Burrow is connected to the Darjeeling Burrow; it's a suburb of ours. That's what I said—a suburb. Listen, I know we're a small place, but where is it written that small places, no matter how small, are not entitled to suburbs? If Grissom can have fourteen suburbs, we can have two. So naturally the Altoona people, white-faced, worried, their mouths opening and closing with aggravation, brought the problem to our Rabbi Joseph Smallman. Nothing was leaking from the cans, they said, but the result of the one test they had conducted was bad: as recommended by the Rabbinical Council of 2135, they had taken a hair from somebody's head and poked it into a hole in a can—and the hair had not visibly curled back out. Did that mean that all the expensive food shipped across space had to be condemned, no seders in the Altoona Burrow?

Well, of course that's what it meant—or would have meant to an ordinary rabbi. Rabbi Smallman looked at them and looked at them, and he scratched the pimple on the right side of his nose. He's a pretty good-looking man, Rabbi Smallman, strong and chunky with a face like a young Ben-Gurion, but he does always seem to have a big red pimple on the side of his nose. Then he got up and went to his bookcase and took out half a dozen volumes of Talmud and the last three volumes of the Proceedings of the Rabbinical Council on Space Travel. And he looked in each book at least once, and he sat and thought for a long time after each passage. Finally he asked a question: "Which hair did you use and from whose head?"

They showed him the hair, a fine, white hair from the head of the oldest great-grandfather in the Altoona Burrow, a hair as thin and as delicate as a baby's first sigh. "So this hair did not curl back," he said, "from a hole in that particular can. So much for your test with a hair of your selection. Now for my test with a hair of my selection." And he called over my oldest boy, Aaron David, and told him to pluck out a hair.

You're not blind, you can see my hair, even at my age, how heavy and coarse it is. And believe me, it's thinning out, it's nothing to what it was. My boy, Aaron David, he has the traditional hair of our family, each one twice, three times as thick as a normal hair, his head always going up into a black explosion. When he comes with me, as helper on a job, the customer usually says something like, "With a head of hair like that, what for do you need to carry around coaxial cable?" I say to them: "Bite your tongue. Maybe Haman or Hitler would have used his hair for coaxial cable, or that unholy pair, Sebastian Pombal and Juan Crevea, they also liked to take our heads as raw material in their terrible factories, but don't you talk like that in the year 2859 to a Jewish father about his Jewish son." The Eternal, blessed be He, may demand my son of me, but to nobody else will I be an Abraham who doesn't defend his Isaac. You know what I mean?

So when Rabbi Smallman picks up a dented can and pokes Aaron David's hair at a hole, the hair comes back right away like a piece of bent wire. What else? And when he tries it with another can, again the hair won't go in. So Rabbi Smallman points to the first can they brought him, the one they tested with the old man's hair, and he says, "I declare the food in this can unfit and unclean. But these others," and he waves his hand at the rest of the shipment, "are perfectly acceptable. Carry them home and enjoy your seder."

They crowd around him with tears in their eyes and they thank him and they thank him. Then they gather the cans together and they hurry back to their burrow—it's getting late and it's time to begin the search for the last bits of *humetz* that you have to do before you can turn to the Pesadikeh food. The Altoona people rush out, in a few minutes, I tell you, it was as it says in the Second book of the Holocaust: "There was none left, not one."

You understand, I hope, wherein lies the greatness of this decision? Jews from all over Venus discussed it and everyone, every-

where, marveled. No. I'm sorry, you're wrong: the greatness did
not lie merely in a decision that made it possible for some poor
Jews to enjoy their own Passover seders in their own homes. That's
based on a simple precept—that it's better to have a Jew without
a beard than a beard without a Jew. Try again. No, that's not right
either: using a thick hair from my son's head was not especially
brilliant—under those particular circumstances, any really good
rabbi would have done the same. For that you don't have to be a
Hillel already; you just have to avoid being a literal-minded Sham-
mai. The point still eludes you, right? *Goyische kop!*

My apologies. I didn't mean to speak in a language you don't
know. What did I say? It was just a simple comment about, well,
how some people are intended to be students of Talmud, and
other people are *not* intended to be students of Talmud. It's kind
of like an old saying amongst us.

Sure I'll explain. Why great? In the *first* place. Almost any decent rabbi would have seen the importance of that food being
found fit and clean. And in the *second* place. A good rabbi, a
first-class rabbi, would have found a way to do it, a hair from my
son, a this, a that, anything. But, in the *third* place, only a truly
great rabbi would have examined that many books and thought
that long and hard about the matter before he announced his
decision. How could they really enjoy the seder unless they had
perfect confidence in his decision? And how could they have perfect confidence unless they had seen him wrestle with it through
nine separate volumes? Now do you see why we called him the
Great Rabbi of Venus, even five years before the Neozionist Congress and the great Bulba scandal?

Now I didn't go so far in Talmudic study myself—a man has a
family to support, and closed-circuit TV repair on a planet like
Venus doesn't exactly help your mind in clearing up the problems
of *Gemara.* But whenever I think of what our congregation here
has in Rabbi Smallman, I think of how the Sages begin their argument: "A man finds a treasure . . ."

You shouldn't get the impression, please, that a treasure is a treasure to everyone. Almost all the Jews on Venus are *Ash-kenazim*—people whose ancestors emigrated from Eastern Europe to America before the Holocaust and who didn't return to Israel after the Ingathering—but there are at least three kinds of Ashkenazim, and only our kind, the Levittown Ashkenazim, call Rabbi Smallman the Great Rabbi of Venus. The Williamsburg Ashkenazim, and there are a lot more of them than there are of us, the black-gabardined Ashkenazim who shake and pray and shake and pray, they call Rabbi Smallman the lox-and-bagels rabbi. And on the other hand, the Miami Ashkenazim, the rich all-right-niks who live in the big IBM Burrow, to them a rabbi is a girl who hasn't yet gotten married and is trying to do something intellectual with herself. It's said that the Williamsburg Ashkenazim believe in miracle-working, that the Levittown Ashkenazim believe it's a miracle when they find work, and that the Miami Ashkenazim don't believe in miracles and don't believe in work, they only believe in the import-export business.

I can see you're remembering I said before that I was through with the appetizer and ready to serve the main dish, the story you came for. And where, in all that I've just been telling you, is the main dish, you want to know? Listen, relax a little. Figure it this way: first I gave you an appetizer, then, after that, for the last few minutes, you've been having a soup course. You're through with the soup? Fine. Now we bring out the main dish.

Only—just a second more. There's something else you have to have first. Call it a salad. Look, it's a very small piece of salad. You'll be finished with it in no time. Now please. You're not the cook; you're only a customer. You want a story that's like a sandwich? Go someplace else. Milchik serves only complete meals.

That night, after the seder, I'm sitting on a bench outside our apartment in the Darjeeling Burrow. To me, this is always the best time. It's quiet, most people have gone to bed, and the corridor doesn't smell from crowds. All through the corridors, the lights are being turned down to half their wattage. That's to let us know it's night on Earth. Exactly *where* it's night on Earth, what part of

Earth, I have no idea. Darjeeling, maybe.

As I sit thinking, Aaron David comes out of the apartment and sits down near me on the bench. "Papa," he says after a while. "That was a great thing Rabbi Smallman did today." I nod, sure, certainly it was a great thing. Aaron David puts his hand up to the part of his head where he pulled the single hair out. He holds his hand tight against the spot and looks across the corridor. "Before this," he says, "I just wanted, but now I more than want. I'm going to be a rabbi."

"Congratulations," I say. "Me, I'm going to be the Viceroy of Venus."

"I'm serious, Papa. I'm really serious."

"I'm joking? I don't think there's a chance I'll one day be appointed by the Council of Eleven Nations Terrestrial, and the Presidents of Titan and Ganymede? I'd do a worse job than that hooligan we got right now, his heart should only explode inside his chest? All right," I say to him, "all right," because now he turns and looks at me, with his eyes that are Sylvia's eyes, and eyes like that, let me tell you, can look. "So you want to be a rabbi. What good is the wanting? Anything you want that I can give, I'll give. You know I have that little insulated screwdriver, the blue one, that was made in Israel over five hundred years ago, when Israel was still a Jewish state. That precious little screwdriver, it's like the bones of my right hand, that I'll give you if you ask for it. But I can't give you tuition money for a yeshiva, and more important, I can't even find the transportation money for a bride. A tradition, now, it's hundreds of years old, ever since the Jews began emigrating into space, and a Levittown bride must come from another planet —and it's not only you, it's also your two brothers. A rational creature, boychik, has to worry in an organized way. First the bride money, then we talk about yeshiva money."

Aaron David is close to crying. "If only—if—" He bites his lip.

"If—," I say. "If—You know what we say about *if*. If your grandmother would have had testicles, she'd have been your grandfather. Consider the problem: if you want to be a rabbi, especially a Levittown rabbi, you have to know three ancient languages even before you begin; you have to know Hebrew, you have to know Aramaic, you have to know Yiddish. So I'll tell you what. *If.* *If* you can learn enough beforehand, maybe *if* the miracle ever happens and we can send you to a yeshiva, you can go through faster than usual, rapid-advance, before the whole family goes bankrupt. *If* Rabbi Smallman, for example, gives you lessons."

"He'll do that," he says excitedly. "He's doing it already!"

"No, I'm not talking about just lessons. I'm talking about *lessons*. The kind you have to pay for. He'll teach you one day after supper, and I'll review with you the next day after supper. That way I'll learn too, I won't be such an ignoramus. You know what the Sages say about studying Talmud: 'Get thee a comrade . . .' You'll be my comrade, and I'll be your comrade, and Rabbi Smallman will be both our comrade. And we'll explain to your mother, when she screams at us, that we're getting a bargain, two for one, a special."

So that's what we did. To make the extra money, I started hauling cargo from the spaceport in my module—you notice it drives now as if it's got a hernia? And I got Aaron David a part-time job down on the eighteenth level, in the boiler room. I figured if Hillel could almost freeze to death on that roof in order to become a scholar, it's no tragedy if my son cooks himself a little bit for the same reason.

It works. My son learns and learns, he begins to have more the walk and talk of a scholar and less the walk and talk of a TV repairman. I learn too, not so much of course, but enough so that I can sweeten my conversation with lines from Ibn Ezra and Mendele Mocher Sforim. I'm not any richer, I'm still a *kasrilik*, a schlemiel, but at least now I'm a bit of an educated schlemiel. And it works also for Rabbi Smallman: he's able to send his family once a year on a vacation to Earth, where they can sit around a piece of lake and see what real water is like in the natural state. I'm happy for him, me and my herniated module. The only thing I'm not happy about is that I still can't see any hope for yeshiva tuition money. But, listen, learning is still learning. As Freud says, just to

see from Warsaw to Minsk, even if you don't see right and you
don't understand what you see, it's still a great thing.

But who, I ask you, can see from here to Rigel? And on the
fourth planet, yet, they'll come here and create such a commotion?

From the Neozionist movement, of course, we had already
heard a long time ago. Jews always hear when other Jews are
getting together to make trouble for them. We'd heard about Dr.
Glickman's book, we'd heard about his being killed by Vegan
Dayanists, we'd heard about his followers organizing all over the
galaxy—listen, we'd even had a collection box installed in our
synagogue by some of his party people here on Venus: "In memory of the heroic Dr. Glickman, and to raise funds to buy back the
Holy Land from the Vegan aliens."

With that I have no particular quarrel; I've even dropped a
couple of coins myself in the *pushke* from time to time. After all,
why shouldn't Milchik the TV man, out of his great wealth, help
to buy back the Holy Land?

But the Neozionist movement is another matter. I'm not a cow-
ard, and show me a real emergency, I'm ready to die for my
people. Outside of an *emergency*—well, we Jews on Venus have
learned to keep the tips of our noses carefully under the surface
of our burrows. It's not that there's anti-Semitism on Venus—who
would ever dream of saying such a thing? When the Viceroy an-
nounces five times a week that the reason Venus has an unfavora-
ble balance of trade with other planets is that the Jews are import-
ing too much kosher food: that's not anti-Semitism, that's pure
economic analysis. And when his Minister of the Interior sets up
a quota for the number of Jews in each burrow and says you can
only move from one place to another if you have special permission: that also is not anti-Semitism, obviously, it's efficient administration. What I say is, why upset a government so friendly to the
Jews?

There's another thing I don't like about Neozionism; and it's
hard to say it out loud, especially to a stranger. This business about

going back to Israel. Where else does a Jew belong but in that particular land? Right? Well, I don't know, maybe. We started out there with Abraham, Isaac, and Jacob. No good. So the first time we came back was with Moses, and that lasted for a while—until the Babylonians threw us out. Then we came back under Zerubbabel, and we stayed there for five hundred years—until Titus burned the Temple and the Romans made us leave again. Two thousand years of wandering around the world with nothing more to show for it than Maimonides and Spinoza, Marx and Einstein, Freud and Chagall, and we said, enough is enough, back to Israel. So back we went with Ben-Gurion and Chaim Weizmann and the rest of them. For a couple of centuries we did all right, we only had to worry about forty million Arabs who wanted to kill us, but that's not enough excitement for what God Himself, Blessed be His Name, called on Mount Sinai a "stiff-necked people." We have to get into an argument—in the middle of the Interplanetary Crisis—with Brazil *and* Argentina.

My feeling, I don't know about the rest of the Jews, but I'm getting tired. If no, is no. If out, is out. If good-bye, is good-bye.

That's not the way the Neozionists see it. They feel we've had our rest. Time for another round. "Let the Third Exile end in our lifetimes. Let the Knesset be rebuilt in our age. Israel for the Jews!"

Good enough. Don't we still say, after all the wine, "Next year in Jerusalem"? Who can argue? Except for the one small thing they overlooked, as you know: Israel and Jerusalem these days isn't even for human beings. The Council of Eleven Nations Terrestrial wants no trouble with the Vegans over a sliver of land like Israel, not in these times with what's going on in the galaxy: if both sides in the Vegan Civil War are going to claim the place as holy territory because the men they call the founders of their religions once walked in it, let the bivalves have it, says the Council, let them fight it out between themselves.

And I, Milchik the TV man, I for one see nothing strange in a bunch of Vegan bivalves basing their religion on the life and legend of a particular Jew like Moshe Dayan and wanting to chop up any other Jews who try to return to the land of their ancestors. In the first place, it's happened to us before: to a Jew such an attitude should by now begin to make sense. Where is it written that a Dayanist should like Dayan's relatives? In the second place, how many Jews protested fifty years ago when the other side, the Vegan Omayyads, claimed all human Mohammedans were guilty of sacrilege and expelled them from Jerusalem? Not, I'll admit, that such a protest would have been as noticeable as a ripple in a saucer of tea . . .

Well, the First Interstellar Neozionist Conference is organized, and it's supposed to meet in Basel, Switzerland, so that, I suppose, history can have a chance to repeat itself. And right away the Dayanist Vegans hear about it and they protest to the Council. Are Vegans honored guests of Earth, or aren't they? Their religion is being mocked, they claim, and they even kill a few Jews to show how aggravated they are. Of course the Jews are accused of inciting a pogrom, and it's announced that in the interests of law and order, not to mention peace and security, no Jewish entrance visas will be honored in spaceports anywhere on Earth. Fair is fair.

Meanwhile delegates to the Conference are on their way from all over the galaxy. If they can't land on Earth, where do they go? And to what site should the Conference be transferred by the authorities?

Where else but to Venus? It's the perfect place for such a conference. The scenery is gorgeous—on the other side of the dust storms—and there's a Viceroy whose administration loves the Jewish people most dearly. Besides, there's a desperate housing shortage on Venus. That will create the kind of problem Jews love to solve: a game of musical burrows.

Listen, it could have been worse. As Esther said to Mordecai when he told her of Haman's plans to massacre all the Jews of Persia—it could have been worse, but I don't for the moment see exactly how.

So the delegates begin arriving in the Solar System, they're

shunted to Venus—and don't ask. Life becomes full of love and
bounce for us all. First, a decree comes down. The delegates can't
use hotel facilities on Venus, even if they've got the money: there
are too many of them, they'll put a strain on the hotel system or
something. Next, the Jews of Venus are responsible for their coreli-
gionists. In other words, not only is a Jew naturally a brother to
every other Jew, he's now also got to be either a boarder or a
landlord.

Stop for a moment and reflect on how many are inflicted on us.
Each and every planet in the galaxy which has a human population has at least a breath, a kiss, of Jewish population. So from this
planet comes two delegates, from that one fifteen delegates, from
that other one—where there are plenty of Jews, they should live
and be healthy, but they disagree with each other; comes a total
of sixty-three delegates, organized in eight separate caucuses. It
may not be nice to number Jews, even if they're delegates, but you
can figure for yourself that by the time the last one has landed at
a Venusian spaceport, we've got more than enough to go around.

We've got plenty. And on Venus, you don't go up on the surface
and throw together a couple of shacks for the visitors.

The Williamsburg Ashkenazim object. To them, some of these
Jews aren't even Jews; they won't let them into their burrows, let
alone their homes. After all, Shomrim in khaki pants whose idea
of a religious service is to stand around singing *Techezachna*,
Reconstructionists who pray from a *siddur* that is rewritten every
Monday and Wednesday, Japanese Hasidim who put on *tefillin*
once a year at sunset in memory of the Great Conversion of 2112
—these are *also* Jews, say the Williamsburg Ashkenazim?

Exactly, these are also Jews, say the government officials of
Venus. Brothers and boarders they are, and you will kindly make
room for them. And they send in police, and they send in troops.
Heads are cracked, beards are torn, life, as I said, is full of love and
bounce.

And if you don't object, you think it helps? Sure it helps—like
a groan it helps. The Levittown Ashkenazim announce we'll coop-

erate with the government, we'll provide housing for the delegates to the limit—beyond the limit, even. So what happens? My
brother and his family and all their neighbors get evicted from the
Kwantung Burrow, it's needed for delegate headquarters says the
government.

An Interstellar Neozionist Congress we had to have?

I look around and I remember the promise made to Abraham,
Isaac, and Israel—"I will multiply your seed as the stars of heaven"
—and I think to myself, "A promise is a promise, but even a
promise can go too far. The stars by themselves are more than
enough, but when each star has maybe ten, twenty planets . . ."

By this time, me and my whole family, we're living in what used
to be the kitchen of our apartment. My brother and his family, it's
a big family, they should live and be well, they're living in the
dining room. In what my wife, Sylvia, calls the parlor, there's the
wonder-working rabbi from Procyon XII and his entire court—
plus, in one corner of the parlor, there's the correspondent from
the *Jewish Sentinel* of Melbourne, Australia, and his wife, and
their dog, an Afghan. In the bedrooms—listen, why should I go on?
In the bedrooms, there are crowds and arguments and cooking
smells that I don't even want to know about.

Enough already? No, I am sorry to tell you, not enough.

One day I go into the bathroom. A man is entitled once in a
while to go into the bathroom of his own apartment? It's nature,
no? And there in the bathtub I see three creatures, each as long
as my arm and as thick as my head. They look like three brown
pillows, all wrinkled and twisted, with some big gray spots on this
side and on that side, and out of each gray spot there is growing
a short gray tentacle. I didn't know what they were, giant cock-
roaches maybe, or some kind of plant that the delegates living
with us brought along as food, but when they moved I let out a
yell.

My son, Aaron David, came running into the bathroom. "What's
the matter, Papa?"

I pointed to the brown pillows. They had some sort of ladder arrangement set up in the bathtub with small shelves in different places, and they were climbing up and down, up and down. "What's the matter, you want to know, when I see things like that in my bathroom?"

"Oh, them. They're the Bulbas."

"Bulbas?"

"Three of the delegates from the fourth planet of the star Rigel. The other three delegates are down the corridor in the Guttenplans' bathroom."

"Delegates? You mean they're Jewish?" I stared at them. "They don't look Jewish."

Aaron David rolled his eyes up to the ceiling of the bathroom. "Papa you're so old-fashioned! You yourself told me that the blue Jews from Aldebaran show how adaptable our people are."

"You should pardon me," I said. "You and your adaptable. A Jew can be blue—I don't say I like it, but who am I to argue with somebody else's color scheme?—and a Jew can be tall or short. He can even be deaf from birth like those Jews from Canopus, Sirius, wherever they come from. But a Jew has to have arms and legs. He has to have a face with eyes, a nose, a mouth. It seems to me that's not too much to ask."

"So their mouths are not exactly like our mouths," Aaron David said excitedly. "Is that a crime? Is that any reason to show prejudice?"

I left him and I went to the bathroom in the synagogue. Call me old-fashioned, all right, but there are still boundaries, there are certain places where I have to stop. Here, I have to say, Milchik cannot force himself to be modern.

Well. You know what happened. It turns out I'm not the only one.

I took the day off and went to the first session of the Conference. "Rich man," my Sylvia says to me. "My breadwinner. Family provider. From political conferences you're going to get brides for your three sons?"

"Sylvia," I say to her. "Once in a lifetime my customers can maybe not have clear reception of the news broadcasts and *Captain Iliad*. Once in a lifetime I can go see representatives from all of the Jews of the Galaxy holding a meeting and getting along with each other."

So I went. Only I can't say they got along so good. First there was the demonstration by the Association of Latter-Day Mea Shearim ("If the Messiah appears and starts going from star to star, only to find that all Jews are already on Earth and in Israel . . ."). When that was quieted down, there was the usual Bronsteinite Trotskyist resolution aimed at the Union of Soviet Uganda and Rhodesia, followed by the usual attempt to excommunicate retroactively the authors of the Simplified Babylonian Talmud that had been published in 2685. Then we had to sit through an hour of discussion about how the very existence of a six-story-high statue of Juan Crevea in Buenos Aires was an affront and an insult and an agony to every Jew, and how we should all boycott Argentinian products until the statue was pulled down. I agreed with what the chairman said when he managed to rule the discussion out of order: "We cannot allow ourselves to be distracted by such ancient agonies, such stale affronts. If we do, where do we begin and where do we stop? Let Argentina have its statue of Crevea, let Düsseldorf have its Adolf Hitler University, let Egypt and Libya continue to maintain the Torquemada Observatory on Pluto. This is not our business here today."

At last, finally, after all the traditional Jewish preliminaries, they got down to the real problems of the opening session: the accreditation of delegates. And there, in no time at all, they got stuck. They got stuck and all mixed up, like bits of lox in a lox omelette.

The Bulbas. The three from my bathroom, the three from Max Guttenplan's bathroom—the total delegation from Rigel IV.

No question about their credentials, said the Committee on Accreditation. Their credentials are in order, and they're certainly delegates. The only thing is, they can't be Jews.

And why can't we be Jews, the six Bulbas wanted to know? And here I had to stand up to get a good look, I could hardly believe my eyes. Because guess who their interpreter was? No one else but my son, my *kaddish*, my Aaron David. Mr. Show-No-Prejudice in person.

"Why can't you be Jews? Because," says the Committee Chairman, stuttering with wet lips and plucking at the air with his right hand, "because Jews can be this, can be that. They can be a lot of things. But, first of all, they have to be human."

"You will kindly point out to us," the Bulbas say through my son, the interpreter, "where it says and in which book that Jews have to be human. Name an authority, provide a quotation."

At this point the Deputy Chairman comes up and apologizes to the Chairman of the Committee. The Deputy Chairman is the kind who wins scholarships and fellowships. "You'll pardon me," he says, "but you're not making it clear. It's a very simple matter, really." He turns to the Bulbas. "No one can be a Jew," he explains to the six of them, "who is not the child of a Jewish mother. That's the most ancient, most fundamental definition of a Jew."

"Aha," say the Bulbas. "And from what do you get the impression that we are *not* the children of Jewish mothers? Will you settle for the copies of our birth certificates that we brought along with us?"

That's when the meeting falls apart. A bunch of delegates in khakis starts cheering and stamping their feet. Another bunch with fur hats and long earlocks begins screaming that this whole colloquy is an abomination. All over the hall arguments break out, little clusters of argument between two and three people, big clusters of argument between twenty and thirty people, arguments on biology, on history, on the *Baba M'tziya*. The man sitting next to me, a fat, squinty-eyed man to whom I haven't said a word, suddenly turns to me and pushes his forefinger into my chest and says: "But if you take that position, my dear fellow, how in the world can you make it compatible with the well-known decision, to mention just one example—"And up on the platform, Bronstein-ite Trotskyists have seized control of the public-address system and are trying to reintroduce their resolution on Uganda and Rhodesia.

By the time some kind of order is restored, two blue Jews have been carried away to the hospital and a lawyer from Ganymede has been arrested for using a hearing aid as a deadly weapon.

Someone calls for a vote, by the entire Congress, on the accreditation of the Bulbas. Accreditation as what—someone else wants to know—as delegates or as Jews? They've been accepted as delegates, and who are we to pass upon them as Jews? I'll accept them as Jews in the religious sense, someone else stands up to point out, but not in the biological sense. What kind of biological sense, he's asked by a delegate from across the hall; you don't mean biology, you mean race, you racist. All right, all right, cries out a little man who's sitting in front of him, but would you want your sister to marry one?

It's obvious that there are as many opinions as there are delegates. And the chairman, up there on the platform, he's standing there and he doesn't know what to do.

Suddenly I notice one of the Bulbas is climbing up on the platform. These little tentacles, they use them for everything, for walking, for eating, for talking, for I don't know what. And this Bulba, he gets to the public-address system, and he vibrates one short tentacle for a while, and finally we hear what he says, faint and very soft. We hear that funny voice, like a piece of paper rustling, all through the hall:

"Modeh ani l'fonecha."

The line, just translated by itself, may not mean so much— "Here I am standing before you" or "I present myself before you" —but what Jew, even with only a fingernail's worth of religious background, could not be moved by it, delivered in such a way and at such a time? *Modeh ani l'fonecha*, the Jew says in the prayer, when he is directly addressing God, blessed be His Name. And that's what we all of us now hear in the hall.

Don't talk to me about race, the Bulba is actually saying, don't talk to me about religion, don't talk to me about any legal or philosophical technicalities. I claim that I am a Jew, whatever a Jew is, essentially and spiritually. As Jews, do you accept me or reject me?

No one can answer.

Of course, all this is not getting the Congress any closer to Israel, to a return from the Third Exile. But it's obvious on the one hand that the matter can't be put on the table, and it's obvious on the other hand that it can't be taken off the table. This is not quite the kind of *pilpul* that our learned ancestors had to deal with. We have to find out: what is a Space Age Jew?

So, by general agreement it is decided that as Moses smote the rock to get water, we're going to smite a High Rabbinical Court to get wisdom.

A High Rabbinical Court is appointed by the Accreditation Committee. It has the kind of membership that will satisfy everybody at least a little bit, even if it means that the members of the Court won't want to talk to each other. You know, a kind of kosher smorgasbord. There's the rabbi his followers call the Gaon of Tau Ceti. There's the president of the Unitarian Jewish Theological Seminary. There's the Borneo Mystic Rabbi. There's a member of the chalutziot rabbinate, with his bare chest and rolled-up sleeves. And so on, and so on. There are two women rabbis, one to satisfy the majority Reconstructionist sect, and the other to keep the Miami Ashkenazim happy. And finally, because this is Venus, there's a rabbi from Venus: Rabbi Joseph Smallman.

You want to know something? It's not only because he's from Venus, no matter what the Committee Chairman says. The Bulbas have been insisting that they're entitled to a rabbi who in some way will represent them, and suddenly they want that to be Rabbi Smallman. I can tell what's going on from where I sit, I can see my son with his big mop of black hair going from one Bulba to another, arguing, explaining, urging. He's talking them into it, that Aaron David of mine. He's become the floor manager at the nominating convention of a political party.

"We did it!" he says to me that night in the apartment. His eyes are dancing like meteors. "We got Rabbi Smallman on the Rabbinical Court."

I try to calm him down. "That by itself is not yet the equivalent of crossing the Red Sea on dry land, or of the oil which renewed itself night after night. Just because Rabbi Smallman can push a black hair into a dent, you think he can push Jews into accepting six lumpy brown pillows as fellow Jews?"

"He can if anyone can."

"And if anyone can, why should he? Why should he even try to do such a thing?"

My son gave me the kind of look you give a doctor who tells you he wants to spray disease germs at the electric fan. "Why, Papa! For the sake of justice."

When a son makes a father feel ashamed of himself, the father has a right to feel proud too. I sat down in a corner of the kitchen while Aaron David went into the bathroom to hold a consultation with his brown Bulbas.

But let me tell you, I also felt sad. The wisdom of The Preacher I don't quite have, but one thing I've learned. Whenever someone uses the word "justice," sooner or later there's going to be a split head or a broken heart.

From that day on, every free second I had, I rushed off to Decatur Burrow to attend the sessions of the High Rabbinical Court. Sylvia found out about it and my life was not easy. "While you're studying this new trade, you and that son of yours," she said, "someone's got to work at the old one. You'll be a judge, he'll be a district attorney, so I'll have to be the TV man. Give me a pair of pliers and the Index to the Printed Circuits, and I'll go out and make a living."

"Woman," I told her, "I'm doing my work and my son's work, and I'm keeping food on the table. If the customers don't complain, why should you? I don't get drunk, I don't take drugs. I'm entitled to nourish my spirit at the feet of scholars and wise men."

Sylvia looked up at the ceiling and clapped her hands together. "He can't nourish first a couple of daughters-in-law into the house?" she asked the ceiling. "That's a procedure that is specifically forbidden by the holy books?"

No, my life was not easy. Why should I tell you otherwise?

But what was going on in the Decatur Burrow was so interesting I could hardly sit still while I listened to it. It was like a legend had come to life, it was like watching the golem taking a stroll one day in downtown Prague, it was like coming across the River Sabbathion and seeing it boil and bubble and throw up stones every day in the week but Saturday. Such history as the Bulbas told the Rabbinical Court!

They'd come to the fourth planet of the star Rigel maybe seven, eight hundred years ago in one of the first star ships. Originally, they had been a small orthodox community living in Paramus, New Jersey, and the whole community had been expelled to make way for a new approach to the George Washington Bridge. So they had to go somewhere, right? So why not Rigel? In those days a trip to another solar system took almost a whole lifetime, children were born on the way, people had to live, you know, close. The star ship foundations were advertising for people who already got along with each other, who were living in groups—political groups, religious groups, village groups. The Paramus, New Jersey, people weren't the only ones who went out in a star ship looking for a quiet place where they'd be left alone. That's how the galaxy came to be so full of Amish and Mennonites, Black Muslims and Bangladesh intellectuals, and these old-fashioned polygamous Mormons who spit three times when you mention Salt Lake City.

The only trouble was that the one halfway comfortable planet in the Rigel system already had an intelligent race living on it, a race of brown creatures with short gray tentacles who called themselves Bulbas. They were mostly peasants living off the land, and they'd just begun their industrial revolution. They had at most a small factory here, a mill or two, and a small smelting plant there. The Jews from Paramus, New Jersey, had been hoping for a planet all to themselves, but the Bulbas made them so welcome, the Bulbas wanted them so much to settle on their planet and bring in trade with the rest of the galaxy, that they looked at each other and they said, why not?

So the Jews settled there. They built a small commercial spaceport, and they built houses, and they fixed up a *shul* and a *heder*
and a teenage recreation center. *Nu*, they called the place home.

At this point in the story, one of the rabbinical judges leaned
forward and interrupted. "But while this was going on, you looked
like Jews? I mean, the kind of Jews we're familiar with?"

"Well, more or less. What we looked like particularly, we understand, was Jews from New Jersey."

"That's close enough. Continue."

For a hundred, a hundred and fifty years, there was happiness
and prosperity. The Jews thrived, the Bulbas thrived, and there
was peace between them. But you know what Isaac Leib Peretz
says about the town of Tzachnovka? "It hangs by nothing." Every
Jewish community, everywhere, hangs by nothing. And, unfortunately, nothing is not so strong. Sooner or later it gives way.

With the Jews to help them, the Bulbas began to become important. They built more factories, more smelting plants, they built
banks and computer centers and automobile junkyards. They began to have big wars, big depressions, big political dictatorships.
And they began to wonder why they were having them.

Is there any other answer to such a question? There's only one
answer. The Jews, naturally. Philosophers and rabble-rousers
pointed out that before the Jews came there'd been no such trouble. The Jews were responsible for everything. So Rigel IV had its
first pogrom.

And after the government had apologized, and helped the Jews
to bury their dead, and even offered to pay for some repairs,
twenty or thirty years later there was a second pogrom. And then
there was a third pogrom, and a fourth pogrom. By this time, the
government was no longer apologizing, and it was the Jews who
were paying for repairs.

Now there came ghettos, there came barring from certain occu-
pations, there even came, from time to time, concentration
camps. Not that it was all terrible: there were pleasant interludes.
A government of murderers would be followed by a halfway de-

cent government, a government, say, of just maimers. The Jews sank into the position of the Jews who lived in Yemen and Morocco a thousand years ago, in the eighteenth and nineteenth centuries. They did the dirtiest, most poorly paid work of all. Everybody spit at them, and they spit at themselves.

But Jews they remained. They continued their religious studies, even though, on the whole planet by this time, there was not one set of the Talmud without missing books, there was not one Torah scroll without empty spaces. And the centuries went by, and they knew wars and tyrannies, devastations and exterminations. Until recently, when a new, enlightened government had come to power over all of Rigel IV. It had restored citizenship to the Jews and allowed them to send a delegation to the Neozionist Congress.

The only trouble was that by this time, after all they'd been through, they looked like just plain Bulbas. And they looked like the weakest, poorest Bulbas of all, Bulbas of the very lowest class.

But in the past couple of months they'd learned that this sort of thing had happened to other Jews, in other places. Jews tended to blend into their environment. After all, hadn't there been blonde Jews in Germany, redheaded Jews in Russia, black Jews—the Falashas—in Ethiopia, tall Mountain Jews in the Caucasus who had been as fine horsemen and marksmen as their neighbors? Hadn't there been Jews who had settled in China far back in the Han Dynasty and who were known in the land as the "T'ai Chin Chiao"? What about the blue Jews sitting in this very Congress? And, for that matter—

Another interruption. "These are normal physiological changes that can be explained on a reasonable genetic basis."

If it's possible for a brown cushion with short gray tentacles to look shocked, this brown cushion with short gray tentacles looked shocked. "Are you suggesting that such Jews—the Chinese Jews, the Russian Jews—intermarried and were allowed to remain within the congregation?"

"No, but there are other possibilities. Rape, for example."

"So much rape? Again and again?"

The judges muttered to each other uncomfortably. Then:

"In other words, despite your appearance, you are asking us to believe that you are Jews, and not Bulbas?"

The brown cushion stretched forward with all of its tentacles. "No, we are asking you to believe that we are Bulbas. *Jewish* Bulbas."

And it explained about the genealogical charts it was offering in evidence. The most prized possession of every Jewish family on Rigel IV was its genealogical chart. These records had been preserved intact through fires and wars and pogroms, no matter what else had been destroyed. No Jewish wedding ever took place on Rigel IV unless both parties could produce thoroughly validated genealogical charts. Through them, each Jewish Bulba could trace his ancestry back to the very first settlers on the planet.

"I, for example," the speaker said proudly, "I, Yitzhak ben Pinchas, am the direct descendant of Melvin Cohen, the assistant manager of a supermarket in Paramus, New Jersey."

And the argument got thicker and thicker. How is it possible, the judges wanted to know, for such tremendous changes to take place? Isn't it more likely that at some time or another all the Jews on Rigel IV were wiped out and that then there was a mass conversion of some sort, similar to the one experienced among the Khazars of the eighth century and the Japanese later? No, said the Bulbas, if you knew what conditions have been like for Jews on Rigel IV you wouldn't talk about mass conversions to Judaism. That would have been mass insanity. All that happened is that we began as ordinary Jews, we had a lot of trouble, a lot of time went by, and when it was all over *this* is what we looked like.

"But that denies the experimental facts of biology!"

The Bulbas were very reproachful. "Who are you going to believe, the experimental facts of biology—or your fellow Jews?"

And that was just the first day. I got back to my apartment and I told my brother all about it. We began discussing the case. He took one side and I took the other. In a few minutes, I was waving my fist in his face and he was screaming that I was "an idiot, an animal!" From the next room we heard the wonder-working rabbi from Procyon XII trying to quiet down a similar argument among the members of his court.

"They want to be Jews," my brother yelled at me, "let them convert to Judaism. Then they'll be Jews. Not before."

"Murderer!" I said to him. "Dolt of dolts! How can they convert to Judaism when they're already Jews? Such a conversion would be a filthy, shameful mockery!"

"Without a conversion I absolutely refuse to go up on the *bima* and read a portion with one of them. Without a conversion they cannot join my *minyan*, even if no matter where I look I can't come up with more than nine men. Without a conversion, even if I'm celebrating a circumcision ceremony for a son—" He broke off, his eyes got suddenly calmer, more thoughtful. "How do they circumcise, do you suppose, Milchik? Where and *what* do they circumcise?"

"They cut off a very little bit from the tip of their shortest tentacle, Uncle Fleischik," said my Aaron David, who'd just walked in. "It's a fold of flesh that looks a lot like a foreskin. Besides, you know, only one drop of blood is required by the Covenant. Blood they got."

"A new speciality," said Sylvia as she put out the supper. "*Now,* God be praised and thanked, my son is a *mohel.*"

Aaron David kissed her. "Put my supper aside until later, Mamma. Me and the Bulbas are going to meet with Rabbi Smallman in his study."

Let me tell you, maybe my son was no longer the interpreter since the Bulbas had found voices, but he was still their floor manager. Every day I could see him jumping from one to the other while the case was being discussed. Something special has to be looked up? They need a copy of Rov Chaim Mordecai Brecher's *Commentary on the Book of Ruth*? Who goes running out of the hall to get it but my Aaron David?

After all, that turns out to be a very important issue. Ruth was a Moabite, and from her came eventually King David. And how about Ezra and the problem of the Jewish men who took Canaanite wives? And where do you fit the Samaritans in all this? Jewish women, you'll remember, were not allowed to marry Samaritans. And what does Maimonides have to say on the subject? Maimonides is always Maimonides.

I tell you, day after day, it was like the dream of my life to listen to all those masters and sages.

And then the Court comes through time to the formation of the Jewish State in the twentieth century. All those problem cases when the Ingathering began. The Bene-Israel Jews, for example, of Bombay. The other Indians called them *Shanwar Teles*, "Saturday oilmen," and they were supposed to have arrived in India as a result of the invasion of Palestine by Antiochus Epiphanes. Almost all they remembered of Judaism was the *Shema*, and there were two castes who didn't intermarry, one white, one black. Were they really Jewish? Were both castes Jewish? And how do you prove it?

And more up-to-date, more complicated discussions. The Japanese and the Conversion of 2112, and the results among Jews of the *Ryo-Ritsu* tractates. The Mars-Sirius controversy and the whole problem of the blue Jews. The attitude of the Lubavitchers toward Sebastian Pombal—let Pombal and Crevea, I say, lie deep, *deep* in the ground—and what that meant to Israel as an independent state.

It all comes down to: What is a Jew?

So one of the Bulbas can say, in that thin, rustling voice: "Do not put me in the position of the Wicked Son in the *Haggadah*. Do not put me in the state of *yotzei min haklal*, one who departs from the Congregation. I have said *we* to my people; I have not said *you.*" So he quotes from the Passover service, and all of us have a catch in our throat and tears on our face. But it still comes down to: What is a Jew? Wherefore is this people different from every other people?

And you know something? That's not an easy question to answer. Not with all the different kinds of Jews you've got around today.

So the Court can move into other, even more tangled-up places. It can weigh the definition of a human being that was worked out by the Council of Eleven Nations Terrestrial, during the Sagittarian War. It can look at Napoleon's questions on intermarriage and the answers of the Paris Sanhedrin of 1807. It can turn at last to *Cabala,* even if three of its members don't want to, and ask about the problem of monster births that are brought on by cohabitation with the Children of Lilith. But in the end it has to decide what a Jew is, once and for all—or it has to find some kind of new way out.

Rabbi Smallman found some kind of new way out. On Venus, I'm telling you, have we got a rabbi!

Since this was a special court, set up under special circumstances, facing a question nobody had ever faced before, I expected more than one decision. I expected sweet and sour decisions, hot decisions and cold decisions, chopped decisions and marinated decisions. I was sure we'd see them "confound there their language, that they may not understand one another's speech." But no. Rabbi Smallman argued with each and all, and he brought them around to one point of view, and he wrote most of what was the final judgment. To bring a bunch of Jews—and learned Jews!—to a single decision, that, my friend, is an achievement that can stand.

All through the case, whenever an argument broke out between the judges, and it looked like we were going to spend a couple of weeks on whether it was a black thread or a white thread, you'd see Rabbi Smallman scratch the red pimple on the side of his nose and say that maybe we could all agree on the fact that at least it was a piece of thread? And I got the impression—I admit it's a father speaking—that he looked at my Aaron David, and that my Aaron David nodded. This was even before they came in with a judgment.

Of course, between us, they knew they had to come in with a *something.* The Congress was at a standstill, the delegates didn't know how many delegates there were, and they were arguing the matter out every day along with the Court. There were fights over the Bulbas, there were factions over the Bulbas, and a lot of people had gone home already saying they were sick and tired of the Bulbas.

So.

The decision reviewed all the evidence, all the commentaries, all the history, from Ezra and Nehemia on. It showed what was to be said for the conservative group in the Court, the group which began and ended with the traditional proposition that a Jew is someone who is provably the child of a Jewish mother. Then it went into what was to be said for the liberal-radical wing, the people who felt that a Jew is anyone who freely accepts the *ol*, the yoke, the burden, of Jewishness. And then the decision discussed a couple of positions in-between, and it pointed out that there was no way to sew them all together.

But do they have to be sewn together? Is there any chance that a human being and a Bulba will mate? And what happens if we go deeper and deeper into space, to another galaxy even, and we find all kinds of strange creatures who want to become Jews? Suppose we find a thinking entity whose body is nothing but waves of energy, do we say, no, you're entirely unacceptable? Do we know for sure that it is?

Look at it another way. Among human beings there are Jews and there are *goyim*, gentiles. Between Jews there are a lot of different types, Reformed, blue, Levittown, Williamsburg, and they don't get along with each other so good, but measure them against *goyim* and they're all Jews. Between Jew and *goy* there are a lot of differences, but measure them against any alien and they're both human beings. The word *goy* does not apply to aliens. *Up to recently.*

We've all seen, in the last century or two, how some creatures from the star Vega have adopted an Earth-type religion, two different Earth-type religions, in fact. They won't let Jews into the land of Israel, they maneuver against us, they persecute us. Are these ordinary aliens, then? Certainly not! They may look nonhuman, like crazy giant oysters, but they definitely have to be put into the category of *goyische* aliens. Aliens may be aliens, but the Vegans are quite different as far as Jews are concerned: the Vegans are alien *goyim*.

Well, if there are alien *goyim*, why can't there be alien Jews? We don't expect human *goyim* to marry alien *goyim*, and we don't expect human Jews to marry alien Jews. But we can certainly face the fact that there are aliens who live as we do, who face problems as we do, and—if you won't mind—who worship as we do. There are aliens who know what a pogrom tastes like, and who also know the sweetness of our Sabbath. Let's put it this way: there are Jews —and there are Jews. The Bulbas belong in the second group.

These are not the exact words of the decision, you understand. It's a kind of free translation, provided for you with no extra charge by Milchik the TV man. But it gives you enough to gnaw on.

Not everyone went along with the decision. Some of the Bulbas complained. And a whole bunch of Williamsburgniks walked out of the Congress saying, Well, what could you expect? But the majority of the delegates were so happy to have the thing settled at last that they voted to let the decision stand and to accept the Bulbas. So the Bulbas were also happy: they were full Jewish delegates.

The only trouble was, just as they were finally getting down to the business of the Congress, an order came down from the Viceroy of Venus abolishing it. He said the Congress had gone on too long and it was stirring up bad feelings. All the delegates were sent packing.

Some excitement for a planet like this, no? Rabbi Smallman is still our rabbi, even though he's famous now. He's always going away on lecture tours, from one end of the galaxy to the other. But he always comes back to us, every year, for the High Holy Days. Well, not exactly, you know how it is, once in a while he can't make it. A celebrity, after all. The Great Rabbi of Venus. He's in demand.

And so's my Aaron David, in a way. He finally made it to a

yeshiva. The Bulbas are paying for it, they sent him to one on the other side of Venus, in the Yoruba Burrow. Once in a while I get a letter from him. What he plans to do, it's the agreement he has with them, he's going to go to Rigel IV and be their rabbi.

But of a possible bride he says nothing. Listen, maybe I'll turn out to be the grandfather of a lumpy brown pillow with short gray tentacles? A grandchild, I guess, is still a grandchild.

I don't know. Let's talk about something cheerful. How many people would you say were killed in that earthquake on Callisto?

AVRAM DAVIDSON

The Golem

The Golem is the Jew's Frankenstein. (Indeed, the Golem legends might have prompted the idea for Mary Shelley's Frankenstein.) Legend has it that the Golem was created out of clay by Rabbi Löw of Prague for the protection of persecuted Jews. Its dreadful corpse is said to be still lying in the attic of a synagogue, ready to be raised again if needed. The Golem is one of the most powerful symbols to come out of Jewish lore. It is a symbol of fear and dread, but also of love and pride, for it was created with God's consent. The Golem is a clay mannikin, an automaton infused with life to become man's servant and, hopefully, an instrument of God's will. Upon its forehead is written the sacred word Shem, *the life-principle. If this word is rubbed out, the Golem will sink into a lump of clay. Thus man retains ultimate power over his clay servant. But each day the Golem increases in strength and size. One day the owner might find that he cannot reach its forehead to erase the sacred word. So the Golem becomes a threat, even when it is dutifully performing good deeds. In the end, the Golem goes mad. The creation of an artificial being becomes a tragedy.*

Avram Davidson has blended the legend into a warm, poignant, sometimes comic story set in a modern land of Jewish make-believe, that warm country called California where everything is stable and quiet and filled with hours of sweet-sad reminiscence. There, white-haired couples who have always been in love can hold hands and count nephews and speak Yiddish. A place of simple expectations and, of course, no surprises. Sometimes.

—J. D.

*

THE GRAY-FACED PERSON CAME ALONG THE STREET where old Mr. and Mrs. Gumbeiner lived. It was afternoon, it was autumn, the sun was warm and soothing to their ancient bones. Anyone who attended the movies in the twenties or the early thirties has seen that street a thousand times. Past these bungalows with their half-double roofs Edmund Lowe walked arm-in-arm with Leatrice Joy, and Harold Lloyd was chased by Chinamen waving hatchets. Under these squamous palm trees Laurel kicked Hardy and Woolsey beat Wheeler upon the head with codfish. Across these pocket-handkerchief-sized lawns the juveniles of the Our Gang Comedies pursued one another and were pursued by angry fat men in golf knickers. On this same street—or perhaps on some other one of five hundred streets exactly like it.

Mrs. Gumbeiner indicated the gray-faced person to her husband.

"You think maybe he's got something the matter?" she asked. "He walks kind of funny, to me."

"Walks like a *golem*," Mr. Gumbeiner said indifferently.

The old woman was nettled.

"Oh, I don't know," she said. "*I* think he walks like your cousin Mendel."

The old man pursed his mouth angrily and chewed on his pipe stem. The gray-faced person turned up the concrete path, walked up the steps to the porch, sat down in a chair. Old Mr. Gumbeiner ignored him. His wife stared at the stranger.

"Man comes in without a hello, good-bye, or howareyou, sits himself down, and right away he's at home. . . . The chair is comfortable?" she asked. "Would you like maybe a glass tea?"

She turned to her husband.

"Say something, Gumbeiner!" she demanded. "What are you, made of wood?"

The old man smiled a slow, wicked, triumphant smile.

"Why should *I* say anything?" he asked the air. "Who am I? Nothing, that's who."

The stranger spoke. His voice was harsh and monotonous. "When you learn who—or rather what—I am, the flesh will melt from your bones in terror." He bared porcelain teeth.

"Never mind about my bones!" the old woman cried. "You've got a lot of nerve talking about my bones!"

"You will quake with fear," said the stranger. Old Mrs. Gumbeiner said that she hoped he would live so long. She turned to her husband once again.

"Gumbeiner, when are you going to mow the lawn?"

"All mankind—" the stranger began.

"*Shah!* I'm talking to my husband. . . . He talks *eppis* kind of funny, Gumbeiner, no?"

"Probably a foreigner," Mr. Gumbeiner said, complacently.

"You think so?" Mrs. Gumbeiner glanced fleetingly at the stranger. "He's got a very bad color in his face, *nebbich*. I suppose he came to California for his health."

"Disease, pain, sorrow, love, grief—all are nought to . . ."

Mr. Gumbeiner cut in on the stranger's statement.

"Gall bladder," the old man said. "Guinzburg down at the *shule* looked exactly the same before his operation. Two professors they had in for him, and a private nurse day and night."

"I am not a human being!" the stranger said loudly.

"Three thousand seven hundred fifty dollars it cost his son, Guinzburg told me. 'For you, Poppa, nothing is too expensive— only get well,' the son told him."

"*I am not a human being!*"

"Ai, is that a son for you!" the old woman said, rocking her head. "A heart of gold, pure gold." She looked at the stranger. "All right, all right, I heard you the first time. Gumbeiner! I asked you a question. When are you going to cut the lawn?"

"On Wednesday, *odder* maybe Thursday, comes the Japaneser to the neighborhood. To cut lawns is *his* profession. *My* profession is to be a glazier—retired."

"Between me and all mankind is an inevitable hatred," the stranger said. "When I tell you what I am, the flesh will melt—"

"You said, you said already," Mr. Gumbeiner interrupted.

"In Chicago where the winters were as cold and bitter as the Czar of Russia's heart," the old woman intoned, "you had strength to carry the frames with the glass together day in and day out. But in California with the golden sun to mow the lawn when your wife asks, for this you have no strength. Do I call in the Japaneser to cook for you supper?"

"Thirty years Professor Allardyce spent perfecting his theories. Electronics, neuronics—"

"Listen, how educated he talks," Mr. Gumbeiner said, admiringly. "Maybe he goes to the University here?"

"If he goes to the University, maybe he knows Bud?" his wife suggested.

"Probably they're in the same class and he came to see him about the homework, no?"

"Certainly he must be in the same class. How many classes are there? Five *in ganzen:* Bud showed me on his program card." She counted off her fingers. "Television Appreciation and Criticism, Small Boat Building, Social Adjustment, The American Dance . . . The American Dance—nu, Gumbeiner—"

"Contemporary Ceramics," her husband said, relishing the syllables. "A fine boy, Bud. A pleasure to have him for a boarder."

"After thirty years spent in these studies," the stranger, who had continued to speak unnoticed, went on, "he turned from the theoretical to the pragmatic. In ten years' time he had made the most titanic discovery in history: he made mankind, *all* mankind, superfluous: he made *me.*"

"What did Tillie write in her last letter?" asked the old man.

The old woman shrugged.

"What should she write? The same thing. Sidney was home from the army, Naomi has a new boy friend—"

"He made Me!"

"Listen, Mr. Whatever-your-name-is," the old woman said, "maybe where you came from is different, but in *this* country you don't interrupt people the while they're talking. . . . Hey. Listen —what do you mean, he *made* you? What kind of talk is that?"

The stranger bared all his teeth again, exposing the too-pink gums.

"In his library, to which I had a more complete access after his sudden and as yet undiscovered death from entirely natural causes, I found a complete collection of stories about androids, from Shelley's *Frankenstein* through Čapek's *R.U.R.* to Asimov's —"

"Frankenstein?" said the old man, with interest. "There used to be Frankenstein who had the soda-*wasser* place on Halstead Street: a Litvack, *nebbich.*"

"What are you talking?" Mrs. Gumbeiner demanded. "His name was Franken*thal,* and it wasn't on Halstead, it was on Roosevelt."

"—clearly showing that all mankind has an instinctive antipathy toward androids and there will be an inevitable struggle between them—"

"Of course, of course!" Old Mr. Gumbeiner clicked his teeth against his pipe. "I am always wrong, you are always right. How could you stand to be married to such a stupid person all this time?"

"I don't know," the old woman said. "Sometimes I wonder, myself. I think it must be his good looks." She began to laugh. Old Mr. Gumbeiner blinked, then began to smile, then took his wife's hand.

"Foolish old woman," the stranger said, "why do you laugh? Do you not know I have come to destroy you?"

"What!" old Mr. Gumbeiner shouted. "Close your mouth, you!"

He darted from his chair and struck the stranger with the flat of his hand. The stranger's head struck against the porch pillar and bounced back.

"When you talk to my wife, talk respectable, you hear?"

Old Mrs. Gumbeiner, cheeks very pink, pushed her husband back in his chair. Then she leaned forward and examined the stranger's head. She clicked her tongue as she pulled aside the flap of gray, skinlike material.

"Gumbeiner, look! He's all springs and wires inside!"

"I *told* you he was a *golem*, but no, you wouldn't listen," the old man said.

"You said he *walked* like a *golem*."

"How could he walk like a *golem* unless he *was* one?"

"All right, all right. . . . You broke him, so now fix him."

"My grandfather, his light shines from Paradise, told me that when MoHaRaL—Moreynu Ha-Rav Löw—his memory for a blessing, made the *golem* in Prague, three hundred? four hundred years ago? he wrote on his forehead the Holy Name."

Smiling reminiscently, the old woman continued, "And the *golem* cut the rabbi's wood and brought his water and guarded the ghetto."

"And one time only he disobeyed the Rabbi Löw, and Rabbi Löw erased the *Shem Ha-Mephorash* from the *golem*'s forehead and the *golem* fell down like a dead one. And they put him up in the attic of the *shule* and he's still there today if the Communisten haven't sent him to Moscow. . . . This is not just a story," he said.

"*Avadda* not!" said the old woman.

"I myself have seen both the *shule and* the rabbi's grave," her husband said, conclusively.

"But I think this must be a different kind *golem*, Gumbeiner. See, on his forehead: nothing written."

"What's the matter, there's a law I can't write something there? Where is that lump clay Bud brought us from his class?"

The old man washed his hands, adjusted his little black skullcap, and slowly and carefully wrote four Hebrew letters on the gray forehead.

"Ezra the Scribe himself couldn't do better," the old woman said, admiringly. "Nothing happens," she observed, looking at the lifeless figure sprawled in the chair.

"Well, after all, am I Rabbi Löw?" her husband asked, deprecatingly. "No," he answered. He leaned over and examined the exposed mechanism. "This spring goes here . . . this wire comes with this one . . ." The figure moved. "But this one goes where? And this one?"

"Let be," said his wife. The figure sat up slowly and rolled its eyes loosely.

"Listen, Reb *Golem,*" the old man said, wagging his finger. "Pay attention to what I say—you understand?"

"Understand. . . ."

"If you want to stay here, you got to do like Mr. Gumbeiner says."

"Do-like-Mr.-Gumbeiner-says. . . ."

"That's the way I like to hear a *golem* talk. Malka, give here the mirror from the pocketbook. Look, you see your face? You see on the forehead, what's written? If you don't do like Mr. Gumbeiner says, he'll wipe out what's written and you'll be no more alive."

"No-more-alive. . . ."

"That's right. Now, listen. Under the porch you'll find a lawnmower. Take it. And cut the lawn. Then come back. Go."

"Go. . . ." The figure shambled down the stairs. Presently the sound of the lawnmower whirred through the quiet air in the street just like the street where Jackie Cooper shed huge tears on Wallace Beery's shirt and Chester Conklin rolled his eyes at Marie Dressler.

"So what will you write to Tillie?" Old Mr. Gumbeiner asked.

"What should I write?" Old Mrs. Gumbeiner shrugged. "I'll write that the weather is lovely out here and that we are both, Blessed be the Name, in good health."

The old man nodded his head slowly, and they sat together on the front porch in the warm afternoon sun.

ISAAC ASIMOV

Unto the Fourth Generation

*The mystique of the assimilated Jew: He's polished, ur-
bane, suburban, modern, middle-class, mildly—if at all—religious, well-educated, politically liberal, socially insecure, and a
second-generation American. He identifies with, and embodies,
American culture. He's Mr. New Yorker, the man on the way up,
the cultural catchall. But his roots are carefully hidden, his links
to the old world and his rich heritage seemingly severed. He must
still come to terms with himself, his modern lifestyle, and his
ancestral culture.*

*So here is a parable for that mythical assimilated Jew, an answer
to the question: assimilation or continuation? Isaac Asimov, one of
science fiction's foremost yarnspinners, blends folk spirit with city
sophistication to create a dream-distant New York where shadows
of the past leave their imprints on Madison Avenue shop windows
and old men can come back for one last look at the young.*

J. D.

*

AT TEN OF NOON, Sam Marten hitched his way out of the taxicab, trying as usual to open the door with one hand, hold his briefcase in another and reach for his wallet with a third. Having only two hands, he found it a difficult job and, again as usual, he thudded his knee against the cab-door and found himself still groping uselessly for his wallet when his feet touched pavement.

The traffic of Madison Avenue inched past. A red truck slowed its crawl reluctantly, then moved on with a rasp as the light changed. White script on its side informed an unresponsive world that its ownership was that of *F. Lewkowitz and Sons, Wholesale Clothiers.*

Levkovich, thought Marten with brief inconsequence, and finally fished out his wallet. He cast an eye on the meter as he clamped his briefcase under his arm. Dollar sixty-five, make that twenty cents more as a tip, two singles gone would leave him only one for emergencies, better break a fiver.

"Okay," he said, "take out one-eighty-five, bud."

"Thanks," said the cabbie with mechanical insincerity and made the change.

Marten crammed three singles into his wallet, put it away, lifted his briefcase and breasted the human currents on the sidewalk to reach the glass doors of the building.

Levkovich? he thought sharply, and stopped. A passerby glanced off his elbow.

"Sorry," muttered Marten, and made for the door again.

Levkovich? That wasn't what the sign on the truck had said. The name had read Lewkowitz, *Loo-koh-itz.* Why did he *think* Levkovich? Even with his college German in the near past changing the w's to v's, where did he get the "-ich" from?

Levkovich? He shrugged the whole matter away roughly. Give it a chance and it would haunt him like a Hit Parade tinkle.

Concentrate on business. He was here for a luncheon appointment with this man, Naylor. He was here to turn a contract into an account and begin, at twenty-three, the smooth business rise which, as he planned it, would marry him to Elizabeth in two years and make him a paterfamilias in the suburbs in ten.

He entered the lobby with grim firmness and headed for the banks of elevators, his eye catching at the white-lettered directory as he passed.

It was a silly habit of his to want to catch suite numbers as he passed, without slowing, or (heaven forbid) coming to a full halt. With no break in his progress, he told himself, he could maintain the impression of belonging, of knowing his way around, and that was important to a man whose job involved dealing with other human beings.

Kulin-etts was what he wanted, and the word amused him. A firm specializing in the production of minor kitchen gadgets, striving manfully for a name that was significant, feminine, and coy, all at once—

His eyes snagged at the M's and moved upward as he walked. Mandel, Lusk, Lippert Publishing Company (two full floors), Lafkowitz, Kulin-etts. There it was—1024. Tenth floor. O.K.

And then, after all, he came to a dead halt, turned in reluctant fascination, returned to the directory, and stared at it as though he were an out-of-towner.

Lafkowitz?

What kind of spelling was that?

It was clear enough. Lafkowitz, Henry J., 701. With an A. That was no good. That was useless.

Useless? Why useless? He gave his head one violent shake as though to clear it of mist. Damn it, what did he care how it was spelled? He turned away, frowning and angry, and hastened to an elevator door, which closed just before he reached it, leaving him flustered.

Another door opened and he stepped in briskly. He tucked his briefcase under his arm and tried to look bright alive—junior executive in its finest sense. He had to make an impression on Alex Naylor, with whom so far he had communicated only by telephone. If he was going to brood about Lewkowitzes and Lafkowitzes—

The elevator slid noiselessly to a halt at seven. A youth in shirt-sleeves stepped off, balancing what looked like a desk-drawer in which were three containers of coffee and three sandwiches.

Then, just as the doors began closing, frosted glass with black lettering loomed before Marten's eyes. It read: 701—HENRY J. LEFKOWITZ—IMPORTER and was pinched off by the inexorable coming together of the elevator doors.

Marten leaned forward in excitement. It was his impulse to say: Take me back down to 7.

But there were others in the car. And after all, he had no reason.

Yet there was a tingle of excitement within him. The Directory *had* been wrong. It wasn't A, it was E. Some fool of a non-spelling menial with a packet of small letters to go on the board and only one hind foot to do it with.

Lefkowitz. Still not right, though.

Again, he shook his head. Twice. Not right for what?

The elevator stopped at ten and Marten got off.

Alex Naylor of Kulin-etts turned out to be a bluff, middle-aged man with a shock of white hair, a ruddy complexion, and a broad smile. His palms were dry and rough, and he shook hands with a considerable pressure, putting his left hand on Marten's shoulder in an earnest display of friendliness.

He said, "Be with you in two minutes. How about eating right here in the building? Excellent restaurant, and they've got a boy who makes a good martini. That sound all right?"

"Fine. Fine." Marten pumped up enthusiasm from a somehow-clogged reservoir.

It was nearer ten minutes than two, and Marten waited with the usual uneasiness of a man in a strange office. He stared at the upholstery on the chairs and at the little cubby-hole within which a young and bored switchboard operator sat. He gazed at the pictures on the wall and even made a half-hearted attempt to glance through a trade journal on the table next to him.

What he did not do was think of Lev—

He did *not* think of it.

The restaurant was good, or it would have been good if Marten had been perfectly at ease. Fortunately, he was freed of the necessity of carrying the burden of the conversation. Naylor talked rapidly and loudly, glanced over the menu with a practiced eye, recommended the Eggs Benedict, and commented on the weather and the miserable traffic situation.

On occasion, Marten tried to snap out of it, to lose that edge of fuzzed absence of mind. But each time the restlessness would return. Something was wrong. The name was wrong. It stood in the way of what he had to do.

With main force, he tried to break through the madness. In sudden verbal clatter, he led the conversation into the subject of wiring. It was reckless of him. There was no proper foundation; the transition was too abrupt.

But the lunch had been a good one; the dessert was on its way; and Naylor responded nicely.

He admitted dissatisfaction with existing arrangements. Yes, he had been looking into Marten's firm and, actually, it seemed to him that, yes, there was a chance, a good chance, he thought, that—

A hand came down on Naylor's shoulder as a man passed behind his chair. "How's the boy, Alex?"

Naylor looked up, grin ready-made and flashing. "Hey, Lefk, how's business?"

"Can't complain. See you at the—" He faded into the distance.

Marten wasn't listening. He felt his knees trembling, as he half-rose. "Who was that man?" he asked, intensely. It sounded more peremptory than he intended.

"Who? Lefk? Jerry Lefkovitz. You know him?" Naylor stared with cool surprise at his lunch companion.

"No. How do you spell his name?"

"L-E-F-K-O-V-I-T-Z, I think. Why?"

"With a V?"

"An F. . . . Oh, there's a V in it, too." Most of the good nature had left Naylor's face.

Marten drove on. "There's a Lefkowitz in the building. With a W. You know, Lef-COW-itz."

"Oh?"

"Room 701. This is not the same one?"

"Jerry doesn't work in this building. He's got a place across the street. I don't know this other one. This is a big building, you know. I don't keep tabs on everyone in it. What is all this, anyway?"

Marten shook his head and sat back. He didn't know what all this was, anyway. Or at least, if he did, it was nothing he dared explain. Could he say: I'm being haunted by all manner of Lefkowitzes today.

He said, "We were talking about wiring."

Naylor said, "Yes. Well, as I said, I've been considering your company. I've got to talk it over with the production boys, you understand. I'll let you know."

"Sure," said Marten, infinitely depressed. Naylor wouldn't let him know. The whole thing was shot.

And yet, through and beyond his depression, there was still that restlessness.

The hell with Naylor. All Marten wanted was to break this up and get on with it. (*Get on with what?* But the question was only a whisper. Whatever did the questioning inside him was ebbing away, dying down. . . .)

The lunch frayed to an ending. If they had greeted each other like long-separated friends at last reunited, they parted like strangers.

Marten felt only relief.

He left with pulses thudding, threading through the tables, out of the haunted building, onto the haunted street.

Haunted? Madison Avenue at 1:20 P.M. in an early fall afternoon with the sun shining brightly and ten thousand men and women be-hiving its long straight stretch.

But Marten felt the haunting. He tucked his briefcase under his arm and headed desperately northward. A last sigh of the normal within him warned him he had a three o'clock appointment on 36th Street. Never mind. He headed uptown. Northward.

At 54th Street, he crossed Madison and walked west, came abruptly to a halt and looked upward.

There was a sign on the window, three stories up. He could make it out clearly: A. S. LEFKOWICH, CERTIFIED ACCOUNTANT.

It had an F and an OW, but it was the first "-ich" ending he had seen. The first one. He was getting closer. He turned north again on Fifth Avenue, hurrying through the unreal streets of an unreal city, panting with the chase of something, while the crowds about him began to fade.

A sign in a ground-floor window, M. R. LEFKOWICZ, M.D.

A small gold-leaf semi-circle of letters in a candy-store window: JACOB LEVKOW.

(Half a name, he thought savagely. Why is he disturbing me with half a name?)

The streets were empty now except for the varying clan of Lefkowitz, Levkowitz, Lefkowicz to stand out in the vacuum.

He was dimly aware of the park ahead, standing out in painted motionless green. He turned west. A piece of newspaper fluttered at the corner of his eyes, the only movement in a dead world. He veered, stooped, and picked it up, without slackening his pace.

It was in Yiddish, a torn half-page.

He couldn't read it. He couldn't make out the blurred Hebrew letters, and could not have read it if they were clear. But one word was clear. It stood out in dark letters in the center of the page, each letter clear in its every serif. And it said Lefkovitsch, he knew, and as he said it to himself, he placed its accent on the second syllable: Lef-KUH-vich.

He let the paper flutter away and entered the empty park.

The trees were still and the leaves hung in odd, suspended attitudes. The sunlight was a dead weight upon him and gave no warmth.

He was running, but his feet kicked up no dust and a tuft of grass on which he placed his weight did not bend.

And there on a bench was an old man; the only man in the desolate park. He wore a dark felt hat, with a visor shading his eyes. From underneath it, tufts of gray hair protruded. His grizzled beard reached the uppermost button of his rough jacket. His old trousers were patched, and a strip of burlap was wrapped about each worn and shapeless shoe.

Marten stopped. It was difficult to breathe. He could only say one word and he used it to ask his question: "Levkovich?"

He stood there, while the old man rose slowly to his feet; brown old eyes peering close.

"Marten," he sighed. "Samuel Marten. You have come." The words sounded with an effect of double exposure, for under the English, Marten heard the faint sigh of a foreign tongue. Under the "Samuel" was the unheard shadow of a "Schmu-el."

The old man's rough, veined hands reached out, then withdrew as though he were afraid to touch. "I have been looking but there are so many people in this wilderness of a city-that-is-to-come. So many Martins and Martines and Mortons and Mertons. I stopped at last when I found greenery, but for a moment only—I would not commit the sin of losing faith. And then you came."

"It is I," said Marten, and knew it was. "And you are Phinehas Levkovich. Why are we here?"

"I am Phinehas ben Jehudah, assigned the name Levkovich by the ukase of the Tsar that ordered family names for all. And we are here," the old man said, softly, "because I prayed. When I was already old, Leah, my only daughter, the child of my old age, left for America with her husband, left the knouts of the old for the hope of the new. And my sons died, and Sarah, the wife of my bosom, was long dead and I was alone. And the time came when I, too, must die. But I had not seen Leah since her leaving for the far country and word had come but rarely. My soul yearned that I might see sons born unto her, sons of my seed, sons in whom my soul might yet live and not die."

His voice was steady and the soundless shadow of sound beneath his words was the stately roll of an ancient language.

"And I was answered and two hours were given me that I might see the first son of my line to be born in a new land and in a new time. My daughter's daughter's daughter's son, have I found you, then, amidst the splendor of this city?"

"But why the search? Why not have brought us together at once?"

"Because there is pleasure in the hope of the seeking, my son," said the old man, radiantly, "and in the delight of the finding. I was given two hours in which I might seek, two hours in which I might find . . . and behold, thou art here, and I have found that which I had not looked to see in life." His voice was old, caressing. "Is it well with thee, my son?"

"It is well, my father, now that I have found thee," said Marten, and dropped to his knees. "Give me thy blessing, my father, that it may be well with me all the days of my life, and with the maid whom I am to take to wife and the little ones yet to be born of my seed and thine."

He felt the old hand resting lightly on his head and there was only the soundless whisper.

Marten rose.

The old man's eyes gazed into his yearningly. Were they losing focus?

"I go to my fathers now in peace, my son," said the old man, and Marten was alone in the empty park.

There was an instant of renewing motion, of the sun taking up its interrupted task, of the wind reviving, and even with that first instant of sensation, all slipped back—

At ten of noon, Sam Marten hitched his way out of the taxicab, and found himself groping uselessly for his wallet while traffic inched on.

A red truck slowed, then moved on. A white script on its side announced: *F. Lewkowitz and Sons, Wholesale Clothiers.*

Marten didn't see it.

CAROL CARR

Look, You Think You've Got Troubles

The delights of humor rest on fear and foible. Its best materials are insecurity, discomfort, frustration, hypocrisy, and nostalgia; its favorite tools are satire, ironic self-mockery, and exaggeration. It is both a foil and a shield, an effective armor against a hostile society.

Quite a bit of contemporary American humor takes its cues from Jewish culture, and Jewish humor—that particular blend of language, style, caricature, and profound alienation—becomes an important societal mirror. Spoken with the tongue of the outsider —the anti-hero—it has the sophistication of the urban middle class and the grit and pith of the ghetto. And it's taken to heart. As Albert Goldman says, "Jewishness itself has become a metaphor for modern life. The individual Jew—the alien in search of identity—has become a symbolic protagonist."

Jewish humor—a term, like science fiction, that is too broad and illusive to pin down—might best be defined by example. Take a nice Jewish couple with a nice Jewish daughter who marries a Martian. He's the ultimate goy, or is he? If love can conquer all, what then happens to tradition and law and culture and despondent parents? Let them be conquered while the reader settles into rocket ships and belly laughs. But watch out for that mythical assimilated Jew peeking around the corner. He's grinning slyly and baring his chest.

J. D.

59

*

To TELL YOU THE TRUTH, in the old days we would have sat shivah for the whole week. My so-called daughter gets married, my own flesh and blood, and not only he doesn't look Jewish, he's not even human.

"Papa," she says to me, two seconds after I refuse to speak to her again in my entire life, "if you know him you'll love him, I promise." So what can I answer—the truth, like I always tell her: "If I know him I'll vomit, that's how he affects me. I can help it? He makes me want to throw up on him."

With silk gloves you have to handle the girl, just like her mother. I tell her what I feel, from the heart, and right away her face collapses into a hundred cracks and water from the Atlantic Ocean makes a soggy mess out of her paper sheath. And that's how I remember her after six months—standing in front of me, sopping wet from the tears and making me feel like a monster—me—when all the time it's her you-should-excuse-the-expression husband who's the monster.

After she's gone to live with him (New Horizon Village, Crag City, Mars), I try to tell myself it's not me who has to—how can I put it?—deal with him intimately; if she can stand it, why should I complain? It's not like I need somebody to carry on the business; my business is to enjoy myself in my retirement. But who can enjoy? Sadie doesn't leave me alone for a minute. She calls me a criminal, a worthless no-good with gallstones for a heart.

"Hector, where's your brains?" she says, having finally given up on my emotions. I can't answer her. I just lost my daughter, I should worry about my brains too? I'm silent as the grave. I can't eat a thing. I'm empty—drained. It's as though I'm waiting for something to happen but I don't know what. I sit in a chair that folds me up like a bee in a flower and rocks me to sleep with electronic rhythms when I feel like sleeping, but who can sleep? I look at my wife and I see Lady Macbeth. Once I caught her whistling as she pushed the button for her bath. I fixed her with a look like an icicle tipped with arsenic.

"What are you so happy about? Thinking of your grandchildren with the twelve toes?"

She doesn't flinch. An iron woman.

When I close my eyes, which is rarely, I see our daughter when she was fourteen years old, with skin just beginning to go pimply and no expression yet on her face. I see her walking up to Sadie and asking her what she should do with her life now she's filling out, and my darling Sadie, my life's mate, telling her why not marry a freak; you got to be a beauty to find a man here, but on Mars you shouldn't know from so many fish. "I knew I could count on you, Mama," she says, and goes ahead and marries a plant with legs.

Things go on like this—impossible—for months. I lose twenty pounds, my nerves, three teeth and I'm on the verge of losing Sadie, when one day the mailchute goes ding-dong and it's a letter from my late daughter. I take it by the tips of two fingers and bring it in to where my wife is punching ingredients for the gravy I won't eat tonight.

"It's a communication from one of your relatives."

"Oh-oh-oh." My wife makes a grab for it, meanwhile punching CREAM-TOMATO-SAUCE-BEEF DRIPPINGS. No wonder I have no appetite.

"I'll give it to you on one condition only," I tell her, holding it out of her trembling reach. "Take it into the bedroom and read it to yourself. Don't even move your lips for once; I don't want to know. If she's God forbid dead, I'll send him a sympathy card."

Sadie has a variety of expressions but the one thing they have in common is they all wish me misfortune in my present and future life.

While she's reading the letter I find suddenly I have nothing to

do. The magazines I read already. Breakfast I ate (like a bird). I'm
all dressed to go out if I felt like, but there's nothing outside I don't
have inside. Frankly, I don't feel like myself—I'm nervous. I say
a lot of things I don't really intend and now maybe this letter
comes to tell me I've got to pay for my meanness. Maybe she got
sick up there; God knows what they eat, the kind of water they
drink, the creatures they run around with. Not wanting to think
about it too much, I go over to my chair and turn it on to brisk
massage. It doesn't take long till I'm dreaming (fitfully).

I'm someplace surrounded by sand, sitting in a baby's crib and
bouncing a diapered kangaroo on my knee. It gurgles up at me
and calls me grandpa and I don't know what I should do. I don't
want to hurt its feelings, but if I'm a grandpa to a kangaroo, I want
no part of it; I only want it should go away. I pull out a dime from
my pocket and put it into its pouch. The pouch is full of tiny insects
which bite my fingers. I wake up in a sweat.

"Sadie! Are you reading, or rearranging the sentences? Bring it
in here and I'll see what she wants. If it's a divorce, I know a
lawyer."

Sadie comes into the room with her I-told-you-so waddle and
gives me a small wet kiss on the cheek—a gold star for acting like
a mensch. So I start to read it, in a loud monotone so she shouldn't
get the impression I give a damn:

"Dear Daddy, I'm sorry for not writing sooner. I suppose I
wanted to give you a chance to simmer down first." (Ingrate! Does
the sun simmer down?) "I know it would have been inconvenient
for you to come to the wedding, but Mor and I hoped you would
maybe send us a letter just to let us know you're okay and still love
me, in spite of everything."

Right at this point I feel a hot sigh followed by a short but
wrenching moan.

"Sadie, get away from my neck. I'm warning you. . . ."

Her eyes are going flick-a-fleck over my shoulder, from the
piece of paper I'm holding to my face, back to the page, flick-a-
fleck, flick-a-fleck.

"All right, already," she shoo-shoos me. "I read it, I know what's in it. Now it's your turn to see what kind of a lousy father you turned out to be." And she waddles back into the bedroom, shutting the door extra careful, like she's handling a piece of snow-white velvet.

When I'm certain she's gone, I sit myself down on the slab of woven dental floss my wife calls a couch and press a button on the arm that reads SEMI-CL.: FELDMAN TO FRIML. The music starts to slither out from the speaker under my left armpit. The right speaker is dead and buried and the long narrow one at the base years ago got drowned from the dog, who to this day hasn't learned to control himself when he hears "Desert Song."

This time I'm lucky; it's a piece by Feldman that comes on. I continue to read, calmed by the music.

"I might as well get to the point, Papa, because for all I know you're so mad you tore up this letter without even reading it. The point is that Mor and I are going to have a baby. Please, please don't throw this into the disintegrator. It's due in July, which gives you over three months to plan the trip up here. We have a lovely house, with a guest room that you and Mama can stay in for as long as you want."

I have to stop here to interject a couple of questions, since my daughter never had a head for logic and it's my strong point.

First of all, if she were in front of me in person right now I would ask right off what means "Mor and I are going to have a baby." Which? Or both? The second thing is, when she refers to it as "it" is she being literal or just uncertain? And just one more thing and then I'm through for good: Just how lovely can a guest room be that has all the air piped in and you can't even see the sky or take a walk on the grass because there is no grass, only simulated this and substituted that?

All the above notwithstanding, I continue to read:

"By the way, Papa, there's something I'm not sure you understand. Mor, you may or may not know, is as human as you and me, in all the important ways—and frankly a bit more intelligent."

I put down the letter for a minute just to give the goosebumps a chance to fly out of my stomach ulcers before I go on with her love and best and kisses and hopes for seeing us soon, Lorinda.

I don't know how she manages it, but the second I'm finished, Sadie is out of the bedroom and breathing hard.

"Well, do I start packing or do I start packing? And when I start packing, do I pack for us or do I pack for me?"

"Never. I should die three thousand deaths, each one with a worse prognosis."

It's a shame a company like Interplanetary Aviation can't afford, with the fares they charge, to give you a comfortable seat. Don't ask how I ever got there in the first place. Ask my wife—she's the one with the mouth. First of all, they only allow you three pounds of luggage, which if you're only bringing clothes is plenty, but we had a few gifts with us. We were only planning to stay a few days and to sublet the house was Sadie's idea, not mine.

The whole trip was supposed to take a month, each way. This is one reason Sadie thought it was impractical to stay for the weekend and then go home, which was the condition on which I'd agreed to go.

But now that we're on our way, I decide I might as well relax. I close my eyes and try to think of what the first meeting will be like.

"How." I put up my right hand in a gesture of friendship and trust. I reach into my pocket and offer him beads.

But even in my mind he looks at me blank, his naked pink antennas waving in the breeze like a worm's underwear. Then I realize there isn't any breeze where we're going. So they stop waving and wilt.

I look around in my mind. We're alone, the two of us, in the middle of a vast plain, me in my business suit and him in his green skin. The scene looks familiar, like something I had experienced, or read about. . . . "We'll meet at Philippi," I think, and stab him with my sword.

Only then am I able to catch a few winks.

The month goes by. When I begin to think I'll never remember how to use a fork, the loudspeaker is turned on and I hear this very smooth, modulated voice, the tranquilized tones of a psychiatrist sucking glycerine, telling us it's just about over, and we should expect a slight jolt upon landing.

That slight jolt starts my life going by so fast I'm missing all the good parts. But finally the ship is still and all you can hear are the wheezes and sighs of the engines—the sounds remind me of Sadie when she's winding down from a good argument. I look around. Everybody is very white. Sadie's five fingers are around my upper arm like a tourniquet.

"We're here," I tell her. "Do I get a hacksaw or can you manage it yourself?"

"Oh, my goodness." She loosens her grip. She really looks a mess —completely pale, not blinking, not even nagging.

I take her by the arm and steer her into customs. All the time I feel that she's a big piece of unwilling luggage I'm smuggling in. There's no cooperation at all in her feet and her eyes are going every which way.

"Sadie, shape up!"

"If you had a little more curiosity about the world you'd be a better person," she says tolerantly.

While we're waiting to be processed by a creature in a suit like ours who surprises me by talking English, I sneak a quick look around.

It's funny. If I didn't know where we are I'd think we're in the backyard. The ground stretches out pure green, and it's only from the leaflet they give you in the ship to keep your mind off the panic that I know it's 100 percent Acrispan we're looking at, not grass. The air we're getting smells good, too, like fresh-cut flowers, but not too sweet.

By the time I've had a good look and a breathe, what's-its-name is handing us back our passports with a button that says to keep Mars beautiful don't litter.

I won't tell you about the troubles we had getting to the house, or the misunderstanding about the tip, because to be honest I wasn't paying attention. But we do manage to make it to the right door, and considering that the visit was a surprise, I didn't really expect they would meet us at the airport. My daughter must have been peeking, though, because she's in front of us even before we have a chance to knock.

"Mother!" she says, looking very round in the stomach. She hugs and kisses Sadie, who starts bawling. Five minutes later, when they're out of the clinch, Lorinda turns to me, a little nervous.

You can say a lot of things about me, but basically I'm a warm person, and we're about to be guests in this house, even if she is a stranger to me. I shake her hand.

"Is he home, or is he out in the back yard, growing new leaves?"

Her face (or what I can see of it through the climate adapter) crumbles a little at the chin line, but she straightens it out and puts her hand on my shoulder.

"Mor had to go out, Daddy—something important came up—but he should be back in an hour or so. Come on, let's go inside."

Actually there's nothing too crazy about the house, or even interesting. It has walls, a floor and a roof, I'm glad to see, even a few relaxer chairs, and after the trip we just had, I sit down and relax. I notice my daughter is having a little trouble looking me straight in the face, which is only as it should be, and it isn't long before she and Sadie are discussing pregnancy, gravitational exercise, labor, hospitals, formulas and sleep-taught toilet training. When I'm starting to feel that I'm getting over-educated, I decide to go into the kitchen and make myself a bite to eat. I could have asked them for a little something but I don't want to interfere with their first conversation. Sadie has all engines going and is interrupting four times a sentence, which is exactly the kind of game they always had back home—my daughter's goal is to say one complete thought out loud. If Sadie doesn't spring back with a non sequitur, Lorinda wins that round. A full-fledged knockout with Sadie still champion is when my daughter can't get a sentence in for a week. Sometimes I can understand why she went to Mars.

Anyway, while they're at the height of their simultaneous mono-logues, I go quietly off to the kitchen to see what I can dig up. (Ripe parts of Mor, wrapped in plastic? Does he really regenerate, I wonder. Does Lorinda fully understand how he works, or one day will she make an asparagus omelet out of one of his appendages, only to learn that's the part that doesn't grow back? "Oh, I'm so *sorry,*" she says. "Can you ever forgive me?")

The refrigerator, though obsolete on Earth, is well stocked—fruits of a sort, steaks, it seems, small chicken-type things that might be stunted pigeons. There's a bowl of a brownish, creamy mess—I can't even bring myself to smell it. Who's hungry, anyway, I think. The rumbling in my stomach is the symptom of a father's love turning sour.

I wander into the bedroom. There's a large portrait of Mor hanging on the wall—or maybe his ancestor. Is it true that, instead of hearts, Martians have a large avocado pit? There's a rumor on Earth that when Martians get old they start to turn brown at the edges, like lettuce.

There's an object on the floor and I bend down and pick it up. A piece of material—at home I would have thought it was a man's handkerchief. Maybe it is a handkerchief. Maybe they have colds like us. They catch a germ, the sap rises to combat the infection, and they have to blow their stamens. I open up a drawer to put the piece of material in (I like to be neat), but when I close it, something gets stuck. Another thing I can't recognize. It's small, round and either concave or convex, depending on how you look at it. It's made of something black and shiny. A cloth bowl? What would a vegetable be doing with a cloth bowl? Some questions are too deep for me, but what I don't know I eventually find out—and not by asking, either.

I go back to the living room.

"Did you find anything to eat?" Lorinda asks. "Or would you like me to fix—"

"Don't even get up," Sadie says quickly. "I can find my way

around any kitchen, I don't care whose."

"I'm not hungry. It was a terrible trip. I thought I'd never wake up from it in one piece. By the way, I heard a good riddle on the ship. What's round and black, either concave or convex, depending on how you look at it, and made out of a shiny material?"

Lorinda blushed. "A skullcap? But that's not funny."

"So who needs funny? Riddles have to be a laugh a minute all of a sudden? You think Oedipus giggled all the way home from seeing the Sphinx?"

"Look, Daddy, I think there's something I should tell you."

"I think there are all sorts of things you should tell me."

"No, I mean about Mor."

"Who do you think *I* mean, the grocery boy? You elope with a cucumber from outer space and you want I should be satisfied because he's human in all the important ways? What's important —that he sneezes and hiccups? If you tell me he snores, I should be ecstatic? Maybe he sneezes when he's happy and hiccups when he's making love and snores because it helps him think better. Does that make him human?"

"Daddy, *please.*"

"Okay, not another word." Actually I'm starting to feel quite guilty. What if she has a miscarriage right on the spot? A man like me doesn't blithely torture a pregnant woman, even if she does happen to be his daughter. "What's so important it can't wait till later?"

"Nothing, I guess. Would you like some chopped liver? I just made some fresh."

"What?"

"Chopped liver—you know, chopped liver."

Oh yes, the ugly mess in the refrigerator. "You made it, that stuff in the bowl?"

"Sure. Daddy, there's something I really have to tell you."

She never does get to tell me, though, because her husband walks in, bold as brass.

I won't even begin to tell you what he looks like. Let me just say he's a good dream cooked up by Mary Shelley. I won't go into it, but if it gives you a small idea, I'll say that his head is shaped like an acorn on top of a stalk of broccoli. Enormous blue eyes, green skin and no hair at all except for a small blue round area on top of his head. His ears are adorable. Remember Dumbo the Elephant? Only a little smaller—I never exaggerate, even for effect. And he looks boneless, like a filet.

My wife, God bless her, I don't have to worry about; she's a gem in a crisis. One look at her son-in-law and she faints dead away. If I didn't know her better, if I wasn't absolutely certain that her simple mind contained no guile, I would have sworn she did it on purpose, to give everybody something to fuss about. Before we know what's happening, we're all in a tight, frantic conversation about what's the best way to bring her around. But while my daughter and her husband are in the bathroom looking for some deadly chemical, Sadie opens both eyes at once and stares up at me from the floor.

"What did I miss?"

"You didn't miss anything—you were only unconscious for fifteen seconds. It was a cat nap, not a coma."

"Say hello, Hector. Say hello to him or so help me I'll close my eyes for good."

"I'm very glad to meet you, Mr. Trumbnick," he says. I'm grateful that he's sparing me the humiliation of making the first gesture, but I pretend I don't see the stalk he's holding out.

"Smutual," I say.

"I beg your pardon?"

"Smutual. How are you? You look better than your pictures." He does, too. Even though his skin is green, it looks like the real thing up close. But his top lip sort of vibrates when he talks, and I can hardly bear to look at him except sideways.

"I hear you had some business this afternoon. My daughter never did tell me what your line is, uh, Morton."

"Daddy, his name is Mor. Why don't you call him Mor?"

"Because I prefer Morton. When we know each other better I'll call him something less formal. Don't rush me, Lorinda; I'm still getting adjusted to the chopped liver."

My son-in-law chuckles and his top lip really goes crazy. "Oh, were you surprised? Imported meats aren't a rarity here, you know. Just the other day one of my clients was telling me about an all-Earth meal he had at home."

"Your client?" Sadie asks. "You wouldn't happen to be a law-yer?" (My wife amazes me with her instant familiarity. She could live with a tyrannosaurus in perfect harmony. First she faints, and while she's out cold everything in her head that was strange becomes ordinary and she wakes up a new woman.)

"No, Mrs. Trumbnick. I'm a—"

"—rabbi, of course," she finishes. "I knew it. The minute Hector found that skullcap I knew it. Him and his riddles. A skullcap is a skullcap and nobody not Jewish would dare wear one—not even a Martian." She bites her lip but recovers like a pro. "I'll bet you were out on a bar mitzvah—right?"

"No, as a matter of fact—"

"—a Bris. I knew it."

She's rubbing her hands together and beaming at him. "A Bris, how *nice*. But why didn't you tell us, Lorinda? Why would you keep such a thing a secret?"

Lorinda comes over to me and kisses me on the cheek, and I wish she wouldn't because I'm feeling myself go soft and I don't want to show it.

"Mor isn't *just* a rabbi, Daddy. He converted because of me and then found there was a demand among the colonists. But he's never given up his own beliefs, and part of his job is to minister to the Kopchopees who camp outside the village. That's where he was earlier, conducting a Kopchopee menopausal rite."

"A what!"

"Look, to each his own," says my wife with the open mind. But me, I want facts, and this is getting more bizarre by the minute.

"Kopchopee. He's a Kopchopee priest to his own race and a rabbi to ours, and that's how he makes his living? You don't feel there's a contradiction between the two, Morton?"

"That's right. They both pray to a strong silent god, in different ways of course. The way my race worships, for instance—"

"Listen, it takes all kinds," says Sadie.

"And the baby, whatever it turns out to be—will it be a Choptapi or a Jew?"

"Jew, shmoo," Sadie says with a wave of dismissal. "All of a sudden it's Hector the Pious—such a megilla out of a molehill." She turns away from me and addresses herself to the others, like I've just become invisible. "He hasn't seen the inside of a synagogue since we got married—what a rain that night—and now he can't take his shoes off in a house until he knows its race, color and creed." With a face full of fury, she brings me back into her sight. "Nudnick, what's got into you?"

I stand up straight to preserve my dignity. "If you'll excuse me, my things are getting wrinkled in the suitcase."

Sitting on my bed (with my shoes on), I must admit I'm feeling a little different. Not that Sadie made me change my mind. Far from it; for many years now her voice is the white sound that lets me think my own thoughts. But what I'm realizing more and more is that in a situation like this a girl needs her father, and what kind of a man is it who can't sacrifice his personal feelings for his only daughter? When she was going out with Herbie the Hemophiliac and came home crying it had to end because she was afraid to touch him, he might bleed, didn't I say pack your things, we're going to Grossingers Venus for three weeks? When my twin brother Max went into kitchen sinks, who was it that helped him out at only four percent? Always, I stood ready to help my family. And if Lorinda ever needed me, it's now when she's pregnant by some religious maniac. Okay—he makes me retch, so I'll talk to him with a tissue over my mouth. After all, in a world that's getting smaller all the time, it's people like me who have to be bigger to make up for it, no?

I go back to the living room and extend my hand to my son-in-law the cauliflower. (Feh.)

AVRAM DAVIDSON

Goslin Day

In Yiddish gozlin *means thief or swindler—a non-professional* gonif. *But what about* goslins *(with an "s") that flicker-snicker and nimblesnitch and create havoc with pious people on hotsticky days, that swim in dusty mirrors and wait for propitious moments to escape through the cracks and swindle, thieve, and connive?*

Kabbalah has provided the mystical soil to grow monsters. It is the crick in the back of rationalistic Jewish thought, a diamondfind of magic, lore, divination, supernal tastes and speculations, and superstition. It is an attempt to achieve mystic unity with God and master (or at least foil) those evil spirits that would stand in the way of the Kabbalists. By offering hope of magical intervention, it assuaged and strengthened countless persecuted Jews from the spirit-withering attacks of the pogrom and the ever-present threat of expulsion.

Manipulation of Hebrew words and numbers—numerology, gematria, noutricon, anagrams, acrostics—became magical tools to divine the secret names of angels, and thus gain limited power over them. The Kabbalistic sorcerer has access to pantheons of angels and evil spirits, to intervening worlds such as Yetzirah— *where the ten orders of angels can be found—and the dead, imperfect worlds that are the sources of evil. God created these imperfect worlds, so Kabbalists tell, and then destroyed them—but not completely, for God's works could not be totally destroyed, only changed.*

From one of these dead worlds come goslin thieves and schemers, swimming and splashing in that darkest part of the subcon-

scious landscape. They are all the hobgoblins and things that go bump in the night come true. They are the sometime shapes we see with peripheral vision, the monsters that hide behind us when we're alone.

J. D.

*

IT WAS A GOSLIN day, no doubt about it; of course it can happen that goslin things can occur, say, once a day for many days. But *this* day was a *goslin* day. From the hour when, properly speaking, the ass brays in his stall, but here instead the kat kvells on the rooftop—to the hour when the cock crows on his roost, but here instead the garbageman bangs on his can—even that early, Faroly realized that it was going to be a goslin day (night? let be night: *It was* evening, *and* [after that] *it was morning: one day.* Yes or no?). In the warbled agony of the shriekscream Faroly had recognized an element present which was more than the usual ketzelkat expression of its painpleasure syndrome. In the agglutinative obscenities which interrupted the bang-crashes of the yuckels emptying eggshells orangerinds coffeegrounds there was (this morning, different from all other mornings) something unlike their mere usual brute pleasure in waking the dead. Faroly sighed. His wife and child were still asleep. He saw the dimlight already creeping in, sat up, reached for the glass and saucer and poured water over his nails, began to whisper his preliminary prayers, already concentrating on his Intention in the name *Unity:* but aware, aware, aware, the hotsticky feeling in the air, the swimmy looks in the dusty corners of windows, mirrors; something a tension, here a twitch and there a twitch. Notgood notgood.

In short: a goslin day.

Faroly decided to seek an expert opinion, went to Crown Heights to consult the kabbalist, Kaplánovics.

Rabbaness Kaplánovics was at the stove, schauming off the soup with an enormous spoon, gestured with a free elbow toward an inner room. There sat the sage, the sharp one, the teacher of our teachers, on his head his beaver hat neatly brushed, on his feet and legs his boots brightly polished, in between his garments well and clean without a fleck or stain as befits a disciple of the wise. He and Faroly shook hands, greeted, blessed the Name. Kaplánovics pushed across several sheets of paper covered with an exquisitely neat calligraphy.

"Already there," the kabbalist said. "I have been through everything three times, twice. The *NY Times*, the *Morgen Dzshornal*, I. F. Stone, Dow-Jones, the *Daph-Yomi*, your name-Text, the weather report, Psalm of the Day. Everything is worked out, by numerology, analogy, gematria, noutricon, anagrams, allegory, procession and precession. So.

"Of course today as any everyday we must await the coming of the Messiah: 'await'—*expect? today?* not today. Today he wouldn't come. Considerations for atmospheric changes, or changes for atmospheric considerations, *not—bad. Not—bad.* Someone gives you an offer for a good air-conditioner, cheap, you could think about it. Read seven capitals of psalms between afternoon and evening prayers. One sequence is enough. The day is favorable for decisions on growth stocks, but avoid closed-end mutual funds. On the corner by the beygal store is an old woman with a pyshka, collecting dowries for orphan girls in Jerusalem: the money, she never sends, this is *her* sin, it's no concern of yours: give her eighteen cents, a very auspicious number: merit, cheaply bought (she has sugar diabetes and the daughter last week gave birth to a weak-headed child by a schwartzer), what else?" They examined the columns of characters.

"Ahah. Ohoh. If you get a chance to buy your house, don't buy it, the Regime will condemn it for a freeway, where are they all *going* so fast?—every man who has two legs thinks he needs three automobiles—besides—where did I write it? oh yes. There. The neighborhood is going to change very soon and if you stay you will be killed in three years and two months, or three months and two years, depending on which system of gematria is used in calculating. You have to warn your brother-in-law his sons should each commence bethinking a marriagematch. Otherwise they will be going to cinemas and watching televisions and putting arms around girls, won't have the proper intentions for their nighttime prayers, won't even read the protective psalms selected by the greatgrandson of the Baalshemtov: and with what results, my dear man? Nocturnal emissions and perhaps worse; is it for nothing that The Chapters of the Principles caution us, 'At age eighteen to the marriage canopy and the performance of good deeds,' hm?"

Faroly cleared his throat. "Something else is on your mind," said the kabbalist. "Speak. Speak." Faroly confessed his concern about goslins. Kaplánovics exclaimed, struck the table. "Goslins! You wanted to talk about goslins? It's already gone past the hour to say the Shema, and I certainly didn't have in mind when I said it to commence constructing a kaméa—" He clicked his tongue in annoyance. "Am I omniscient?" he demanded. "Why didn't you let me know you were coming? Man walks in off the street, expects to find—"

But it did not take long to soothe and smooth him—Who is strong? He who can control his own passion.

And now to first things first, or, in this case, last things first, for it was the most recent manifestation of goslinness which Faroly wished to talk about. The kabbalist listened politely but did not seem in agreement with nor impressed by his guest's recitation of the signs by which a goslin day might make itself known. " 'Show simônim,' " he murmured, with a polite nod. "This one loses an object, that one finds it, let the claimant come and 'show simônim,' let him cite the signs by which his knowledge is demonstrated, and, hence, his ownership . . ." But this was mere polite fumfutting, and Faroly knew that the other knew that both knew it.

On Lexington a blackavised goslin slipped out from a nexus of cracked mirrors reflecting dust at each other in a disused nightclub, snatched a purse from a young woman emerging from a ribs joint; in Bay Ridge another, palepink and blond, snatched a purse

from an *old* woman right in front of Suomi Evangelical Lutheran.
Both goslins flickersnickered and were sharply gone. In Totten-
ville, a third one materialized in the bedroom of an honest young
woman still half asleep in bed just a second before her husband
came back from the nightshift in Elizabeth, New Jersey; uttered
a goslin cry and jumped out the window holding his shirt. Naturally the husband never believed her—would *you?* Two more
slipped in and out of a crucial street corner on the troubled bor-
dermarches of Italian Harlem, pausing only just long enough to
exchange exclamations of *guineabastard! goddamnigger!* and goslin looks out of the corners of their goslin eyes. Goslin cabdrivers
curseshouted at hotsticky pregnant women dumb enough to try
and cross at pedestrian crossings. The foul air grew fouler, thicker,
hotter, tenser, muggier, murkier: and the goslins, smelling it from
afar, came leapsniffing through the vimveil to nimblesnitch, torment, buffet, burden, uglylook, poke, makestumble, maltreat, and
quickshmiggy back again to gezzle guzzle goslinland.

The kabbalist had grown warm in discussion, eagerly inscribed
circles in the air with downhooked thumb apart from fist, " '. . .
they have the forms of men and also they have the lusts of men,' "
he quoted.

"You are telling me what every schoolchild knows," protested
Faroly. "But from *which* of the other three of the four worlds of
Emanation, Creation, Formation, and Effectation—from *which*
do they come? And why more often, and more and more often,
and more and more and more often, and—"

Face wrinkled to emphasize the gesture of waving these words
away, Kaplánovics said, "If Yesod goes, how can Hod remain? If
there is no Malchuth, how can there be Qether? Thus one throws
away with the hand the entire configuration of Adam Qadmon,
the Tree of Life, the Ancient of Days. Men tamper with the very
vessels themselves, as if they don't know what happened with the
Bursting of the Vessels before, as though the Husks, the Shards,
even a single shattered Cortex, doesn't still plague and vex and
afflict us to this day. They look down into the Abyss, and they say,

'This is high,' and they look up to an Eminence and they say, 'This is low.' . . . And not thus alone! And not thus alone! Not just with complex deenim, as, for example, those concerning the fluxes of women—no! no! But the simplest of the simple of the Six Hundred and Thirteen Commandments: to place a parapet around a roof to keep someone from falling off and be killed. What can be simpler? What can be more obvious? What can be easier?

"—but do they do it? What, was it only three weeks ago, or four? a Puertorican boy didn't fall off the roof of an apartment house near here? Dead, perished. Go talk to the wall. Men don't want to know. Talk to them *Ethics,* talk to them *Brotherhood,* talk to them *Ecumenical Dialogue,* talk to them any kind of nonsenseness: they'll listen. But talk to them: It's written, textually, in the Torah, to build a parapet around your rooftop to prevent blood being shed—no: to this they won't listen. They would neither hear nor understand. They don't know *Torah,* don't know *Text,* don't know *parapet; roof*—this they never heard of either—"

He paused. "Come tomorrow and I'll have prepared for you a kaméa against goslins." He seemed suddenly weary.

Faroly got up. Sighed. "And tomorrow will you also have prepared a kaméa against goslins for everyone else?"

Kaplánovics didn't raise his eyes. "Don't blame the rat," he said. "Blame the rat-hole."

Downstairs Faroly noticed a boy in a green and white skullcap, knotted crispadin coming up from inside under his shirt to dangle over his pants. "Let me try a sortilegy," he thought to himself. "Perhaps it will give me some remez, or hint . . ." Aloud, he asked, "Youngling, tell me, what text did you learn today in school?"

The boy stopped twisting one of his stroobley earlocks, and turned up his phlegm-green eyes. " 'Three things take a man out of this world,' " he yawned. " 'Drinking in the morning, napping in the noon, and putting a girl on a winebarrel to find out if she's a virgin.' "

Faroly clicked his tongue, fumbled for a handkerchief to wipe his heatprickled face. "You are mixing up the texts," he said.

The boy raised his eyebrows, pursed his lips, stuck out his lower jaw. "Oh indeed. You ask me a question, then you give me an answer. How do you know I'm mixing up the texts? Maybe I cited a text which you never heard before. What are you, the Vilna Gaon?"

"Brazen face—look, look, how you've gotten your crispadin all snarled," Faroly said, slightly amused, fingering the cinctures passed through one belt-loop—then, feeling his own horrified amazement and, somehow, *knowing . . . knowing . . .* as one *knows* the refrigerator is going to stop humming one half second before it does stop, yet—"What is this? What is this? The cords of your crispadin are tied in *pairs?*"

The filthgreen eyes slid to their corners, still holding Faroly's. "Hear, O Israel," chanted the child; "the Lord our God, the Lord is Two."

The man's voice came out agonyshrill. "Dualist. Heresiarch. Sectary. Ah. Ah ah *ah—goslin!*"

"Take ya hands outa my pants!" shrieked the pseudo-child, and, with a cry of almost totally authentic fear, fled. Faroly, seeing people stop, faces changing, flung up his arms and ran for his life. The goslin-child, wailing and slobbering, trampled up steps into an empty hallway where the prismatic edge of a broken windowpane caught the sunlight and winkyflashed rainbow changes. The goslin stretched thin as a shadow and vanished into the bright edge of the shard.

Exhausted, all but prostrated by the heat, overcome with humiliation, shame, tormented with fear and confusion, Faroly stumbled through the door of his home. His wife stood there, looking at him. He held to the doorpost, too weary even to raise his hand to kiss the mazuzah, waiting for her to exclaim at his appearance. But she said nothing. He opened his mouth, heard his voice click in his throat. "Solomon," his wife said. He moved slowly into the room. "Solomon," she said.

"Listen—"

"Solomon, we were in the park, and at first it was so hot, then we sat under a tree and it was so *cool*—"

"Listen . . ."

". . . I think I must have fallen asleep . . . Solomon, you're so quiet. . . . Now you're home, I can give the Heshy his bath. Look at him, Solomon! Look, look!"

Already things were beginning to get better. *"And the High Priest shall pray for the peace of himself and his house.* Tanya Rabbanan:—*and his house.* This means, his wife. He who has no wife, has no home." Small sighs, stifled sobs, little breaks of breath, Faroly moved forward into the apartment. Windows and mirrors were still, dark, quiet. The goslin day was almost over. She had the baby ready for the bath. Faroly moved his eyes, squinting against the last sunlight, to look at the flesh of his first born, unique son, his Kaddish. What child was this, sallow, squinting back, scrannel, preternaturally sly—? Faroly heard his own voice screaming screaming changeling! changeling!

—Goslin!

ROBERT SILVERBERG

The Dybbuk of Mazel Tov IV

The Diaspora (exile) has become a thread of fear running through Jewish history and fiction. Born out of suffering, it has evolved into myth. It is the torn house of the wandering Jew, the voice of his modern fears, a synonym for his alienation.

Robert Silverberg gives flesh to the legend (a legend that history has recorded as terrible reality) and sets it afire once again. The story has an authenticity—an attention to detail and human reaction—that twists itself into satire, not the freewheeling, distorting satire of the fantast, but the satire of reflected history. Images of our mythical selves attend to their legends inside perfect mirrors turned this way and that. Another twist and the images unravel —myth is being used to dispel myth. Where, then, is the real Jew? Is that him there with his hopes, failings, prejudices, and pretensions? And where lies the glory of God? Is it in death's bright angels or a wink and a nod?

J. D.

EDITOR'S NOTE: *This is an original story written expressly for this volume.*

*

MY GRANDSON DAVID will have his bar mitzvah next spring. No one in our family has undergone that rite in at least three hundred years—certainly not since we Levins settled in Old Israel, the Israel on Earth, soon after the European Holocaust. My friend Eliahu asked me not long ago how I feel about David's bar mitzvah, whether the idea of it angers me, whether I see it as a disturbing element. No, I replied: the boy is a Jew, after all, let him have a bar mitzvah if he wants one. These are times of transition and upheaval, as all times are. David is not bound by the attitudes of his ancestors.

"Since when is a Jew not bound by the attitudes of his ancestors?" Eliahu asked.

"You know what I mean," I said.

Indeed he did. We are bound but yet free. If anything governs us out of the past it is the tribal bond itself, not the philosophies of our departed kinsmen. We accept what we choose to accept; nevertheless we remain Jews. I come from a family that has liked to say—especially to Gentiles—that we are Jews but not Jewish, that is, we acknowledge and cherish our ancient heritage but we do not care to entangle ourselves in outmoded rituals and folkways. This is what my forefathers declared, as far back as those secular-minded Levins who fought, three centuries ago, to win and guard the freedom of the land of Israel. (Old Israel, I mean.) I would say the same here, if there were any Gentiles on this world to whom such things had to be explained. But of course in this New Israel in the stars we have only ourselves, no Gentiles within a dozen light-years, unless you count our neighbors the Kunivaru as

Gentiles. (Can creatures that are not human rightly be called Gentiles? I'm not sure the term applies. Besides, the Kunivaru now insist that they are Jews. My mind spins. It's an issue of Talmudic complexity, and, God knows, I'm no Talmudist. Hillel, Akiva, Rashi, help me!) Anyway, come the fifth day of Sivan my son's son will have his bar mitzvah, and I'll play the proud grandpa as pious old Jews have done for six thousand years.

All things are connected. That my grandson would have a bar mitzvah is merely the latest link in a chain of events that goes back to—when? To the day the Kunivaru decided to embrace Judaism? To the day the dybbuk entered Seul the Kunivar? To the day we refugees from Earth discovered the fertile planet that we sometimes call New Israel and sometimes call Mazel Tov IV? To the day of the Final Pogrom on Earth? Reb Yossele the Hassid might say that David's bar mitzvah was determined on the day the Lord God fashioned Adam out of dust. But I think that would be overdoing things.

The day the dybbuk took possession of the body of Seul the Kunivar was probably where it really started. Until then things were relatively uncomplicated here. The Hassidim had their settlement, we Israelis had ours, and the natives, the Kunivaru, had the rest of the planet; and generally we all kept out of one another's way. After the dybbuk everything changed. It happened more than forty years ago, in the first generation after the Landing, on the ninth day of Tishri in the year 6302. I was working in the fields, for Tishri is a harvest month. The day was hot, and I worked swiftly, singing and humming. As I moved down the long rows of crackle-pods, tagging those that were ready to be gathered, a Kunivar appeared at the crest of the hill that overlooks our kibbutz. It seemed to be in some distress, for it came staggering and lurching down the hillside with extraordinary clumsiness, tripping over its own four legs as if it barely knew how to manage them. When it was about a hundred meters from me it cried out, "Shimon! Help me, Shimon! In God's name help me!"

There were several strange things about this outcry, and I perceived them gradually, the most trivial first. It seemed odd that a Kunivar would address me by my given name, for they are a formal people. It seemed more odd that a Kunivar would speak to me in quite decent Hebrew, for at that time none of them had learned our language. It seemed most odd of all—but I was slow to discern it—that a Kunivar would have the very voice, dark and resonant, of my dear dead friend Joseph Avneri.

The Kunivar stumbled into the cultivated part of the field and halted, trembling terribly. Its fine green fur was pasted into hummocks by perspiration and its great golden eyes rolled and crossed in a ghastly way. It stood flat-footed, splaying its legs out under the four corners of its chunky body like the legs of a table, and clasped its long powerful arms around its chest. I recognized the Kunivar as Seul, a sub-chief of the local village, with whom we of the kibbutz had had occasional dealings.

"What help can I give you?" I asked. "What has happened to you, Seul?"

"Shimon—Shimon—" A frightful moan came from the Kunivar. "Oh, God, Shimon, it goes beyond all belief! How can I bear this? How can I even comprehend it?"

No doubt of it. The Kunivar was speaking in the voice of Joseph Avneri.

"Seul?" I said hesitantly.

"My name is Joseph Avneri."

"Joseph Avneri died a year ago last Elul. I didn't realize you were such a clever mimic, Seul."

"Mimic? You speak to me of mimicry, Shimon? It's no mimicry. I am your Joseph, dead but still aware, thrown for my sins into this monstrous alien body. Are you Jew enough to know what a dybbuk is, Shimon?"

"A wandering ghost, yes, who takes possession of the body of a living being."

"I have become a dybbuk."

"There are no dybbuks. Dybbuks are phantoms out of medieval folklore," I said.

"You hear the voice of one."

"This is impossible," I said.

"I agree, Shimon, I agree." He sounded calmer now. "It's entirely impossible. I don't believe in dybbuks either, any more than I believe in Zeus, the Minotaur, werewolves, gorgons, or golems. But how else do you explain me?"

"You are Seul the Kunivar, playing a clever trick."

"Do you really think so? Listen to me, Shimon: I knew you when we were boys in Tiberias. I rescued you when we were fishing in the lake and our boat overturned. I was with you the day you met Leah whom you married. I was godfather to your son Yigal. I studied with you at the university in Jerusalem. I fled with you in the fiery days of the Final Pogrom. I stood watch with you aboard the Ark in the years of our flight from Earth. Do you remember, Shimon? Do you remember Jerusalem? The Old City, the Mount of Olives, the Tomb of Absalom, the Western Wall? Am I a Kunivar, Shimon, to know of the Western Wall?"

"There is no survival of consciousness after death," I said stubbornly.

"A year ago I would have agreed with you. But who am I if I am not the spirit of Joseph Avneri? How can you account for me any other way? Dear God, do you think I *want* to believe this, Shimon? You know what a scoffer I was. But it's real."

"Perhaps I'm having a very vivid hallucination."

"Call the others, then. If ten people have the same hallucination, is it still a hallucination? Be reasonable, Shimon! Here I stand before you, telling you things that only I could know, and you deny that I am—"

"Be reasonable?" I said. "Where does reason enter into this? Do you expect me to believe in ghosts, Joseph, in wandering demons, in dybbuks? Am I some superstition-ridden peasant out of the Polish woods? Is this the Middle Ages?"

"You called me Joseph," he said quietly.

"I can hardly call you Seul when you speak in that voice."

"Then you believe in me!"

"No."

"Look, Shimon, did you ever know a bigger skeptic than Joseph Avneri? I had no use for the Torah, I said Moses was fictional, I ploughed the fields on Yom Kippur, I laughed in God's nonexistent face. What is life, I said? And I answered: a mere accident, a transient biological phenomenon. Yet here I am. I remember the moment of my death. For a full year I've wandered this world, bodiless, perceiving things, unable to communicate. And today I find myself cast into this creature's body, and I know myself for a dybbuk. If *I* believe, Shimon, how can you dare disbelieve? In the name of our friendship, have faith in what I tell you!"

"You have actually become a dybbuk?"

"I have become a dybbuk," he said.

I shrugged. "Very well, Joseph. You're a dybbuk. It's madness, but I believe." I stared in astonishment at the Kunivar. Did I believe? Did I believe that I believed? How could I not believe? There was no other way for the voice of Joseph Avneri to be coming from the throat of a Kunivar. Sweat streamed down my body. I was face to face with the impossible, and all my philosophy was shattered. Anything was possible now. God might appear as a burning bush. The sun might stand still. No, I told myself. Believe only one irrational thing at a time, Shimon. Evidently there are dybbuks; well, then, there are dybbuks. But everything else pertaining to the Invisible World remains unreal until it manifests itself.

I said, "Why do you think this has happened to you?"

"It could only be as a punishment."

"For what, Joseph?"

"My experiments. You knew I was doing research into the Kunivaru metabolism, didn't you?"

"Yes, certainly. But—"

"Did you know I performed surgical experiments on live Kunivaru in our hospital? That I used patients, without informing them or anyone else, in studies of a forbidden kind? It was vivisection, Shimon."

"*What?*"

"There were things I needed to know, and there was only one way I could discover them. The hunger for knowledge led me into sin. I told myself that these creatures were ill, that they would shortly die anyway, and that it might benefit everyone if I opened them while they still lived, you see? Besides, they weren't human beings, Shimon, they were only animals, very intelligent animals, true, but still only—"

"No, Joseph. I can believe in dybbuks more readily than I can believe this. You, doing such a thing? My calm rational friend, my scientist, my wise one?" I shuddered and stepped a few paces back from him. "Auschwitz!" I cried. "Buchenwald! Dachau! Do those names mean anything to you? 'They weren't human beings,' the Nazi surgeon said, 'they were only Jews, and our need for scientific knowledge is such that—' That was only three hundred years ago, Joseph. And you, a Jew, a Jew of all people, to—"

"I know, Shimon, I know. Spare me the lecture. I sinned terribly, and for my sins I've been given this grotesque body, this gross, hideous, heavy body, these four legs which I can hardly coordinate, this crooked spine, this foul hot furry pelt. I still don't believe in a God, Shimon, but I think I believe in some sort of compensating force that balances accounts in this universe, and the account has been balanced for me, oh, yes, Shimon! I've had six hours of terror and loathing today such as I never dreamed could be experienced. To enter this body, to fry in this heat, to wander these hills trapped in such a mass of flesh, to feel myself being bombarded with the sensory perceptions of a being so alien—it's been hell, I tell you that without exaggeration. I would have died of shock in the first ten minutes if I didn't already happen to be dead. Only now, seeing you, talking to you, do I begin to get control of myself. Help me, Shimon."

"What do you want me to do?"

"Get me out of here. This is torment. I'm a dead man; I'm entitled to rest the way the other dead ones rest. Free me, Shimon."

"How?"

"How? How? Do I know? Am I an expert on dybbuks? Must I direct my own exorcism? If you knew what an effort it is simply to hold this body upright, to make its tongue form Hebrew words, to say things in a way you'll understand—" Suddenly the Kunivar sagged to his knees, a slow, complex folding process that reminded me of the manner in which the camels of Old Earth lowered themselves to the ground. The alien creature began to sputter and moan and wave his arms about; foam appeared on his wide rubbery lips. "God in Heaven, Shimon," Joseph cried, "set me free!"

I called for my son Yigal and he came running swiftly from the far side of the fields, a lean healthy boy, only eleven years old but already long-legged, strong-bodied. Without going into details I indicated the suffering Kunivar and told Yigal to get help from the kibbutz. A few minutes later he came back leading seven or eight men—Abrasha, Itzhak, Uri, Nahum, and some others. It took the full strength of all of us to lift the Kunivar into the hopper of a harvesting machine and transport him to our hospital. Two of the doctors—Moshe Shiloah and someone else—began to examine the stricken alien, and I sent Yigal to the Kunivaru village to tell the chief that Seul had collapsed in our fields.

The doctors quickly diagnosed the problem as a case of heat prostration. They were discussing the sort of injection the Kunivar should receive when Joseph Avneri, breaking a silence that had lasted since Seul had fallen, announced his presence within the Kunivar's body. Uri and Nahum had remained in the hospital room with me; not wanting this craziness to become general knowledge in the kibbutz, I took them outside and told them to forget whatever ravings they had heard. When I returned, the doctors were busy with their preparations and Joseph was patiently explaining to them that he was a dybbuk who had involuntarily taken possession of the Kunivar. "The heat has driven the poor creature insane," Moshe Shiloah murmured, and rammed a huge needle into one of Seul's thighs.

"Make them listen to me," Joseph said.

"You know that voice," I told the doctors. "Something very unusual has happened here."

But they were no more willing to believe in dybbuks than they were in rivers that flow uphill. Joseph continued to protest, and the doctors continued methodically to fill Seul's body with sedatives and restoratives and other potions. Even when Joseph began to speak of last year's kibbutz gossip—who had been sleeping with whom behind whose back, who had illicitly been peddling goods from the community storehouse to the Kunivaru—they paid no attention. It was as though they had so much difficulty believing that a Kunivar could speak Hebrew that they were unable to make sense out of what he was saying, and took Joseph's words to be Seul's delirium. Suddenly Joseph raised his voice for the first time, calling out in a loud, angry tone, "You, Moshe Shiloah! Aboard the Ark I found you in bed with the wife of Teviah Kohn, remember? Would a Kunivar have known such a thing?"

Moshe Shiloah gasped, reddened, and dropped his hypodermic. The other doctor was nearly as astonished.

"What is this?" Moshe Shiloah asked. "How can this be?"

"Deny me now!" Joseph roared. "Can you deny me?"

The doctors faced the same problems of acceptance that I had had, that Joseph himself had grappled with. We were all of us rational men in this kibbutz, and the supernatural had no place in our lives. But there was no arguing the phenomenon away. There was the voice of Joseph Avneri emerging from the throat of Seul the Kunivar, and the voice was saying things that only Joseph would have said, and Joseph had been dead more than a year. Call it a dybbuk, call it hallucination, call it anything: Joseph's presence could not be ignored.

Locking the door, Moshe Shiloah said to me, "We must deal with this somehow."

Tensely we discussed the situation. It was, we agreed, a delicate and difficult matter. Joseph, raging and tortured, demanded to be exorcised and allowed to sleep the sleep of the dead; unless we placated him, he would make us all suffer. In his pain, in his fury, he might say anything, he might reveal everything he knew about our private lives; a dead man is beyond all of society's rules of common decency. We could not expose ourselves to that. But what could we do about him? Chain him in an outbuilding and hide him in solitary confinement? Hardly. Unhappy Joseph deserved better of us than that; and there was Seul to consider, poor supplanted Seul, the dybbuk's unwilling host. We could not keep a Kunivar in the kibbutz, imprisoned or free, even if his body did house the spirit of one of our own people, nor could we let the shell of Seul go back to the Kunivaru village with Joseph as a furious passenger trapped inside. What to do? Separate soul from body, somehow: restore Seul to wholeness and send Joseph to the limbo of the dead. But how? There was nothing in the standard pharmacopoeia about dybbuks. What to do? What to do?

I sent for Shmarya Asch and Yakov Ben-Zion, who headed the kibbutz council that month, and for Shlomo Feig, our rabbi, a shrewd and sturdy man, very unorthodox in his Orthodoxy, almost as secular as the rest of us. They questioned Joseph Avneri extensively, and he told them the whole tale, his scandalous secret experiments, his postmortem year as a wandering spirit, his sudden painful incarnation within Seul. At length Shmarya Asch turned to Moshe Shiloah and snapped, "There must be some therapy for such a case."

"I know of none."

"This is schizophrenia," said Shmarya Asch in his firm, dogmatic way. "There are cures for schizophrenia. There are drugs, there are electric shock treatments, there are—you know these things better than I, Moshe."

"This is not schizophrenia," Moshe Shiloah retorted. "This is a case of demonic possession. I have no training in treating such maladies."

"Demonic possession?" Shmarya bellowed. "Have you lost your mind?"

"Peace, peace, all of you," Shlomo Feig said, as everyone began to shout at once. The rabbi's voice cut sharply through the tumult and silenced us all. He was a man of great strength, physical as well

as moral, to whom the entire kibbutz inevitably turned for guid-
ance although there was virtually no one among us who observed
the major rites of Judaism. He said, "I find this as hard to comprehend as any of you. But the evidence triumphs over my skepticism. How can we deny that Joseph Avneri has returned as a
dybbuk? Moshe, you know no way of causing this intruder to leave
the Kunivar's body?"

"None," said Moshe Shiloah.

"Maybe the Kunivaru themselves know a way," Yakov Ben-Zion
suggested.

"Exactly," said the rabbi. "My next point. These Kunivaru are
a primitive folk. They live closer to the world of magic and witchcraft, of demons and spirits, than we do whose minds are schooled
in the habits of reason. Perhaps such cases of possession occur
often among them. Perhaps they have techniques for driving out
unwanted spirits. Let us turn to them, and let them cure their
own."

Before long Yigal arrived, bringing with him six Kunivaru, including Gyaymar, the village chief. They wholly filled the little
hospital room, bustling around in it like a delegation of huge furry
centaurs; I was oppressed by the acrid smell of so many of them
in one small space, and although they had always been friendly to
us, never raising an objection when we appeared as refugees to
settle on their planet, I felt fear of them now as I had never felt
before. Clustering about Seul, they asked questions of him in their
own supple language, and when Joseph Avneri replied in Hebrew
they whispered things to each other unintelligible to us. Then,
unexpectedly, the voice of Seul broke through, speaking in halting
spastic monosyllables that revealed the terrible shock his nervous
system must have received; then the alien faded and Joseph Avneri spoke once more with the Kunivar's lips, begging forgiveness,
asking for release.

Turning to Gyaymar, Shlomo Feig said, "Have such things happened on this world before?"

"Oh, yes, yes," the chief replied. "Many times. When one of us dies having a guilty soul, repose is denied, and the spirit may undergo strange migrations before forgiveness comes. What was the nature of this man's sin?"

"It would be difficult to explain to one who is not Jewish," said the rabbi hastily, glancing away. "The important question is whether you have a means of undoing what has befallen the unfortunate Seul, whose sufferings we all lament."

"We have a means, yes," said Gyaymar the chief.

The six Kunivaru hoisted Seul to their shoulders and carried him from the kibbutz; we were told that we might accompany them, if we cared to do so. I went along, and Moshe Shiloah, and Shmarya Asch, and Yakov Ben-Zion, and the rabbi, and perhaps some others. The Kunivaru took their comrade not to their village but to a meadow several kilometers to the east, down in the direction of the place where the Hassidim lived. Not long after the Landing the Kunivaru had let us know that the meadow was sacred to them, and none of us had ever entered it.

It was a lovely place, green and moist, a gently sloping basin crisscrossed by a dozen cool little streams. Depositing Seul beside one of the streams, the Kunivaru went off into the woods bordering the meadow to gather firewood and herbs. We remained close by Seul. "This will do no good," Joseph Avneri muttered more than once. "A waste of time, a foolish expense of energy." Three of the Kunivaru started to build a bonfire. Two sat nearby, shredding the herbs, making heaps of leaves, stems, roots. Gradually more of their kind appeared, until the meadow was filled with them; it seemed that the whole village, some four hundred Kunivaru, was turning out to watch or to participate in the rite. Many of them carried musical instruments, trumpets and drums, rattles and clappers, lyres, lutes, small harps, percussive boards, wooden flutes, everything intricate and fanciful of design; we had not suspected such cultural complexity. The priests—I assume they were priests, Kunivaru of stature and dignity—wore ornate ceremonial helmets and heavy golden mantles of sea-beast fur. The ordinary townsfolk carried ribbons and streamers, bits of bright fabric, polished mirrors of stone, and other ornamental devices. When he saw how elaborate a function it was going to be, Moshe Shiloah, an amateur anthropologist at heart, ran back to the kibbutz to fetch camera and recorder. He returned, breathless, just as the rite commenced.

And a glorious rite it was: incense, a grandly blazing bonfire, the pungent fragrance of freshly picked herbs, some heavy-footed quasi-orgiastic dancing, and a choir punching out harsh, sharp-edged arhythmic melodies. Gyaymar and the high priest of the village performed an elegant antiphonal chant, uttering long curling intertwining melismas and sprinkling Seul with a sweet-smelling pink fluid out of a baroquely carved wooden censer. Never have I beheld such stirring pageantry. But Joseph's gloomy prediction was correct; it was all entirely useless. Two hours of intensive exorcism had no effect. When the ceremony ended—the ultimate punctuation marks were five terrible shouts from the high priest —the dybbuk remained firmly in possession of Seul. "You have not conquered me," Joseph declared in a bleak tone.

Gyaymar said, "It seems we have no power to command an Earthborn soul."

"What will we do now?" demanded Yakov Ben-Zion of no one in particular. "Our science and their witchcraft both fail."

Joseph Avneri pointed toward the east, toward the village of the Hassidim, and murmured something indistinct.

"No!" cried Rabbi Shlomo Feig, who stood closest to the dybbuk at that moment.

"What did he say?" I asked.

"It was nothing," the rabbi said. "It was foolishness. The long ceremony has left him fatigued, and his mind wanders. Pay no attention."

I moved nearer to my old friend. "Tell me, Joseph."

"I said," the dybbuk replied slowly, "that perhaps we should send for the Baal Shem."

"Foolishness!" said Shlomo Feig, and spat.

"Why this anger?" Shmarya Asch wanted to know. "You, Rabbi

Shlomo, you were one of the first to advocate employing Kunivaru sorcerers in this business. You gladly bring in alien witch doctors, rabbi, and grow angry when someone suggests that your fellow Jew be given a chance to drive out the demon? Be consistent, Shlomo!"

Rabbi Shlomo's strong face grew mottled with rage. It was strange to see this calm, even-tempered man becoming so excited. "I will have nothing to do with Hassidim!" he exclaimed.

"I think this is a matter of professional rivalries," Moshe Shiloah commented.

The rabbi said, "To give recognition to all that is most superstitious in Judaism, to all that is most irrational and grotesque and outmoded and medieval? No! No!"

"But dybbuks *are* irrational and grotesque and outmoded and medieval," said Joseph Avneri. "Who better to exorcise one than a rabbi whose soul is still rooted in ancient beliefs?"

"I forbid this!" Shlomo Feig sputtered. "If the Baal Shem is summoned I will—I will—"

"Rabbi," Joseph said, shouting now, "this is a matter of my tortured soul against your offended spiritual pride. Give way! Give way! Get me the Baal Shem!"

"I refuse!"

"Look!" called Yakov Ben-Zion. The dispute had suddenly become academic. Uninvited, our Hassidic cousins were arriving at the sacred meadow, a long procession of them, eerie prehistoric-looking figures clad in their traditional long black robes, wide-brimmed hats, heavy beards, dangling side-locks, and at the head of the group marched their tzaddik, their holy man, their prophet, their leader, Reb Shmuel the Baal Shem.

It was certainly never our idea to bring Hassidim with us when we fled out of the smouldering ruins of the Land of Israel. Our intention was to leave Earth and all its sorrows far behind, to start anew on another world where we could at last build an enduring Jewish homeland, free for once of our eternal Gentile enemies and free, also, of the religious fanatics among our own kind whose presence had long been a drain on our vitality. We needed no mystics, no ecstatics, no weepers, no moaners, no leapers, no chanters; we needed only workers, farmers, machinists, engineers, builders. But how could we refuse them a place on the Ark? It was their good fortune to come upon us just as we were making the final preparations for our flight. The nightmare that had darkened our sleep for three centuries had been made real: the Homeland lay in flames, our armies had been shattered out of ambush, Philistines wielding long knives strode through our devastated cities. Our ship was ready to leap to the stars. We were not cowards but simply realists, for it was folly to think we could do battle any longer, and if some fragment of our ancient nation were to survive, it could only survive far from that bitter world Earth. So we were going to go; and here were suppliants asking us for succor, Reb Shmuel and his thirty followers. How could we turn them away, knowing they would certainly perish? They were human beings, they were Jews. For all our misgivings, we let them come on board.

And then we wandered across the heavens year after year, and then we came to a star that had no name, only a number, and then we found its fourth planet to be sweet and fertile, a happier world than Earth, and we thanked the God in whom we did not believe for the good luck that He had granted us, and we cried out to each other in congratulation, Mazel tov! Mazel tov! Good luck, good luck, good luck! And someone looked in an old book and saw that *mazel* once had had an astrological connotation, that in the days of the Bible it had meant not only "luck" but a lucky star, and so we named our lucky star Mazel Tov, and we made our landfall on Mazel Tov IV, which was to be the New Israel. Here we found no enemies, no Egyptians, no Assyrians, no Romans, no Cossacks, no Nazis, no Arabs, only the Kunivaru, kindly people of a simple nature, who solemnly studied our pantomimed explanations and replied to us in gestures, saying, Be welcome, there is more land here than we will ever need. And we built our kibbutz.

But we had no desire to live close to those people of the past, the Hassidim, and they had scant love for us, for they saw us as pagans, godless Jews who were worse than Gentiles, and they went off to build a muddy little village of their own. Sometimes on clear nights we heard their lusty singing, but otherwise there was scarcely any contact between us and them.

I could understand Rabbi Shlomo's hostility to the idea of intervention by the Baal Shem. These Hassidim represented the mystic side of Judaism, the dark uncontrollable Dionysiac side, the skeleton in the tribal closet; Shlomo Feig might be amused or charmed by a rite of exorcism performed by furry centaurs, but when Jews took part in the same sort of supernaturalism it was distressing to him. Then, too, there was the ugly fact that the sane, sensible Rabbi Shlomo had virtually no followers at all among the sane, sensible secularized Jews of our kibbutz, whereas Reb Shmuel's Hassidim looked upon him with awe, regarding him as a miracle-worker, a seer, a saint. Still, Rabbi Shlomo's understandable jealousies and prejudices aside, Joseph Avneri was right: dybbuks were vapors out of the realm of the fantastic, and the fantastic was the Baal Shem's kingdom.

He was an improbably tall, angular figure, almost skeletal, with gaunt cheekbones, a soft, thickly curling beard, and gentle dreamy eyes. I suppose he was about fifty years old, though I would have believed it if they said he was thirty or seventy or ninety. His sense of the dramatic was unfailing; now—it was late afternoon—he took up a position with the setting sun at his back, so that his long shadow engulfed us all, and spread forth his arms, and said, "We have heard reports of a dybbuk among you."

"There is no dybbuk!" Rabbi Shlomo retorted fiercely.

The Baal Shem smiled. "But there is a Kunivar who speaks with an Israeli voice?"

"There has been an odd transformation, yes," Rabbi Shlomo conceded. "But in this age, on this planet, no one can take dybbuks seriously."

"That is, *you* cannot take dybbuks seriously," said the Baal Shem.

"I do!" cried Joseph Avneri in exasperation. "I! I! I am the dybbuk! I, Joseph Avneri, dead a year ago last Elul, doomed for my sins to inhabit this Kunivar carcass. A Jew, Reb Shmuel, a dead Jew, a pitiful sinful miserable Yid. Who'll let me out? Who'll set me free?"

"There is no dybbuk?" the Baal Shem said amiably.

"This Kunivar has gone insane," said Shlomo Feig.

We coughed and shifted our feet. If anyone had gone insane it was our rabbi, denying in this fashion the phenomenon that he himself had acknowledged as genuine, however reluctantly, only a few hours before. Envy, wounded pride, and stubbornness had unbalanced his judgment. Joseph Avneri, enraged, began to bellow the Aleph Beth Gimel, the Shma Yisroel, anything that might prove his dybbukhood. The Baal Shem waited patiently, arms outspread, saying nothing. Rabbi Shlomo, confronting him, his powerful stocky figure dwarfed by the long-legged Hassid, maintained energetically that there had to be some rational explanation for the metamorphosis of Seul the Kunivar.

When Shlomo Feig at length fell silent, the Baal Shem said, "There is a dybbuk in this Kunivar. Do you think, Rabbi Shlomo, that dybbuks ceased their wanderings when the shtetls of Poland were destroyed? Nothing is lost in the sight of God, Rabbi. Jews go to the stars; the Torah and the Talmud and the Zohar have gone also to the stars; dybbuks too may be found in these strange worlds. Rabbi, may I bring peace to this troubled spirit and to this weary Kunivar?"

"Do whatever you want," Shlomo Feig muttered in disgust, and strode away scowling.

Reb Shmuel at once commenced the exorcism. He called first for a minyan. Eight of his Hassidim stepped forward. I exchanged a glance with Shmarya Asch, and we shrugged and came forward too, but the Baal Shem, smiling, waved us away and beckoned two more of his followers into the circle. They began to sing; to my everlasting shame I have no idea what the singing was about, for the words were Yiddish of a Galitsianer sort, nearly as alien to me as the Kunivaru tongue. They sang for ten or fifteen minutes; the Hassidim grew more animated, clapping their hands, dancing about their Baal Shem; suddenly Reb Shmuel lowered his arms to his sides, silencing them, and quietly began to recite Hebrew phrases, which after a moment I recognized as those of the 91st Psalm: The Lord is my refuge and my fortress, in him will I trust. The psalm rolled melodiously to its comforting conclusion, its promise of deliverance and salvation. For a long moment all was still. Then in a terrifying voice, not loud but immensely command- ing, the Baal Shem ordered the spirit of Joseph Avneri to quit the body of Seul the Kunivar. "Out! Out! In God's name out, and off to your eternal rest!" One of the Hassidim handed Reb Shmuel a shofar. The Baal Shem put the ram's horn to his lips and blew a single titanic blast.

Joseph Avneri whimpered. The Kunivar that housed him took three awkward, toppling steps. "Oy, mama, mama," Joseph cried. The Kunivar's head snapped back; his arms shot straight out at his sides; he tumbled clumsily to his four knees. An eon went by. Then Seul rose—smoothly, this time, with natural Kunivaru grace—and went to the Baal Shem, and knelt, and touched the tzaddik's black robe. So we knew the thing was done.

Instants later the tension broke. Two of the Kunivaru priests rushed toward the Baal Shem, and then Gyaymar, and then some of the musicians, and then it seemed the whole tribe was pressing close upon him, trying to touch the holy man. The Hassidim, looking worried, murmured their concern, but the Baal Shem, towering over the surging mob, calmly blessed the Kunivaru, stroking the dense fur of their backs. After some minutes of this the Kunivaru set up a rhythmic chant, and it was a while before I realized what they were saying. Moshe Shiloah and Yakov Ben- Zion caught the sense of it about the same time I did, and we began to laugh, and then our laughter died away.

"What do their words mean?" the Baal Shem called out.

"They are saying," I told him, "that they are convinced of the power of your god. They wish to become Jews."

For the first time Reb Shmuel's poise and serenity shattered. His eyes flashed ferociously and he pushed at the crowding Kunivaru, opening an avenue between them. Coming up to me, he snapped, "Such a thing is an absurdity!"

"Nevertheless, look at them. They worship you, Reb Shmuel."

"I refuse their worship."

"You worked a miracle. Can you blame them for adoring you and hungering after your faith?"

"Let them adore," said the Baal Shem. "But how can they become Jews? It would be a mockery."

I shook my head. "What was it you told Rabbi Shlomo? Nothing is lost in the sight of God. There have always been converts to Judaism; we never invite them, but we never turn them away if they're sincere, eh, Reb Shmuel? Even here in the stars, there is continuity of tradition, and tradition says we harden not our hearts to those who seek the truth of God. These are a good people: let them be received into Israel."

"No," the Baal Shem said. "A Jew must first of all be human."

"Show me that in the Torah."

"The Torah! You joke with me. A Jew must first of all be human. Were cats allowed to become Jews? Were horses?"

"These people are neither cats nor horses, Reb Shmuel. They are as human as we are."

"No! No!"

"If there can be a dybbuk on Mazel Tov IV," I said, "then there can also be Jews with six limbs and green fur."

"No. No. No. *No!*"

The Baal Shem had had enough of this debate. Shoving aside the clutching hands of the Kunivaru in a most unsaintly way, he gathered his followers and stalked off, a tower of offended dignity, bidding us no farewells.

But how can true faith be denied? The Hassidim offered no encouragement, so the Kunivaru came to us; they learned Hebrew and we loaned them books, and Rabbi Shlomo gave them religious instruction, and in their own time and in their own way they entered into Judaism. All this was years ago, in the first generation after the Landing. Most of those who lived in those days are dead now—Rabbi Shlomo, Reb Shmuel the Baal Shem, Moshe Shiloah, Shmarya Asch. I was a young man then. I know a good deal more now, and if I am no closer to God than I ever was, perhaps He has grown closer to me. I eat meat and butter at the same meal, and I plough my land on the Sabbath, but those are old habits that have little to do with belief or the absence of belief.

We are much closer to the Kunivaru, too, than we were in those early days; they no longer seem like alien beings to us, but merely neighbors whose bodies have a different form. The younger ones of our kibbutz are especially drawn to them. The year before last Rabbi Lhaoyir the Kunivar suggested to some of our boys that they come for lessons to the Talmud Torah, the religious school, that he runs in the Kunivaru village; since the death of Shlomo Feig there has been no one in the kibbutz to give such instruction. When Reb Yossele, the son and successor of Reb Shmuel the Baal Shem, heard this, he raised strong objections. If your boys will take instruction, he said, at least send them to us, and not to green monsters. My son Yigal threw him out of the kibbutz. We would rather let our boys learn the Torah from green monsters, Yigal told Reb Yossele, than have them raised to be Hassidim.

And so my son's son has had his lessons at the Talmud Torah of Rabbi Lhaoyir the Kunivar, and next spring he will have his bar mitzvah. Once I would have been appalled by such goings-on, but now I say only, How strange, how unexpected, how interesting! Truly the Lord, if He exists, must have a keen sense of humor. I like a god who can smile and wink, who doesn't take himself too seriously. The Kunivaru are Jews! Yes! They are preparing David for his bar mitzvah! Yes! Today is Yom Kippur, and I hear the sound of the shofar coming from their village! Yes! Yes. So be it. So be it, yes, and all praise be to Him.

HORACE L. GOLD

Trouble with Water

Yiddish, once supposed to be a dying language, is very much alive in America. The patois of city sophistication, it has become the familiar shtik *of the showman and stand-up comic. And it provides its own special vocabulary to describe today's hero —the non-hero. He's the shnook, the* shlepper, the shmo *(and the* shmendrick, shlemiel, shlub, shlump, shlimazel)—*the born loser, the meek passive patsy, the milquetoast; he's repressed, inadequate, alienated, and plagued with inferiority and virility complexes.*

In short, he's the victim, the man-who-couldn't-make-it. By dramatizing this archetypical shnook, Jewish fiction exorcises contemporary man's most popular fear: failure. But underlying the poor shnook's clumsiness and apparent weakness lies a bedrock of thwarted strength so twisted that it can only express itself as bland stoicism. He is the true tragic figure, but his troubles are so grotesque that they elicit chuckles of sympathy. Giggles replace tears. As the author says, "It wasn't meant to be funny. If it is, it's because humor and tragedy are so inseparable, and what happens to my protagonist is tragic financially, religiously and culturally. Go ahead, laugh. See if I care."

—J. D.

*

GREENBERG DID NOT DESERVE HIS SURROUNDINGS. He was the
first fisherman of the season, which guaranteed him a fine catch;
he sat in a dry boat—one without a single leak—far out on a lake
that was ruffled only enough to agitate his artificial fly. The sun was
warm, the air was cool; he sat comfortably on a cushion; he had
brought a hearty lunch; and two bottles of beer hung over the
stern in the cold water.

Any other man would have been soaked with joy to be fishing
on such a splendid day. Normally, Greenberg himself would have
been ecstatic, but instead of relaxing and waiting for a nibble, he
was plagued by worries.

This short, slightly gross, definitely bald, eminently respectable
businessman lived a gypsy life. During the summer, he lived in a
hotel with kitchen privileges in Rockaway; winters he lived in a
hotel with kitchen privileges in Florida; and in both places he
operated concessions. For years now, rain had fallen on schedule
every week end, and there had been storms and floods on Decora-
tion Day, July 4th and Labor Day. He did not love his life, but it
was a way of making a living.

He closed his eyes and groaned. If he had only had a son instead
of his Rosie! Then things would have been mighty different—

For one thing, a son could run the hot dog and hamburger
griddle, Esther could draw beer, and he would make soft drinks.
There would be small difference in the profits, Greenberg admitted to himself; but at least those profits could be put aside for old
age, instead of toward a dowry for his miserably ugly, dumpy,
pitifully eager Rosie.

"All right—so what do I care if she don't get married?" he had cried to his wife a thousand times. "I'll support her. Other men can set up boys in candy stores with soda fountains that have only two spigots. Why should I have to give a boy a regular International Casino?"

"May your tongue rot in your head, you no-good piker!" she would scream. "It ain't right for a girl to be an old maid. If we have to die in the poorhouse, I'll get my poor Rosie a husband. Every penny we don't need for living goes to her dowry!"

Greenberg did not hate his daughter, nor did he blame her for his misfortunes; yet, because of her, he was fishing with a broken rod that he had to tape together.

That morning, his wife opened her eyes and saw him packing his equipment. She instantly came awake. "Go ahead!" she shrilled —speaking in a conversational tone was not one of her accomplishments—"Go fishing, you loafer! Leave me here alone. I can connect the beer pipes and the gas for soda water. I can buy ice cream, frankfurters, rolls, syrup, and watch the gas and electric men at the same time. Go ahead—go fishing!"

"I ordered everything," he mumbled soothingly. "The gas and electric won't be turned on today. I only wanted to go fishing— it's my last chance. Tomorrow we open the concession. Tell the truth, Esther, can I go fishing after we open?"

"I don't care about that. Am I your wife or ain't I, that you should go ordering everything without asking me—"

He defended his actions. It was a tactical mistake. While she was still in bed, he should have picked up his equipment and left. By the time the argument got around to Rosie's dowry, she stood facing him.

"For myself I don't care," she yelled. "What kind of a monster are you that you can go fishing while your daughter eats her heart out? And on a day like this yet! You should only have to make supper and dress Rosie up. A lot you care that a nice boy is coming to supper tonight and maybe take Rosie out, you no-good father, you!"

From that point it was only one hot protest and a shrill curse to find himself clutching half a broken rod, with the other half being flung at his head.

Now he sat in his beautifully dry boat on an excellent game lake far out on Long Island, desperately aware that any average fish might collapse his taped rod.

What else could he expect? He had missed his train; he had had to wait for the boathouse proprietor; his favorite dry fly was missing; and, since morning, not a fish struck at the bait. Not a single fish!

And it was getting late. He had no more patience. He ripped the cap off a bottle of beer and drank it, in order to gain courage to change his fly for a less sporting bloodworm. It hurt him, but he wanted a fish.

The hook and the squirming worm sank. Before it came to rest, he felt a nibble. He sucked in his breath exultantly and snapped the hook deep into the fish's mouth. Sometimes, he thought philosophically, they just won't take artificial bait. He reeled in slowly.

"Oh, Lord," he prayed, "a dollar for charity—just don't let the rod bend in half where I taped it!"

It was sagging dangerously. He looked at it unhappily and raised his ante to five dollars; even at that price it looked impossible. He dipped his rod into the water, parallel with the line, to remove the strain. He was glad no one could see him do it. The line reeled in without a fight.

"Have I—God forbid!—got an eel or something not kosher?" he mumbled. "A plague on you—why don't you fight?"

He did not really care what it was—even an eel—anything at all.

He pulled in a long, pointed, brimless green hat.

For a moment he glared at it. His mouth hardened. Then, viciously, he yanked the hat off the hook, threw it on the floor and trampled on it. He rubbed his hands together in anguish.

"All day I fish," he wailed, "two dollars for train fare, a dollar for a boat, a quarter for bait, a new rod I got to buy—and a five-dollar mortgage charity has got on me. For what? For you, you hat, you!"

Out in the water an extremely civil voice asked politely: "May I have my hat, please?"

Greenberg glowered up. He saw a little man come swimming vigorously through the water toward him: small arms crossed with enormous dignity, vast ears on a pointed face propelling him quite rapidly and efficiently. With serious determination he drove through the water, and, at the starboard rail, his amazing ears kept him stationary while he looked gravely at Greenberg.

"You are stamping on my hat," he pointed out without anger.

To Greenberg this was highly unimportant. "With the ears you're swimming," he grinned in a superior way. "Do you look funny!"

"How else could I swim?" the little man asked politely.

"With the arms and legs, like a regular human being, of course."

"But I am not a human being. I am a water gnome, a relative of the more common mining gnome. I cannot swim with my arms, because they must be crossed to give an appearance of dignity suitable to a water gnome; and my feet are used for writing and holding things. On the other hand, my ears are perfectly adapted for propulsion in water. Consequently, I employ them for that purpose. But please, my hat—there are several matters requiring my immediate attention, and I must not waste time."

Greenberg's unpleasant attitude toward the remarkably civil gnome is easily understandable. He had found someone he could feel superior to, and, by insulting him, his depressed ego could expand. The water gnome certainly looked inoffensive enough, being only two feet tall.

"What you got that's so important to do, Big Ears?" he asked nastily.

Greenberg hoped the gnome would be offended. He was not, since his ears, to him, were perfectly normal, just as you would not be insulted if a member of a race of atrophied beings were to call you "Big Muscles." You might even feel flattered.

"I really must hurry," the gnome said, almost anxiously. "But if I have to answer your questions in order to get back my hat—we are engaged in restocking the Eastern waters with fish. Last year there was quite a drain. The bureau of fisheries is coöperating with us to some extent, but, of course, we cannot depend too much on them. Until the population rises to normal, every fish has instructions not to nibble."

Greenberg allowed himself a smile, an annoyingly skeptical smile.

"My main work," the gnome went on resignedly, "is control of the rainfall over the Eastern seaboard. Our fact-finding committee, which is scientifically situated in the meteorological center of the continent, coördinates the rainfall needs of the entire continent; and when they determine the amount of rain needed in particular spots of the East, I make it rain to that extent. Now may I have my hat, please?"

Greenberg laughed coarsely. "The first lie was big enough—about telling the fish not to bite. You make it rain like I'm President of the United States!" He bent toward the gnome slyly. "How's about proof?"

"Certainly, if you insist." The gnome raised his patient, triangular face toward a particularly clear blue spot in the sky, a trifle to one side of Greenberg. "Watch that bit of the sky."

Greenberg looked up humorously. Even when a small dark cloud rapidly formed in the previously clear spot, his grin remained broad. It could have been coincidental. But then large drops of undeniable rain fell over a twenty-foot circle; and Greenberg's mocking grin shrank and grew sour.

He glared hatred at the gnome, finally convinced. "So you're the dirty crook who makes it rain on week ends!"

"Usually on week ends during the summer," the gnome admitted. "Ninety-two percent of water consumption is on weekdays. Obviously we must replace that water. The week ends, of course, are the logical time."

"But, you thief!" Greenberg cried hysterically, "you murderer! What do you care what you do to my concession with your rain? It ain't bad enough business would be rotten even without rain, you got to make floods!"

"I'm sorry," the gnome replied, untouched by Greenberg's rhetoric. "We do not create rainfall for the benefit of men. We are here to protect the fish.

"Now please give me my hat. I have wasted enough time, when I should be preparing the extremely heavy rain needed for this coming week end."

Greenberg jumped to his feet in the unsteady boat. "Rain this week end—when I can maybe make a profit for a change! A lot you care if you ruin business. May you and your fish die a horrible, lingering death."

And he furiously ripped the green hat to pieces and hurled them at the gnome.

"I'm really sorry you did that," the little fellow said calmly, his huge ears treading water without the slightest increase of pace to indicate his anger. "We Little Folk have no tempers to lose. Nevertheless, occasionally we find it necessary to discipline certain of your people, in order to retain our dignity. I am not malignant; but, since you hate water and those who live in it, water and those who live in it will keep away from you."

With his arms still folded in great dignity, the tiny water gnome flipped his vast ears and disappeared in a neat surface dive.

Greenberg glowered at the spreading circles of waves. He did not grasp the gnome's final restraining order; he did not even attempt to interpret it. Instead he glared angrily out of the corner of his eye at the phenomenal circle of rain that fell from a perfectly clear sky. The gnome must have remembered it at length, for a moment later the rain stopped. Like shutting off a faucet, Greenberg unwillingly thought.

"Good-by, week end business," he growled. "If Esther finds out I got into an argument with the guy who makes it rain—"

He made an underhand cast, hoping for just one fish. The line flew out over the water; then the hook arched upward and came to rest several inches above the surface, hanging quite steadily and without support in the air.

"Well, go down in the water, damn you!" Greenberg said viciously, and he swished his rod back and forth to pull the hook down from its ridiculous levitation. It refused.

Muttering something incoherent about being hanged before he'd give in, Greenberg hurled his useless rod at the water. By this time he was not surprised when it hovered in the air above the lake. He merely glanced red-eyed at it, tossed out the remains of the gnome's hat, and snatched up the oars.

When he pulled back on them to row to land, they did not touch the water—naturally. Instead they flashed unimpeded through the air, and Greenberg tumbled into the bow.

"A-ha!" he grated. "Here's where the trouble begins." He bent over the side. As he had suspected, the keel floated a remarkable distance above the lake.

By rowing against the air, he moved with maddening slowness toward shore, like a medieval conception of a flying machine. His main concern was that no one should see him in his humiliating position.

At the hotel, he tried to sneak past the kitchen to the bathroom. He knew that Esther waited to curse him for fishing the day before opening, but more especially on the very day that a nice boy was coming to see her Rosie. If he could dress in a hurry, she might have less to say—

"Oh, there you are, you good-for-nothing!"

He froze to a halt.

"Look at you!" she screamed shrilly. "Filthy—you stink from fish!"

"I didn't catch anything, darling," he protested timidly.

"You stink anyhow. Go take a bath, may you drown in it! Get dressed in two minutes or less, and entertain the boy when he gets here. Hurry!"

He locked himself in, happy to escape her voice, started the water in the tub, and stripped from the waist up. A hot bath, he hoped, would rid him of his depressed feeling.

First, no fish; now, rain on week ends! What would Esther say —if she knew, of course. And, of course, he would not tell her.

"Let myself in for a lifetime of curses!" he sneered. "Ha!"

He clamped a new blade into his razor, opened the tube of shaving cream, and stared objectively at the mirror. The dominant feature of the soft, chubby face that stared back was its ugly black stubble; but he set his stubborn chin and glowered. He really looked quite fierce and indomitable. Unfortunately, Esther never saw his face in that uncharacteristic pose, otherwise she would speak more softly.

"Herman Greenberg never gives in!" he whispered between savagely hardened lips. "Rain on week ends, no fish—anything he wants; a lot I care! Believe me, he'll come crawling to me before I go to him."

He gradually became aware that his shaving brush was not getting wet. When he looked down and saw the water dividing into streams that flowed around it, his determined face slipped and grew desperately anxious. He tried to trap the water—by catching it in his cupped hands, by creeping up on it from behind, as if it were some shy animal, and shoving his brush at it—but it broke and ran away from his touch. Then he jammed his palm against the faucet. Defeated, he heard it gurgle back down the pipe, probably as far as the main.

"What do I do now?" he groaned. "Will Esther give it to me if I don't take a shave! But how? . . . I can't shave without water."

Glumly, he shut off the bath, undressed, and stepped into the tub. He lay down to soak. It took a moment of horrified stupor to realize that he was completely dry and that he lay in a waterless bathtub. The water, in one surge of revulsion, had swept out onto the floor.

"Herman, stop splashing!" his wife yelled. "I just washed that floor. If I find one little puddle I'll murder you!"

Greenberg surveyed the instep-deep pool over the bathroom floor. "Yes, my love," he croaked unhappily.

With an inadequate washrag he chased the elusive water, hoping to mop it all up before it could seep through to the apartment below. His washrag remained dry, however, and he knew that the ceiling underneath was dripping. The water was still on the floor.

In despair, he sat on the edge of the bathtub. For some time he sat in silence. Then his wife banged on the door, urging him to come out. He started and dressed moodily.

When he sneaked out and shut the bathroom door tightly on the flood inside, he was extremely dirty and his face *was* raw where he had experimentally attempted to shave with a dry razor.

"Rosie!" he called in a hoarse whisper. "Sh! Where's mamma?"

His daughter sat on the studio couch and applied nail-polish to her stubby fingers. "You look terrible," she said in a conversational tone. "Aren't you going to shave?"

He recoiled at the sound of her voice, which, to him, roared out like a siren. "Quiet, Rosie! Sh!" And for further emphasis, he shoved his lips out against a warning finger. He heard his wife striding heavily around the kitchen. "Rosie," he cooed, "I'll give you a dollar if you'll mop up the water I spilled in the bathroom."

"I can't papa," she stated firmly. "I'm all dressed."

"Two dollars, Rosie—all right, two and a half, you blackmailer."

He flinched when he heard her gasp in the bathroom; but, when she came out with soaked shoes, he fled downstairs. He wandered aimlessly toward the village.

Now he was in for it, he thought; screams from Esther, tears from Rosie—plus a new pair of shoes for Rosie and two and a half dollars. It would be worse, though, if he could not get rid of his whiskers—

Rubbing the tender spots where his dry razor had raked his face, he mused blankly at a drugstore window. He saw nothing to help him, but he went inside anyhow and stood hopefully at the drug counter. A face peered at him through a space scratched in the wall case mirror, and the druggist came out. A nice-looking, intelligent fellow, Greenberg saw at a glance.

"What you got for shaving that I can use without water?" he asked.

"Skin irritation, eh?" the pharmacist replied. "I got something very good for that."

"No. It's just—Well, I don't like to shave with water."

The druggist seemed disappointed. "Well, I got brushless shav-

ing cream." Then he brightened. "But I got an electric razor—
much better."

"How much?" Greenberg asked cautiously.

"Only fifteen dollars, and it lasts a lifetime."

"Give me the shaving cream," Greenberg said coldly.

With the tactical science of a military expert, he walked around
until some time after dark. Only then did he go back to the hotel,
to wait outside. It was after seven, he was getting hungry, and the
people who entered the hotel he knew as permanent summer
guests. At last a stranger passed him and ran up the stairs.

Greenberg hesitated for a moment. The stranger was scarcely
a boy, as Esther had definitely termed him, but Greenberg reasoned that her term was merely wish-fulfillment, and he jauntily
ran up behind him.

He allowed a few minutes to pass, for the man to introduce
himself and let Esther and Rosie don their company manners.
Then, secure in the knowledge that there would be no scene until
the guest left, he entered.

He waded through a hostile atmosphere, urbanely shook hands
with Sammie Katz, who was a doctor—probably, Greenberg
thought shrewdly, in search of an office—and excused himself.

In the bathroom, he carefully read the direction for using brushless shaving cream. He felt less confident when he realized that he
had to wash his face thoroughly with soap and water, but without
benefit of either, he spread the cream on, patted it, and waited for
his beard to soften. It did not, as he discovered while shaving. He
wiped his face dry. The towel was sticky and black, with whiskers
suspended in paste, and, for that, he knew, there would be more
hell to pay. He shrugged resignedly. He would have to spend
fifteen dollars for an electric razor after all; this foolishness was
costing him a fortune!

That they were waiting for him before beginning supper, was,
he knew, only a gesture for the sake of company. Without changing her hard, brilliant smile, Esther whispered: "Wait! I'll get you
later—"

He smiled back, his tortured, slashed face creasing painfully. All that could be changed by his being enormously pleasant to Rosie's young man. If he could slip Sammie a few dollars—more expense, he groaned—to take Rosie out, Esther would forgive everything.

He was too engaged in beaming and putting Sammie at ease to think of what would happen after he ate caviar canapes. Under other circumstances Greenberg would have been repulsed by Sammie's ultra-professional waxed mustache—an offensively small, pointed thing—and his commercial attitude toward poor Rosie; but Greenberg regarded him as a potential savior.

"You open an office yet, Doctor Katz?"

"Not yet. You know how things are. Anyhow, call me Sammie."

Greenberg recognized the gambit with satisfaction, since it seemed to please Esther so much. At one stroke Sammie had ingratiated himself and begun bargaining negotiations.

Without another word, Greenberg lifted his spoon to attack the soup. It would be easy to snare this eager doctor. *A doctor!* No wonder Esther and Rosie were so puffed with joy.

In the proper company way, he pushed his spoon away from him. The soup spilled onto the tablecloth.

"Not so hard, you dope," Esther hissed.

He drew the spoon toward him. The soup leaped off it like a live thing and splashed over him—turning, just before contact, to fall on the floor. He gulped and pushed the bowl away. This time the soup poured over the side of the plate and lay in a huge puddle on the table.

"I didn't want any soup anyhow," he said in a horrible attempt at levity. Lucky for him, he thought wildly, that Sammie was there to pacify Esther with his smooth college talk—not a bad fellow, Sammie, in spite of his mustache; he'd come in handy at times.

Greenberg lapsed into a paralysis of fear. He was thirsty after having eaten the caviar, which beats herring any time as a thirst raiser. But the knowledge that he could not touch water without having it recoil and perhaps spill, made his thirst a monumental craving. He attacked the problem cunningly.

The others were talking rapidly and rather hysterically. He waited until his courage was equal to his thirst; then he leaned

over the table with a glass in his hand. "Sammie, do you mind—
a little water, huh?"

Sammie poured from a pitcher while Esther watched for more
of his tricks. It was to be expected, but still he was shocked when
the water exploded out of the glass directly at Sammie's only suit.

"If you'll excuse me," Sammie said angrily, "I don't like to eat
with lunatics."

And he left, though Esther cried and begged him to stay. Rosie
was too stunned to move. But when the door closed, Greenberg
raised his agonized eyes to watch his wife stalk murderously toward him.

Greenberg stood on the boardwalk outside his concession and
glared blearily at the peaceful, blue, highly unpleasant ocean. He
wondered what would happen if he started at the edge of the
water and strode out. He could probably walk right to Europe on
dry land.

It was early—much too early for business—and he was tired.
Neither he nor Esther had slept; and it was practically certain that
the neighbors hadn't either. But above all he was incredibly
thirsty.

In a spirit of experimentation, he mixed a soda. Of course, its
high water content made it slop onto the floor. For breakfast he
had surreptitiously tried fruit juice and coffee, without success.

With his tongue dry to the point of furriness, he sat weakly on
a boardwalk bench in front of his concession. It was Friday morning, which meant that the day was clear, with a promise of intense
heat. Had it been Saturday, it naturally would have been raining.

"This year," he moaned, "I'll be wiped out. If I can't mix sodas,
why should beer stay in a glass for me? I thought I could hire a boy
for ten dollars a week to run the hot-dog griddle; I could make
sodas, and Esther could draw beer. All I can do is make hot dogs,
Esther can still draw beer; but twenty or maybe twenty-five a
week I got to pay a sodaman. I won't even come out square—a
fortune I'll lose!"

The situation really was desperate. Concessions depend on too many factors to be anything but capriciously profitable.

His throat was fiery and his soft brown eyes held a fierce glaze when the gas and electric were turned on, the beer pipes connected, the tank of carbon dioxide hitched to the pump, and the refrigerator started.

Gradually, the beach was filling with bathers. Greenberg writhed on his bench and envied them. They could swim and drink without having liquids draw away from them as if in horror. They were not thirsty—

And then he saw his first customers approach. His business experience was that morning customers buy only soft drinks. In a mad haste he put up the shutters and fled to the hotel.

"Esther!" he cried. "I got to tell you! I can't stand it—"

Threateningly, his wife held her broom like a baseball bat. "Go back to the concession, you crazy fool. Ain't you done enough already?"

He could not be hurt more than he had been. For once he did not cringe. "You got to help me, Esther."

"Why didn't you shave, you no-good bum? Is that any way—"

"That's what I got to tell you. Yesterday I got into an argument with a water gnome—"

"A what?" Esther looked at him suspiciously.

"A water gnome," he babbled in a rush of words. "A little man so high, with big ears that he swims with, and he makes it rain—"

"Herman!" she screamed. "Stop that nonsense. You're crazy!"

Greenberg pounded his forehead with his fist. "I *ain't* crazy. Look, Esther. Come with me into the kitchen."

She followed him readily enough, but her attitude made him feel more helpless and alone than ever. With her fists on her plump hips and her feet set wide, she cautiously watched him try to fill a glass of water.

"Don't you see?" he wailed. "It won't go in the glass. It spills over. It runs away from me."

She was puzzled. "What happened to you?"

Brokenly, Greenberg told of his encounter with the water

gnome, leaving out no single degrading detail. "And now I can't touch water," he ended. "I can't drink it. I can't make sodas. On top of it all, I got such a thirst, it's killing me."

Esther's reaction was instantaneous. She threw her arms around him, drew his head down to her shoulder, and patted him comfortingly as if he were a child. "Herman, my poor Herman!" she breathed tenderly. "What did we ever do to deserve such a curse?"

"What shall I do, Esther?" he cried helplessly.

She held him at arm's length. "You got to go to a doctor," she said firmly. "How long can you go without drinking? Without water you'll die. Maybe sometimes I am a little hard on you, but you know I love you—"

"I know, mamma," he sighed. "But how can a doctor help me?"

"Am I a doctor that I should know? Go anyhow. What can you lose?"

He hesitated. "I need fifteen dollars for an electric razor," he said in a low, weak voice.

"So?" she replied. "If you got to, you got to. Go, darling. I'll take care of the concession."

Greenberg no longer felt deserted and alone. He walked almost confidently to a doctor's office. Manfully, he explained his symptoms. The doctor listened with professional sympathy, until Greenberg reached his description of the water gnome.

Then his eyes glittered and narrowed. "I know just the thing for you, Mr. Greenberg," he interrupted. "Sit there until I come back."

Greenberg sat quietly. He even permitted himself a surge of hope. But it seemed only a moment later that he was vaguely conscious of a siren screaming toward him; and then he was overwhelmed by the doctor and two interns who pounced on him and tried to squeeze him into a bag.

He resisted, of course. He was terrified enough to punch wildly. "What are you doing to me?" he shrieked. "Don't put that thing on me!"

"Easy now," the doctor soothed. "Everything will be all right."

It was on that humiliating scene that the policeman, required by law to accompany public ambulances, appeared. "What's up?" he asked.

"Don't stand there, you fathead," an intern shouted. "This man's crazy. Help us get him into this strait jacket."

But the policeman approached indecisively. "Take it easy, Mr. Greenberg. They ain't gonna hurt you while I'm here. What's it all about?"

"Mike!" Greenberg cried, and clung to his protector's sleeve. "They think I'm crazy—"

"Of course he's crazy," the doctor stated. "He came in here with a fantastic yarn about a water gnome putting a curse on him."

"What kind of a curse, Mr. Greenberg?" Mike asked cautiously.

"I got into an argument with the water gnome who makes it rain and takes care of the fish," Greenberg blurted. "I tore up his hat. Now he won't let water touch me. I can't drink, or anything—"

The doctor nodded. "There you are. Absolutely insane."

"Shut up." For a long moment Mike stared curiously at Greenberg. Then: "Did any of you scientists think of testing him? Here, Mr. Greenberg." He poured water into a paper cup and held it out.

Greenberg moved to take it. The water backed up against the cup's far lip; when he took it in his hand, the water shot out into the air.

"Crazy, is he?" Mike asked with heavy irony. "I guess you don't know there's things like gnomes and elves. Come with me, Mr. Greenberg."

They went out together and walked toward the boardwalk. Greenberg told Mike the entire story and explained how, besides being so uncomfortable to him personally, it would ruin him financially.

"Well, doctors can't help you," Mike said at length. "What do they know about the Little Folk? And I can't say I blame you for sassing the gnome. You ain't Irish or you'd have spoke with more respect to him. Anyhow, you're thirsty. Can't you drink *anything?*"

"Not a thing," Greenberg said mournfully.

They entered the concession. A single glance told Greenberg that business was very quiet, but even that could not lower his feelings more than they already were. Esther clutched him as soon as she saw them.

"Well?" she asked anxiously.

Greenberg shrugged in despair. "Nothing. He thought I was crazy."

Mike stared at the bar. Memory seemed to struggle behind his reflective eyes. "Sure," he said after a long pause. "Did you try beer, Mr. Greenberg? When I was a boy my old mother told me all about elves and gnomes and the rest of the Little Folk. She knew them, all right. They don't touch alcohol, you know. Try drawing a glass of beer—"

Greenberg trudged obediently behind the bar and held a glass under the spigot. Suddenly his despondent face brightened. Beer creamed into the glass—and stayed there! Mike and Esther grinned at each other as Greenberg threw back his head and furiously drank.

"Mike!" he crowed. "I'm saved. You got to drink with me!"

"Well—" Mike protested feebly.

By late afternoon, Esther had to close the concession and take her husband and Mike to the hotel.

The following day, being Saturday, brought a flood of rain. Greenberg nursed an imposing hang-over that was constantly aggravated by his having to drink beer in order to satisfy his recurring thirst. He thought of forbidden ice bags and alkaline drinks in an agony of longing.

"I can't stand it!" he groaned. "Beer for breakfast—phooey!"

"It's better than nothing," Esther said fatalistically.

"So help me, I don't know if it is. But, darling, you ain't mad at me on account of Sammie, are you?"

She smiled gently, "Poo! Talk dowry and he'll come back quick."

"That's what I thought. But what am I going to do about my curse?"

Cheerfully, Mike furled an umbrella and strode in with a little old woman, whom he introduced as his mother. Greenberg enviously saw evidence of the effectiveness of ice bags and alkaline drinks, for Mike had been just as high as he the day before.

"Mike told me about you and the gnome," the old lady said. "Now I know the Little Folk well, and I don't hold you to blame for insulting him, seeing you never met a gnome before. But I suppose you want to get rid of your curse. Are you repentant?"

Greenberg shuddered. "Beer for breakfast! Can you ask?"

"Well, just you go to this lake and give the gnome proof."

"What kind of proof?" Greenberg asked eagerly.

"Bring him sugar. The Little Folk love the stuff—"

Greenberg beamed. "Did you hear that, Esther? I'll get a barrel—"

"They love sugar, but they can't eat it," the old lady broke in. "It melts in water. You got to figure out a way so it won't. Then the little gentleman'll know you're repentant for real."

"A-ha!" Greenberg cried. "I knew there was a catch!"

There was a sympathetic silence while his agitated mind attacked the problem from all angles. Then the old lady said in awe: "The minute I saw your place I knew Mike had told the truth. I never seen a sight like it in my life—rain coming down, like the flood, everywhere else; but all around this place, in a big circle, it's dry as a bone!"

While Greenberg scarcely heard her, Mike nodded and Esther seemed peculiarly interested in the phenomenon. When he admitted defeat and came out of his reflected stupor, he was alone in the concession, with only a vague memory of Esther's saying she would not be back for several hours.

"What am I going to do?" he muttered. "Sugar that won't melt—" He drew a glass of beer and drank it thoughtfully. "Particular they got to be yet. Ain't it good enough if I bring simple sirup —that's sweet."

He pottered about the place, looking for something to do. He could not polish the fountain on the bar, and the few frankfurters boiling on the griddle probably would go to waste. The floor had already been swept. So he sat uneasily and worried his problem.

"Monday, no matter what," he resolved, "I'll go to the lake. It don't pay to go tomorrow. I'll only catch a cold because it'll rain."

At last Esther returned, smiling in a strange way. She was extremely gentle, tender and thoughtful; and for that he was appreciative. But that night and all day Sunday he understood the reason for her happiness.

She had spread word that, while it rained in every other place all over town, their concession was miraculously dry. So, besides a headache that made his body throb in rhythm to its vast pulse, Greenberg had to work like six men satisfying the crowd who mobbed the place to see the miracle and enjoy the dry warmth.

How much they took in will never be known. Greenberg made it a practice not to discuss such personal matters. But it is quite definite that not even in 1929 had he done so well over a single week end.

Very early Monday morning he was dressing quietly, not to disturb his wife. Esther, however, raised herself on her elbow and looked at him doubtfully.

"Herman," she called softly, "do you really have to go?"

He turned, puzzled. "What do you mean—do I have to go?"

"Well—" She hesitated. Then: "Couldn't you wait until the end of the season, Herman, darling?"

He staggered back a step, his face working in horror. "What kind of an idea is that for my own wife to have?" he croaked. "Beer I have to drink instead of water. How can I stand it? Do you think I *like* beer? I can't wash myself. Already people don't like to stand near me; and how will they act at the end of the season? I go around looking like a bum because my beard is too tough for an electric razor, and I'm all the time drunk—the first Greenberg to be a drunkard. I want to be respected—"

"I know, Herman, darling," she sighed. "But I thought for the sake of our Rosie—Such a business we've never done like we did this week end. If it rains every Saturday and Sunday, but not on our concession, we'll make a *fortune!*"

"Esther!" Herman cried, shocked. "Doesn't my health mean anything?"

"Of course, darling. Only I thought maybe you could stand it for—"

He snatched his hat, tie and jacket, and slammed the door. Outside, though, he stood indeterminedly. He could hear his wife crying, and he realized that, if he succeeded in getting the gnome to remove the curse, he would forfeit an opportunity to make a great deal of money.

He finished dressing more slowly. Esther was right, to a certain extent. If he could tolerate his waterless condition—

"No!" he gritted decisively. "Already my friends avoid me. It isn't right that a respectable man like me should always be drunk and not take a bath. So we'll make less money. Money isn't everything—"

And with great determination, he went to the lake.

But that evening, before going home, Mike walked out of his way to stop in at the concession. He found Greenberg sitting on a chair, his head in his hands, and his body rocking slowly in anguish.

"What is it, Mr. Greenberg?" he asked gently.

Greenberg looked up. His eyes were dazed. "Oh, you, Mike," he said blankly. Then his gaze cleared, grew more intelligent, and he stood up and led Mike to the bar. Silently, they drank beer. "I went to the lake today," he said hollowly. "I walked all around it hollering like mad. The gnome didn't stick his head out of the water once."

"I know," Mike nodded sadly. "They're busy all the time."

Greenberg spread his hands imploringly. "So what can I do? I can't write him a letter or send him a telegram; he ain't got a door to knock on or a bell for me to ring. How do I get him to come up and talk?"

His shoulders sagged. "Here, Mike. Have a cigar. You been a real good friend, but I guess we're licked."

They stood in an awkward silence. Finally Mike blurted: "Real hot, today. A regular scorcher."

"Yeah. Esther says business was pretty good, if it keeps up."

Mike fumbled at the cellophane wrapper. Greenberg said: "Anyhow, suppose I did talk to the gnome. What about the sugar?"

The silence dragged itself out, became tense and uncomfortable. Mike was distinctly embarrassed. His brusque nature was not adapted for comforting discouraged friends. With immense concentration he rolled the cigar between his fingers and listened for a rustle.

"Day like this's hell on cigars," he mumbled, for the sake of conversation. "Dries them like nobody's business. This one ain't, though."

"Yeah," Greenberg said abstractedly. "Cellophane keeps them—"

They looked suddenly at each other, their faces clean of expression.

"Holy smoke!" Mike yelled.

"Cellophane on sugar!" Greenberg choked out.

"Yeah," Mike whispered in awe. "I'll switch my day off with Joe, and I'll go to the lake with you tomorrow. I'll call for you early."

Greenberg pressed his hand, too strangled by emotion for speech. When Esther came to relieve him, he left her at the concession with only the inexperienced griddle boy to assist her, while he searched the village for cubes of sugar wrapped in cellophane.

The sun had scarcely risen when Mike reached the hotel, but Greenberg had long been dressed and stood on the porch waiting impatiently. Mike was genuinely anxious for his friend. Greenberg staggered along toward the station, his eyes almost crossed with the pain of a terrific hang-over.

They stopped at a cafeteria for breakfast. Mike ordered orange juice, bacon and eggs, and coffee half-and-half. When he heard the order, Greenberg had to gag down a lump in his throat.

"What'll you have?" the counterman asked.

Greenberg flushed. "Beer," he said hoarsely.

"You kidding me?" Greenberg shook his head, unable to speak. "Want anything with it? Cereal, pie, toast—"

"Just beer." And he forced himself to swallow it. "So help me," he hissed at Mike, "another beer for breakfast will kill me!"

"I know how it is," Mike said around a mouthful of food.

On the train they attempted to make plans. But they were faced by a phenomenon that neither had encountered before, and so they got nowhere. They walked glumly to the lake, fully aware that they would have to employ the empirical method of discarding tactics that did not work.

"How about a boat?" Mike suggested.

"It won't stay in the water with me in it. And you can't row it."

"Well, what'll we do then?"

Greenberg bit his lip and stared at the beautiful blue lake. There the gnome lived, so near to them. "Go through the woods along the shore, and holler like hell. I'll go the opposite way. We'll pass each other and meet at the boathouse. If the gnome comes up, yell for me."

"O.K.," Mike said, not very confidently.

The lake was quite large and they walked slowly around it, pausing often to get the proper stance for particularly emphatic shouts. But two hours later, when they stood opposite each other with the full diameter of the lake between them, Greenberg heard Mike's hoarse voice: "Hey, gnome!"

"Hey, gnome!" Greenberg yelled. "Come on up!"

An hour later they crossed paths. They were tired, discouraged, and their throats burned; and only fishermen disturbed the lake's surface.

"The hell with this," Mike said. "It ain't doing any good. Let's go back to the boathouse."

"What'll we do?" Greenberg rasped. "I can't give up!"

They trudged back around the lake, shouting half-heartedly. At the boathouse, Greenberg had to admit that he was beaten. The boathouse owner marched threateningly toward him.

"Why don't you maniacs get away from here?" he barked. "What's the idea of hollering and scaring away the fish? The guys are sore—"

"We're not going to holler any more," Greenberg said. "It's no use."

When they bought beer and Mike, on an impulse, hired a boat, the owner cooled off with amazing rapidity, and went off to unpack bait.

"What did you get a boat for?" Greenberg asked. "I can't ride in it."

"You're not going to. You're gonna walk."

"Around the lake again?" Greenberg cried.

"Nope. Look, Mr. Greenberg. Maybe the gnome can't hear us through all that water. Gnomes ain't hardhearted. If he heard us and thought you were sorry, he'd take his curse off you in a jiffy."

"Maybe." Greenberg was not convinced. "So where do I come in?"

"The way I figure it, some way or other you push water away, but the water pushes you away just as hard. Anyhow, I hope so. If it does, you can walk on the lake." As he spoke, Mike had been lifting large stones and dumping them on the bottom of the boat. "Give me a hand with these."

Any activity, however useless, was better than none, Greenberg felt. He helped Mike fill the boat until just the gunwales were above water. Then Mike got in and shoved off.

"Come on," Mike said. "Try to walk on the water."

Greenberg hesitated. "Suppose I can't?"

"Nothing'll happen to you. You can't get wet; so you won't drown."

The logic of Mike's statement reassured Greenberg. He stepped out boldly. He experienced a peculiar sense of accomplishment when the water hastily retreated under his feet into pressure bowls, and an unseen, powerful force buoyed him upright across the lake's surface. Though his footing was not too secure, with care he was able to walk quite swiftly.

"Now what?" he asked, almost happily.

Mike had kept pace with him in the boat. He shipped his oars and passed Greenberg a rock. "We'll drop them all over the lake —make it damned noisy down there and upset the place. That'll get him up."

They were more hopeful now, and their comments, "Here's one that'll wake him," and "I'll hit him right on the noodle with this one," served to cheer them still further. And less than half the rocks had been dropped when Greenberg halted, a boulder in his hands. Something inside him wrapped itself tightly around his heart and his jaw dropped.

Mike followed his awed, joyful gaze. To himself, Mike had to admit that the gnome, propelling himself through the water with his ears, arms folded in tremendous dignity, was a funny sight.

"Must you drop rocks and disturb us at our work?" the gnome asked.

Greenberg gulped. "I'm sorry, Mr. Gnome," he said nervously. "I couldn't get you to come up by yelling."

The gnome looked at him. "Oh. You are the mortal who was disciplined. Why did you return?"

"To tell you that I'm sorry, and I won't insult you again."

"Have you proof of your sincerity?" the gnome asked quietly.

Greenberg fished furiously in his pocket and brought out a handful of sugar wrapped in cellophane, which he tremblingly handed to the gnome.

"Ah, very clever, indeed," the little man said, unwrapping a cube and popping it eagerly into his mouth. "Long time since I've had some."

A moment later Greenberg spluttered and floundered under the surface. Even if Mike had not caught his jacket and helped him up, he could almost have enjoyed the sensation of being able to drown.

PAMELA SARGENT

Gather Blue Roses

Auschwitz-Birkenau, Belzec, Treblinka, Majdanek, Sobibor, Chelmo—the deathfurnaces of the Holocaust, open wounds in the confused conscience of a civilized, modern world. Their fires, still stoked by kindlings of anti-Semitism, illuminate what lies below and beyond civilization's fragile constructions.

The Jew carries this burden of the past into a hostile present. Reluctantly, he passes it on to his children. Here is a story about those children, a melancholy prose-poem made up of fleeting after-images, a bad dream that finds its own reality. It is a slow descent into a cold future buried in the present, a present where only love and the strength of children can insure survival.

J. D.

*

I CANNOT REMEMBER EVER HAVING asked my mother outright about the tattooed numbers. We must have known very early that we should not ask; perhaps my brother Simon or I had said something inadvertently as very small children and had seen the look of sorrow on her face at the statement; perhaps my father had told us never to ask.

Of course, we were always aware of the numbers. There were those times when the weather was particularly warm, and my mother would not button her blouse at the top, and she would lean over us to hug us or pick us up, and we would see them written across her, an inch above her breasts.

(By the time I reached my adolescence, I had heard all the horror stories about the death camps and the ovens; about those who had to remove gold teeth from the bodies; the women used, despite the Reich's edicts, by the soldiers and guards. I then regarded my mother with ambivalence, saying to myself, I would have died first, I would have found some way rather than suffering such dishonor, wondering what had happened to her and what secret sins she had on her conscience, and what she had done to survive. An old man, a doctor, had said to me once, "The best ones of us died, the most honorable, the most sensitive." And I would thank God I had been born in 1949; there was no chance that I was the daughter of a Nazi rape.)

By the time I was four, we had moved to an old frame house in the country, and my father had taken a job teaching at a small junior college nearby, turning down his offers from Columbia and Chicago, knowing how impossible that would be for mother. We had a lot of elms and oaks and a huge weeping willow that hovered sadly over the house. Our pond would be invaded in the early spring and late fall by a few geese, which would usually keep their distance before flying on. ("You can tell those birds are Jewish," my father would say; "they go to Miami in the winter," and Simon and I would imagine them lying on a beach, coating their feathers with Coppertone and ordering lemonades from the waitresses; we hadn't heard of Collinses yet.)

Even out in the country, there were often those times when we would see my mother packing her clothes in a small suitcase, and she would tell us that she was going away for a while, just a week, just to get away, to find solitude. One time it was to an old camp in the Adirondacks that one of my aunts owned, another time to a cabin that a friend of my father's loaned her, always alone, always to an isolated place. Father would say that it was "nerves," although we wondered, since we were so isolated as it was. Simon and I thought she didn't love us, that mother was somehow using this means to tell us that we were being rejected. I would try very hard to behave; when mother was resting, I would tiptoe and whisper. Simon reacted more violently. He could contain himself for a while; but then, in a desperate attempt at drawing attention to himself, would run through the house, screaming horribly, and hurl himself, headfirst, at one of the radiators. On one occasion, he threw himself through one of the large living room windows, smashing the glass. Fortunately, he was uninjured, except for cuts and bruises, but after that incident, my father put chicken wire over the windows on the inside of the house. Mother was very shaken by that incident, walking around for a couple of days, her body aching all over, then going away to my aunt's place for three weeks this time. Simon's head must have been strong; he never sustained any damage from the radiators worse than a few bumps and a headache, but the headaches would often keep mother in bed for days.

(I pick up my binoculars to check the forest again from my tower, seeing the small lakes like puddles below, using my glasses to focus on a couple in a small boat near one of the islands, and then turn away from them, not wanting to invade their privacy, envying the girl and boy who can so freely, without fear of consequences, exchange and share their feelings, and yet not share them, not at least in the way that would destroy a person such as myself. I do not think anyone will risk climbing my mountain today, as the sky is overcast, cirro-cumulus clouds slowly chasing each other, a large storm cloud in the west. I hope no one will come; the family who picnicked beneath my observation tower yesterday bothered me; one child had a headache and another indigestion, and I lay in my cabin taking aspirins all afternoon and nursing the heaviness in my stomach. I hope no one will come today.)

Mother and father did not send us to school until we were as old as the law would allow. We went to the small public school in town. An old yellow bus would pick us up in front of the house. I was scared the first day and was glad Simon and I were twins so that we could go together. The town had built a new school; it was a small, square brick building, and there were fifteen of us in the first grade. The high school students went to classes in the same building. I was afraid of them and was glad to discover that their classes were all on the second floor; so we rarely saw them during the day, except when they had gym classes outside. Sitting at my desk inside, I would watch them, wincing every time someone got hit with a ball, or got bruised. (Only three months in school, thank God, before my father got permission to tutor me at home, three months was too much of the constant pains, the turmoil of emotions; I am sweating now and my hands shake, when I remember it all.)

The first day was boring to me for the most part; Simon and I had been reading and doing arithmetic at home for as long as I could remember. I played dumb and did as I was told; Simon was aggressive, showing off, knowing it all. The other kids giggled, pointing at me, pointing at Simon, whispering. I felt some of it, but not enough to bother me too much; I was not then as I am now, not that first day.

Recess: kids yelling, running, climbing the jungle gym, swinging and chinning themselves on bars, chasing a basketball. I was with two girls and a piece of chalk on the blacktop; they taught me hopscotch, and I did my best to ignore the bruises and bumps of the other students.

It was at the end of the second week that the incident occurred during recess.

(I need the peace, the retreat from easily communicated pain. How strange, I think objectively, that our lives are such that discomfort, pain, sadness and hatred are so easily conveyed and so frequently felt. Love and contentment are only soft veils which do not protect me from bludgeons; and with the strongest loves, one can still sense the more violent undercurrents of fear, hate and jealousy.)

It was at the end of the second week that the incident occurred during recess. I was, again, playing hopscotch, and Simon had come over to look at what we were doing before joining some other boys. Five older kids came over, I guess they were in third or fourth grade, and they began their taunts.

"Greeeenbaum," at Simon and me. We both turned toward them, I balancing on one foot on the hopscotch squares we had drawn, Simon clenching his fists.

"Greeeeenbaum, Esther Greeeeenbaum, Simon Greeeeenbaum," whinnying the green, thundering the baum.

"My father says you're Yids."

"He says you're the Yid's kids." One boy hooted and yelled, "Hey, they're Yid kids." Some giggled, and then they chanted, "Yid kid, Yid kid," as one of them pushed me off my square.

"You leave my sister alone," Simon yelled and went for the boy, fists flying, and knocked him over. The boy sat down suddenly, and I felt pain in my lower back. Another boy ran over and punched Simon. Simon whacked him back, and the boy hit him in the nose, hard. It hurt like hell and I started crying from the pain, holding my nose, pulled away my hand and saw blood. Simon's nose was bleeding, and then the other kids started in, trying to pummel my brother, one guy holding him, another guy punching. "Stop it," I screamed, "stop it," as I curled on the ground, hurting, seeing the teachers run over to pull them apart. Then I fainted, mercifully, and came to in the nurse's office. They kept me there until it was time to go home that day.

Simon was proud of himself, boasting, offering self-congratulations. "Don't tell mother," I said when we got off the bus, "don't, Simon, she'll get upset and go away again, please. Don't make her sad."

(When I was fourteen, during one of the times mother was away, my father got drunk downstairs in the kitchen with Mr. Arnstead, and I could hear them talking, as I hid in my room with my books and records, father speaking softly, Mr. Arnstead bellowing.

"No one, no one, should ever have to go through what Anna did. We're beasts anyway, all of us, Germans, Americans, what's the difference."

Slamming of a glass on the table and a bellow: "God damn it, Sam, you Jews seem to think you have a monopoly on suffering. What about the guy in Harlem? What about some starving guy in Mexico? You think things are any better for them?"

"It was worse for Anna."

"No, not worse, no worse than the guy in some street in Calcutta. Anna could at least hope she would be liberated, but who's gonna free that guy?"

"No one," softly, "no one is ever freed from Anna's kind of suffering."

I listened, hiding in my room, but Mr. Arnstead left after that; and when I came downstairs, father was just sitting there, staring at his glass; and I felt his sadness softly drape itself around me as I stood there, and then the soft veil of love over the sadness, making it bearable.)

I began to miss school at least twice a week, hurting, unable to speak to mother, wanting to say something to father but not having the words. Mother was away a lot then, and this made me more depressed (I'm doing it, I'm sending her away), the depression endurable only because of the blanket of comfort that I felt resting over the house.

They had been worried, of course, but did not have their worst fears confirmed until Thanksgiving was over and December arrived (snow drifting down from a grey sky, father bringing in wood for the fireplace, mother polishing the menorah, Simon and me counting up our saved allowances, plotting what to buy for them when father drove us to town). I had been absent from school for a week by then, vomiting every morning at the thought that I might have to return. Father was reading and Simon was outside, trying to climb one of our trees. I was in the kitchen, cutting cookies and decorating them while mother rolled the dough, humming, white flour on her apron, looking away and smiling when I sneaked small pieces of dough and put them in my mouth.

And then I fell off my chair onto the floor, holding my leg, moaning, "Mother, it hurts," blood running from my nose. She picked me up, clutching me to her, and put me on the chair, blotted my nose with a tissue. Then we heard Simon yelling outside, and then his banging on the back door. Mother went and pulled him inside, his nose bleeding. "I fell outa the tree," and, as she picked him up, she looked back at me; and I knew that she understood, and felt her fear and her sorrow as she realized that she and I were the same, that I would always feel the knife thrusts of other people's pain, draw their agonies into myself, and, perhaps, be shattered by them.

(Remembering: Father and mother outside, after a summer storm, standing under the willow, father putting his arm around her, brushing her black hair back and kissing her gently on the forehead. Not for me, too much shared anguish with love for me. I am always alone, with my mountain, my forest, my lakes like puddles. The young couple's boat is moored at the island.)

I hear them downstairs.

"Anna, the poor child, what can we do?"

"It is worse for her, Samuel," sighing, the sadness reaching me and becoming a shroud, "it will be worse with her, I think, than it was for me."

BERNARD MALAMUD

The Jewbird

Jewish fiction has always been at home with humor. Perhaps it is a natural propensity to exaggerate and twist reality—the kind of fancy that soars to the logical end of the ludicrous, that attacks and promotes itself under an umbrella of cynicism and resignation. Even the most realistically layered stories seem to be punctuated with those odd fancies and impossible details that contrast brightly with their sober themes.

While Pamela Sargent transmutes flying geese into rich Jews wintering in Miami Beach, "coating their feathers with Coppertone and ordering lemonades from the waitresses," Bernard Malamud converts crows into Jewbirds that doven with passion, speak a passable Yiddish, prefer matjes herring to schmaltz, and must flee from the "Anti-Semeets." He exaggerates, celebrates, underplays, shouts, whispers, teases, rejoices, and pulls mundane reality apart like Coney Island taffy. And the impossibly possible Jewbird named Schwartz complains, entertains, suffers, endures, and chokes until the reader stops laughing.

But who are the "Anti-Semeets"? Where are the "Anti-Semeets"? Out there, of course, but they're in here, too, in the kosher homes with Friday night candles flickering in dining rooms, in the trades where Yiddish slang operates best, in small neighborhood synagogues, on the Long Island Expressway where the "Queen-Bride" of the Sabbath rides in Cadillacs, and in the media mirror of laughs and insecurities.

As Gabriel Pierson put it so well: "A Jew fares as badly with his own Jewishness as the non-Jew: he is his own 'anti-semit.' "

J. D.

*

THE WINDOW WAS OPEN so the skinny bird flew in. Flappity-flap
with its frazzled black wings. That's how it goes. It's open, you're
in. Closed, you're out and that's your fate. The bird wearily flapped
through the open kitchen window of Harry Cohen's top-floor
apartment on First Avenue near the lower East River. On a rod
on the wall hung an escaped canary cage, its door wide open, but
this black-type long-beaked bird—its ruffled head and small dull
eyes, crossed a little, making it look like a dissipated crow—landed
if not smack on Cohen's thick lamb chop, at least on the table close
by. The frozen foods salesman was sitting at supper with his wife
and young son on a hot August evening a year ago. Cohen, a heavy
man with hairy chest and beefy shorts; Edie, in skinny yellow
shorts and red halter; and their ten-year-old Morris (after her
father)—Maurie, they called him, a nice kid though not overly
bright—were all in the city after two weeks out, because Cohen's
mother was dying. They had been enjoying Kingston, New York,
but drove back when Mama got sick in her flat in the Bronx.

"Right on the table," said Cohen, putting down his beer glass
and swatting at the bird. "Son of a bitch."

"Harry, take care with your language," Edie said, looking at
Maurie, who watched every move.

The bird cawed hoarsely and with a flap of its bedraggled wings
—feathers tufted this way and that—rose heavily to the top of the
open kitchen door, where it perched staring down.

"Gevalt, a pogrom!"

"It's a talking bird," said Edie in astonishment.

"In Jewish," said Maurie.

"Wise guy," muttered Cohen. He gnawed on his chop, then put down the bone. "So if you can talk, say what's your business. What do you want here?"

"If you can't spare a lamb chop," said the bird, "I'll settle for a piece of herring with a crust of bread. You can't live on your nerve forever."

"This ain't a restaurant," Cohen replied. "All I'm asking is what brings you to this address?"

"The window was open," the bird sighed; adding after a moment, "I'm running. I'm flying but I'm also running."

"From whom?" asked Edie with interest.

"Anti-Semeets."

"Anti-Semites?" they all said.

"That's from who."

"What kind of anti-Semites bother a bird?" Edie asked.

"Any kind," said the bird, "also including eagles, vultures, and hawks. And once in a while some crows will take your eyes out."

"But aren't you a crow?"

"Me? I'm a Jewbird."

Cohen laughed heartily. "What do you mean by that?"

The bird began dovening. He prayed without Book or tallith, but with passion. Edie bowed her head though not Cohen. And Maurie rocked back and forth with the prayer, looking up with one wide-open eye.

When the prayer was done Cohen remarked, "No hat, no phylacteries?"

"I'm an old radical."

"You're sure you're not some kind of a ghost or dybbuk?"

"Not a dybbuk," answered the bird, "though one of my relatives had such an experience once. It's all over now, thanks God. They freed her from a former lover, a crazy jealous man. She's now the mother of two wonderful children."

"Birds?" Cohen asked slyly.

"Why not?"

"What kind of birds?"

"Like me. Jewbirds."

Cohen tipped back in his chair and guffawed. "That's a big laugh. I've heard of a Jewfish but not a Jewbird."

"We're once removed." The bird rested on one skinny leg, then on the other. "Please, could you spare maybe a piece of herring with a small crust of bread?"

Edie got up from the table.

"What are you doing?" Cohen asked her.

"I'll clear the dishes."

Cohen turned to the bird. "So what's your name, if you don't mind saying?"

"Call me Schwartz."

"He might be an old Jew changed into a bird by somebody," said Edie, removing a plate.

"Are you?" asked Harry, lighting a cigar.

"Who knows?" answered Schwartz. "Does God tell us everything?"

Maurie got up on his chair. "What kind of herring?" he asked the bird in excitement.

"Get down, Maurie, or you'll fall," ordered Cohen.

"If you haven't got matjes, I'll take schmaltz," said Schwartz.

"All we have is marinated, with slices of onion—in a jar," said Edie.

"If you'll open for me the jar I'll eat marinated. Do you have also, if you don't mind, a piece of rye bread—the spitz?"

Edie thought she had.

"Feed him out on the balcony," Cohen said. He spoke to the bird. "After that, take off."

Schwartz closed both bird eyes. "I'm tired and it's a long way."

"Which direction are you headed, north or south?"

Schwartz, barely lifting his wings, shrugged.

"You don't know where you're going?"

"Where there's charity I'll go."

"Let him stay, papa," said Maurie. "He's only a bird."

"So stay the night," Cohen said, "but no longer."

In the morning Cohen ordered the bird out of the house but Maurie cried, so Schwartz stayed for a while. Maurie was still on vacation from school and his friends were away. He was lonely and Edie enjoyed the fun he had, playing with the bird.

"He's no trouble at all," she told Cohen, "and besides his appetite is very small."

"What'll you do when he makes dirty?"

"He flies across the street in a tree when he makes dirty, and if nobody passes below, who notices?"

"So all right," said Cohen, "but I'm dead set against it. I warn you he ain't gonna stay here long."

"What have you got against the poor bird?"

"Poor bird, my ass. He's a foxy bastard. He thinks he's a Jew."

"What difference does it make what he thinks?"

"A Jewbird, what a chuzpah. One false move and he's out on his drumsticks."

At Cohen's insistence Schwartz lived out on the balcony in a new wooden birdhouse Edie had bought him.

"With many thanks," said Schwartz, "though I would rather have a human roof over my head. You know how it is at my age. I like the warm, the windows, the smell of cooking. I would also be glad to see once in a while the *Jewish Morning Journal* and have now and then a schnapps because it helps my breathing, thanks God. But whatever you give me, you won't hear complaints."

However, when Cohen brought him a bird feeder full of dried corn, Schwartz said, "Impossible."

Cohen was annoyed. "What's the matter, crosseyes, is your life getting too good for you? Are you forgetting what it means to be migratory? I'll bet a helluva lot of crows you happen to be acquainted with, Jews or otherwise, would give their eyeteeth to eat this corn."

Schwartz did not answer. What can you say to a grubber yung?

"Not for my digestion," he later explained to Edie. "Cramps. Herring is better even if it makes you thirsty. At least rainwater don't cost anything." He laughed sadly in breathy caws.

And herring, thanks to Edie, who knew where to shop, was what Schwartz got, with an occasional piece of potato pancake, and even a bit of soupmeat when Cohen wasn't looking.

When school began in September, before Cohen would once again suggest giving the bird the boot, Edie prevailed on him to wait a little while until Maurie adjusted.

"To deprive him right now might hurt his school work, and you know what trouble we had last year."

"So okay, but sooner or later the bird goes. That I promise you."

Schwartz, though nobody had asked him, took on full responsibility for Maurie's performance in school. In return for favors granted, when he was let in for an hour or two at night, he spent most of his time overseeing the boy's lessons. He sat on top of the dresser near Maurie's desk as he laboriously wrote out his homework. Maurie was a restless type and Schwartz gently kept him to his studies. He also listened to him practice his screechy violin, taking a few minutes off now and then to rest his ears in the bathroom. And they afterwards played dominoes. The boy was an indifferent checker player and it was impossible to teach him chess. When he was sick, Schwartz read him comic books though he personally disliked them. But Maurie's work improved in school and even his violin teacher admitted his playing was better. Edie gave Schwartz credit for these improvements though the bird pooh-poohed them.

Yet he was proud there was nothing lower than C minuses on Maurie's report card, and on Edie's insistence celebrated with a little schnapps.

"If he keeps up like this," Cohen said, "I'll get him in an Ivy League college for sure."

"Oh I hope so," sighed Edie.

But Schwartz shook his head. "He's a good boy—you don't have to worry. He won't be a shicker or a wifebeater, God forbid, but a scholar he'll never be, if you know what I mean, although maybe a good mechanic. It's no disgrace in these times."

"If I were you," Cohen said, angered, "I'd keep my big snoot out of other people's private business."

"Harry, please," said Edie.

"My goddamn patience is wearing out. That crosseyes butts into everything."

Though he wasn't exactly a welcome guest in the house, Schwartz gained a few ounces although he did not improve in appearance. He looked bedraggled as ever, his feathers unkempt, as though he had just flown out of a snowstorm. He spent, he admitted, little time taking care of himself. Too much to think about. "Also outside plumbing," he told Edie. Still there was more glow to his eyes so that though Cohen went on calling him crosseyes he said it less emphatically.

Liking his situation, Schwartz tried tactfully to stay out of Cohen's way, but one night when Edie was at the movies and Maurie was taking a hot shower, the frozen foods salesman began a quarrel with the bird.

"For Christ sake, why don't you wash yourself sometimes? Why must you always stink like a dead fish?"

"Mr. Cohen, if you'll pardon me, if somebody eats garlic he will smell from garlic. I eat herring three times a day. Feed me flowers and I will smell like flowers."

"Who's obligated to feed you anything at all? You're lucky to get herring."

"Excuse me, I'm not complaining," said the bird. "You're complaining."

"What's more," said Cohen, "even from out on the balcony I can hear you snoring away like a pig. It keeps me awake at night."

"Snoring," said Schwartz, "isn't a crime, thanks God."

"All in all you are a goddamn pest and free loader. Next thing you'll want to sleep in bed next to my wife."

"Mr. Cohen," said Schwartz, "on this rest assured. A bird is a bird."

"So you say, but how do I know you're a bird and not some kind of a goddamn devil?"

"If I was a devil you would know already. And I don't mean because of your son's good marks."

"Shut up, you bastard bird," shouted Cohen.

"Grubber yung," cawed Schwartz, rising to the tips of his talons, his long wings outstretched.

Cohen was about to lunge for the bird's scrawny neck but Maurie came out of the bathroom, and for the rest of the evening until Schwartz's bedtime on the balcony, there was pretended peace.

But the quarrel had deeply disturbed Schwartz and he slept badly. His snoring woke him, and awake, he was fearful of what would become of him. Wanting to stay out of Cohen's way, he kept to the birdhouse as much as possible. Cramped by it, he paced back and forth on the balcony ledge, or sat on the birdhouse roof, staring into space. In the evenings, while overseeing Maurie's lessons, he often fell asleep. Awakening, he nervously hopped around exploring the four corners of the room. He spent much time in Maurie's closet, and carefully examined his bureau drawers when they were left open. And once when he found a large paper bag on the floor, Schwartz poked his way into it to investigate what possibilities were. The boy was amused to see the bird in the paper bag.

"He wants to build a nest," he said to his mother.

Edie, sensing Schwartz's unhappiness, spoke to him quietly.

"Maybe if you did some of the things my husband wants you, you would get along better with him."

"Give me a for instance," Schwartz said.

"Like take a bath, for instance."

"I'm too old for baths," said the bird. "My feathers fall out without baths."

"He says you have a bad smell."

"Everybody smells. Some people smell because of their thoughts or because who they are. My bad smell comes from the food I eat. What does his come from?"

"I better not ask him or it might make him mad," said Edie.

In late November Schwartz froze on the balcony in the fog and cold, and especially on rainy days he woke with stiff joints and could barely move his wings. Already he felt twinges of rheumatism. He would have liked to spend more time in the warm house, particularly when Maurie was in school and Cohen at work. But though Edie was goodhearted and might have sneaked him in, in the morning, just to thaw out, he was afraid to ask her. In the meantime Cohen, who had been reading articles about the migration of birds, came out on the balcony one night after work when Edie was in the kitchen preparing pot roast, and peeking into the birdhouse, warned Schwartz to be on his way soon if he knew what was good for him. "Time to hit the flyways."

"Mr. Cohen, why do you hate me so much?" asked the bird. "What did I do to you?"

"Because you're an A-number-one trouble maker, that's why. What's more, whoever heard of a Jewbird? Now scat or it's open war."

But Schwartz stubbornly refused to depart so Cohen embarked on a campaign of harassing him, meanwhile hiding it from Edie and Maurie. Maurie hated violence and Cohen didn't want to leave a bad impression. He thought maybe if he played dirty tricks on the bird he would fly off without being physically kicked out. The vacation was over, let him make his easy living off the fat of somebody else's land. Cohen worried about the effect of the bird's departure on Maurie's schooling but decided to take the chance, first, because the boy now seemed to have the knack of studying —give the black bird-bastard credit—and second, because Schwartz was driving him bats by being there always, even in his dreams.

The frozen foods salesman began his campaign against the bird by mixing watery cat food with the herring slices in Schwartz's dish. He also blew up and popped numerous paper bags outside the birdhouse as the bird slept, and when he had got Schwartz good and nervous, though not enough to leave, he brought a full-grown cat into the house, supposedly a gift for little Maurie, who had always wanted a pussy. The cat never stopped springing

up at Schwartz whenever he saw him, one day managing to claw
out several of his tailfeathers. And even at lesson time, when the
cat was usually excluded from Maurie's room, though somehow or
other he quickly found his way in at the end of the lesson,
Schwartz was desperately fearful of his life and flew from pinnacle
to pinnacle—light fixture to clothes-tree to door-top—in order to
elude the beast's wet jaws.

Once when the bird complained to Edie how hazardous his
existence was, she said, "Be patient, Mr. Schwartz. When the cat
gets to know you better he won't try to catch you any more."

"When he stops trying we will both be in Paradise," Schwartz
answered. "Do me a favor and get rid of him. He makes my whole
life worry. I'm losing feathers like a tree loses leaves."

"I'm awfully sorry but Maurie likes the pussy and sleeps with it."

What could Schwartz do? He worried but came to no decision,
being afraid to leave. So he ate the herring garnished with cat
food, tried hard not to hear the paper bags bursting like fire crack-
ers outside the birdhouse at night, and lived terror-stricken closer
to the ceiling than the floor, as the cat, his tail flicking, endlessly
watched him.

Weeks went by. Then on the day after Cohen's mother had died
in her flat in the Bronx, when Maurie came home with a zero on
an arithmetic test, Cohen, enraged, waited until Edie had taken
the boy to his violin lesson, then openly attacked the bird. He
chased him with a broom on the balcony and Schwartz frantically
flew back and forth, finally escaping into his birdhouse. Cohen
triumphantly reached in, and grabbing both skinny legs, dragged
the bird out, cawing loudly, his wings wildly beating. He whirled
the bird around and around his head. But Schwartz, as he moved
in circles, managed to swoop down and catch Cohen's nose in his
beak, and hung on for dear life. Cohen cried out in great pain,
punched the bird with his fist, and tugging at its legs with all his
might, pulled his nose free. Again he swung the yawking Schwartz
around until the bird grew dizzy, then with a furious heave, flung
him into the night. Schwartz sank like stone into the street. Cohen

then tossed the birdhouse and feeder after him, listening at the ledge until they crashed on the sidewalk below. For a full hour, broom in hand, his heart palpitating and nose throbbing with pain, Cohen waited for Schwartz to return but the brokenhearted bird didn't.

That's the end of that dirty bastard, the salesman thought and went in. Edie and Maurie had come home.

"Look," said Cohen, pointing to his bloody nose swollen three times its normal size, "what that sonofabitchy bird did. It's a permanent scar."

"Where is he now?" Edie asked, frightened.

"I threw him out and he flew away. Good riddance."

Nobody said no, though Edie touched a handkerchief to her eyes and Maurie rapidly tried the nine-times table and found he knew approximately half.

In the spring when the winter's snow had melted, the boy, moved by a memory, wandered in the neighborhood, looking for Schwartz. He found a dead black bird in a small lot near the river, his two wings broken, neck twisted, and both bird-eyes plucked clean.

"Who did it to you, Mr. Schwartz?" Maurie wept.

"Anti-Semeets," Edie said later.

GEO. ALEC EFFINGER

Paradise Last

The nightmonsters of satire bathe happily in Jewish love.
They're the happy endings that laugh at themselves, the sour faces
that turn into prunes, last decade's reruns on the late-late show,
dirty jokes that come true, traditional sadnesses, horrors muted
with glibness, true love and happy days as witnessed by the
Borscht Belt, Rube Goldberg, S. J. Perelman, and The Marx Brothers.

Herewith a science fiction story, a satire with self-consistent
details and extrapolations—and, of course, loaded premises, pur-
posely rooted in quicksand. A story of Jewless Jews, bright children, problematical machines with almost all the answers, subtle
diasporas, planets with turquoise grass, and movie-media emotions.

J. D.

EDITOR'S NOTE: *This is an original story written expressly for this volume.*

*

THERE WERE FIVE MEN who ran the world. They were called
Representatives, though democratic elections had long ago been
eliminated as "too inaccurate." There was a Representative of
North America, one of South America, one each from Europe,
Asia, and Africa. They had all been in power for a long time, and
they seemed to enjoy it. The citizens of their continental domains
were glad of that. The last thing the overburdened people needed
was a war.

Helping the Representatives in their duties was TECT. More
comprehensive than just a calculating device, TECT was an immense machine buried far beneath the surface of the earth. It
contained the sum total of everything mankind had yet learned
about the universe; but, of course, so did several private and public
computer installations throughout the world. TECT had special
powers and abilities, though, which set it apart from other species
of machine. It *understood.* Questions could be asked of it which
were impossible to translate into basic computer binary input.
TECT could interpret all human languages; if a built-in impreci-
sion of common speech led to ambiguity, TECT would query the
speaker. One might ask, "What is the difference between right
and wrong?" and expect a quick reply. The machine's answer
would not be merely a philosophic abstract compiled from the vast
recorded literature of the human race; that is what one would
receive from the other, more accessible computers. No, from
TECT there would be a slight pause, and then a closely reasoned,
"personal" opinion made on the basis of TECT's current measure
of data. Such questions were rarely asked, of course; even from

TECT, the answers were never conclusive, always impractical. And it was a very practical world.

What else was going on? Well, the population of the world was becoming joyfully homogeneous. Representatives had come and gone, but all their strategies were to one end; the idea was that the more people were alike, the better they'd all get along. And naturally the better everyone got along, the more power the Representatives would have. Of course, the great masses of people were aware that they were being exploited and manipulated. They understood it, at least on a subconscious level. But people *do* want to get along; it's really so much pleasanter that way. And, too, the Representatives had so much power already, there wasn't any other choice.

That didn't mean that there weren't still pockets of diversity. In the many generations of Representative rule, the distinctions among the races had not been entirely obliterated. The genetic laws of nature insisted at rare intervals on producing individuals with identifiably Negroid or Oriental features. These people often took government-sponsored jobs as "slum-dwellers," living as their ancestors had done before the era of the Representatives. Small ghettos were organized on a strictly voluntary basis, in order to preserve museum-like tableaux of moribund cultures.

Less popular with the state and their fellow citizens were those who clung to cultural differences, as opposed to mere mistakes of breeding. Such groups as intellectuals, artists, homosexuals, and Communists, all of which had enjoyed greater freedom of expression before the Representative regime, were openly attacked. Perhaps the most extensive cultural enclave, and one of the most abused, were the Jews. Their ancient heritage of loyalty to family and to doctrinal ideals had preserved them from total assimilation; the other citizens worried that this would upset the Representatives and cause violent social repercussions. The citizens made their anxiety and their displeasure evident; but, far from being angered by the Jews' persistence, the Representatives frequently made statements honoring the minority's courageous and heartwarming tenacity. Still, the other citizens were not mollified.

Into this world, then, a boy named Murray Rose was born to Jewish parents. They weren't *very* Jewish; they didn't observe the Sabbath in any particular way, they were frequently startled by the arrival of Holy Days, and they were openly amused by their conservative friends' attention to kashrut, the traditional dietary laws. The Rose family maintained a tenuous link to their heritage, more out of sentiment than anything else. But they were careful not to be identified as one of the "troublesome" Jews.

When Murray was ten years old, his grandfather came to visit. Murray was excited; he had never met Grandpa Zalman, but he had often heard the old man's name mentioned. Murray's parents were more anxious than excited. When the old man arrived, the three adults stood facing each other uncomfortably, while Murray hid behind his father. Grandpa Zalman looked different than the boy had imagined; the old man's great gray eyebrows and long beard gave him a fierce look that confused Murray. He had always been told that Grandpa Zalman was odd, but very gentle.

"Hello, Julie," said the old man. He kissed his daughter and shook hands with his son-in-law.

"It's nice to see you again," said Murray's father. There was a long, tense silence.

"This must be Murray," said Grandpa Zalman. Murray's father took the boy's wrist and presented him to his grandfather. Murray said hello and shook hands. He was dismayed by how huge and rough Grandpa Zalman's hands were.

In the next few days Murray spent a lot of time with his grandfather. Murray's father was gone all day at work, and his mother was much too busy with housework to entertain her father. The old man and the boy took walks around the neighborhood together and talked. At first Murray was a little timid, but after a while he realized that Grandpa Zalman was different than his parents in a way that was both foreign and strangely pleasant.

It was chilly and overcast one afternoon when Murray and Grandpa Zalman were sitting on a bench in the park. Murray had grown fond of his grandfather. He knew from their actions that his parents did not like Grandpa Zalman as well. The longer he stayed, the less he talked. Now they sat under a heavy sky, and Grandpa Zalman said nothing at all.

"What's in the bag, Grandpa?" asked Murray.

Grandpa Zalman stared at the brick path. The boy's question startled him from his thoughts. He shook the brown paper sack; its contents rustled. "Crumbs," he said. "I brought crumbs for the birds."

"Will they let you feed the pigeons?"

Grandpa Zalman sighed. "I don't know," he said. "They used to. I used to feed the birds every day. It made me feel better. We used to get along very well, the pigeons and I. I gave them food; they pretended that they liked me. They were truly grateful for the crumbs. That's more than people will admit."

"Can I feed them?" asked Murray.

"Let me do it first," said Grandpa Zalman. "Then if the CAS police come running with their clubs, it'll just be me, an old man, who gets beaten."

"Okay," said Murray.

Grandpa Zalman opened the bag and tossed a handful of crumbs on the bricks. Several pigeons landed immediately and began pecking frantically at the offering. The old man gave the bag to Murray, who sprinkled more crumbs around his feet. "Are they bread crumbs?" he asked.

"No," said Grandpa Zalman, "they're matzo."

"What's that?"

The grandfather watched Murray sadly. "Matzo. Don't you know what next week is? Passover?"

Murray looked up at Grandpa Zalman. "Passover?" he said.

"A Holy Day. A celebration."

"Like Skirt Day?" asked Murray, puzzled.

"Come on, Murray," said Grandpa Zalman. "I feel like walking." Murray spilled the rest of the matzo crumbs in a heap for the pigeons and ran after the old man. They left the park and walked homeward. After a while the grandfather stopped to examine the display in the window of a small fichestore. He had said nothing to the boy since leaving the park; now he silently held the door open, and Murray preceded him into the dark shop.

"Can I help you?" asked the proprietor, looking skeptically at Grandpa Zalman's beard and strange clothes.

"I want the afternoon tectape," said the old man. "And I wonder if you have any fiches, maybe, on the history of the Jews. Their customs."

The proprietor frowned. "We got a small section for religion," he said. "The Representative's office isn't crazy about selling that kind of stuff. They're cracking down now, you know. I don't know what they're worried about. It doesn't move very good, anyway. If we got any Jewish stuff, it'll be in there, but I think it's mostly Moslem and Christian myths. A couple of artfiches."

"Thank you," said Grandpa Zalman. He went to the small bin that the store's owner had indicated. There were a couple of dozen plastic microfiches, each one a microminiature book, designed to be read with the aid of a fichereader or projector. None interested the old man. He glanced at Murray, who had never been in a fichestore; the boy was wandering from bin to bin, picking up random fiches and holding them to the light, vainly trying to read them unenlarged. "Would you like one?" asked Grandpa Zalman.

"No, I don't think so," said Murray. "We don't have a reader at home, anyway. Dad says we'll buy one when I get to high school." Grandpa Zalman shrugged and paid for the newstape, printed out by the store's small tect console. As they left the store a CAS officer brushed by the old man. The policeman scowled and shoved Grandpa Zalman out of the way.

"You guys ought to be more careful," said the CAS man. "You ain't got much time left, the way it is."

Grandpa Zalman said nothing. He took Murray's hand and walked off in the other direction. "The world is filling up with hoodlums," he said at last.

"They don't like you, do they, Grandpa Zalman?"

"No, they don't like me. And they don't like you, either. They don't like *anybody.*"

"Is it because we're Jewish?" asked Murray.

"No," said Grandpa Zalman slowly. "No, I don't think that has anything to do with it. Maybe a little." Then they went home. Grandpa Zalman read his tectape, and Murray went out to play knockerball with his friends. Two days later the boy's father took Grandpa Zalman to the public teletrans tect. Murray never saw his grandfather again.

But the old man had had his effect on the boy. In the guest room Murray found three fiches, which Grandpa Zalman had forgotten or left intentionally. Murray took them to school, where he browsed through them on one of the library's fichereaders. They were the first fiches that he had ever had all to his own; they weren't textfiches, but they weren't picturefiches, either. One was a long collection of Jewish lore that Murray found fascinating. He wondered what had happened to all the curious laws and customs. He asked his mother, and she said, "They're still around. Not here, but around. There's still plenty of people like your grandfather. But they're learning, slow but sure. The Representatives are doing their best for us, and it's people like Grandpa Zalman who make it harder. They're learning, though." Murray was doubtful. It seemed to him a sad thing that all the old Jewish ways were being neglected.

As Murray got older he took more interest in his education. After he read the three leftover fiches, he explored the school's library and saved his money to buy more. When Murray was fourteen he learned that Grandpa Zalman had died; Murray was filled with grief for the first time in his life. He felt that he had never thanked his grandfather for all the old man had shown him. Murray was determined to repay Grandpa Zalman, and to make some sort of memorial to the old man, whom Murray's parents were gratefully forgetting as quickly as possible.

Tenth-year Tests were scheduled for Murray's class in the middle of February; Murray had just turned fifteen. Through the first six years of his schooling he had seemed to be just another unexceptional student, destined for the army or the CAS work legions. But then, after his grandfather's visit, he showed a sudden and dramatic improvement. Murray entered the Test room anxiously, unaware of the envious glances he drew from his fellow students. The Test lasted six hours, and he was one of the first to complete his tapes. The next day he was ordered to the office of the school's master.

"Come in, Mr. Rose," said Master Jennings. "Get comfortable. I have some good news for you."

Murray relaxed. He always felt terribly guilty when he was called into the office, even though he knew he hadn't done anything wrong. He sat in a chair opposite the master's desk and waited.

"This afternoon TECT finished evaluating the Tenth-year Tests. You did very well yesterday, Mr. Rose. In fact, you finished first in our school. Congratulations." Murray smiled; he was proud, and happy that in a small way he had repaid Grandpa Zalman. "More importantly," said Master Jennings, "your score led everyone else in the district. This is the first time our school has had that distinction. Of course, you can understand how grateful we are for that honor. More to the point, though, is the reward you've won for yourself."

Murray knew that the higher scores earned special privileges from the Representatives and TECT. "When you called me in," he said, "I began to think that perhaps something special had happened. I've been hoping for a new fichereader."

The master laughed. "You'll be getting a lot better than that," he said. "As a district winner, you're entitled to a Mark VII tect unit, installed in your home. That comes with complete infotape, newstape, computape, and entertainment capabilities. Everything but the teletrans unit. Only the continental winners get the big one. And you're still in the running for that; many of the other districts haven't had their Tenth-year Tests as yet. The final winner will be announced next week."

Murray was astonished. He would have his own tect, right in the house! That meant access to virtually every facet of TECT itself, except the data classified for security purposes. Of course, he'd still have to use the public teletrans tect facilities. But that was hardly a disappointment. . . .

As promised, the continental winner was named several days later. It wasn't Murray; he wasn't at all let down, for on the same afternoon his own prize, the Mark VII tect, was installed in his house. His parents were proud and a little amazed. They weren't imaginative enough to understand all that the tect represented. Murray stayed up well into the night asking the console questions, having it project pages of books on many esoteric subjects, playing games of go and chess against TECT's Level Nine Opposition.

In the following years, of course, the unit helped Murray even further in his studies. He excelled in high school, and produced a brilliant score on his Twelfth-year Test. He was curious about what kind of prize he would win for that. Nothing was mentioned the next day. Murray was very disappointed. All through the final three weeks before graduation, Murray hoped that he would be called into Master Jennings' office again. That did not happen, either. Murray graduated from school, receiving a huge ovation from the audience when he went to take his diploma. At home that afternoon, a message was waiting for him on the tect's CRT readout. It said:

> **ROSE, Murray S.**   *RepNA Dis9 Sec14 Loc58-NY-337*
> *M154-62-485-39Min*
>
> *12:48:36 9July 467 YR*   *ProgQuery*   *ReplReq***
>
> **ROSE, Murray S.:**
> *Results of Twelfth-year Test earn planet from list*
> *(following)***
> **ROSE, Murray S.:**
> *Accept?***

The tect's *Advise* light was flashing, meaning that TECT had been asking for an immediate answer since quarter to one. It was now nearly four. He identified himself and the light went out. "Reply to 12:48:36 Query, 9 July, 467. Reply affirm." Then, to be safe, he typed in *yes* after *Accept?*** on the tect's screen. He had no idea what the real circumstances were, but it seemed to him that TECT was offering Murray a planet. The boy had never heard of such a thing. In a few seconds the promised list appeared:

> ***ROSE, Murray S.:*

> *15:52:28 9July 467 YR   ProgCat***

> ***ROSE, Murray S.:*
> *Choice to be made from current available planetary*
> *bodies***

> > ***Print list:*

Lalande 8760	Planet C
Lalande 8760	Planet D
Tau Ceti	Planet C
Wolf 359	Planet B
Struve 2398	Planet B
Struve 2398	Planet C
Struve 2398	Planet D

And so on. The tectscreen filled with hundreds of entries in TECT's master star catalogue. But none of the planets were described; Murray, still not fully appreciating that he was being given an entire world, had nothing useful on which to base his choice. The list went on, ending at last with:

> *Walsung 832   Planet C***

> ***ROSE, Murray S.:*
> *Choice?***

"Query," he said.

> ***ROSE, Murray S.:*
> *?***

"According to contemporary standards," said Murray, "rate the planets on the list, insofar as the following criteria are concerned: comfort of climate and terrain, probability of cultivating normal dietary constituents, minimum at least of aesthetic pleasures, lack of serious dangers consisting of animal, vegetable, mineral, geological, and meteorological threats, at least one potential homesite with optimum conditions implied by the above and entailing what we understand to be essential for normal life and human happiness. Narrow the list to three choices."

TECT ransacked its memories for nearly a minute. Finally the original list of worlds on the CRT vanished, replaced by *Epsilon Eridani, Planet D; Tau Ceti, Planet C;* and *Pasogh 1874, Planet C.*

> ***ROSE, Murray S.:*
> *Choice?***

"Print data on the three choices. Request hard copy." Immediately, full profiles of the three planets appeared in the form of fiches, through a slot beneath the CRT screen. Murray studied the material for a couple of hours. Just before dinner he went to the tect. After *Choice?*** he typed, *Pasogh 1874, Planet C.* Then he went out and told his parents, who laughed skeptically. The next morning another message on the tect waited for him. It said:

> ***ROSE, Murray S.   RepNA Dis9 Sec14 Loc58-NY-337*
> *M154-62-485-39Min*
>
> *08:38:06 10July 467 YR   RepGreet   MANDATORY***

> ***ROSE, Murray S.:*
> *Greetings from the Representative of North America*
> *(text follows) (conditions follow) (commands follow)***
> ***ROSE, Murray S.:*
> *The Representative of North America congratulates*
> *you on your superlative score in the Twelfth-year*

Test, and on your award. Your planet, Pasogh 1874,
Planet C, has been readied for you, according to
current standards and the wishes of the Representative.
You are to report to TECT TELETRANS Main Substation
by 12:00:00 11July 467 YR. Failure to do so will
*be considered Contempt of RepWish***
**ROSE, Murray S.:*
You are enjoined against worry, for your planet
has been prepared with more than enough material
for all sustenance and a generous share of luxury.
You are advised to terminate all business and to
appoint an agent to govern those affairs that cannot
*be brought to a conclusion by noon tomorrow***
**ROSE, Murray S.:*
*Name agent***

"Rose, Gordon J.," said Murray.

> **ROSE, Murray S.:*
> *State relationship to agent***

"He's my father."

> **ROSE, Murray S.:*
> *Congratulations once more. Good luck***

And that was it. Murray stared at the console for several seconds, still futilely trying to understand what had happened. He had been given a planet. That in itself was unbelievable enough; but he was expected—no, he was *compelled*—to settle on the un-known place in a matter of hours. He thought about how he would break the news to his parents. He went back to the tect. He identified himself to the console and waited for the *?** to appear. When it did, he said, "Request."

> **ROSE, Murray S.:*
> *State request***

"I'd like a printout of all material relayed through this console since 10July 467 YR RepGreet." In a few seconds a fiche appeared in the slot. Murray took the fiche into the living room and explained the situation to his parents. Their skepticism of the previous day turned first to wonder, then to pride, and at last to horror.

"Tomorrow?" cried Murray's mother. "What kind of a thing is that? Tomorrow?"

"You're going away? Where?" asked his father, who couldn't comprehend the magnitude of the situation.

"I'm going to another planet," said Murray wearily. "Somewhere out in space. By another star. They gave it to me."

"But what about us?" asked his mother, sobbing. "What about you? What about college? Are you going all by yourself?"

"I guess so," said Murray. He hadn't thought about it that way, the only human being on an entire world. He felt cold suddenly, frightened and lonely.

"Who are these Representatives?" said his father. "How can they tear a family apart like this? How can they ruin a fine boy's life?"

"You don't understand," said Murray. "It's an honor. Not even the Representatives themselves have a whole planet to govern. It's a special award, because of how well I did in school."

"I want you *here*, Murray," said his mother. Murray just sighed. He explained to his father about the job of acting as Murray's agent; then Murray went back to his room to pack.

The next day he awoke early, dressed, made himself a small breakfast, and checked his suitcases again. His father came into Murray's room and shook his son's hand. "Your mother's upset," he said. "I gave her a pill last night, so she won't wake up until after you're gone."

"Okay," said Murray. "I'll miss her. I'll miss you."

"It's a hell of an opportunity, I suppose," said Murray's father.

"I have to get down to the Substation. It's getting late." Murray loaded his luggage into his small car. His father stood on the driveway, looking worried and sad. Just before Murray began backing out of the drive, his father came to the car and shook hands again. Murray said nothing.

There were only a few people in the Substation. Teletrans was an expensive way to travel; people made long journeys by train, or they saved their money for the trip by tect. There didn't seem to be anyone to meet Murray. He went up to a uniformed CAS guard and explained his predicament.

"Certainly, Mr. Rose," said the guard. He spoke with more deference than Murray had ever experienced. "Just check in at the TECT desk over there." Murray began to wrestle his suitcases across the broad, polished floor, but to his surprise the guard offered to carry one of the bags. Murray nodded, and carried the other suitcase to the TECT control station.

"Mr. Rose?" asked one of the uniformed women there. Murray nodded. "Just sign here, and step through. You'll have to leave those bags behind."

"But I'll need—"

"I'm sorry, Mr. Rose," said the woman. "The office of the Representative specified 'No Luggage.' It costs too much to ship it through, and they've taken care of all your needs on the other side." Murray shrugged and signed the release form.

"Through here?" he asked, pointing to a small door in the building's wall, apparently leading back out to the parking lot. The woman waved him away impatiently. Murray took a deep breath, opened the door, and walked through.

He was on another world.

Behind him there was the sound of the door sighing closed. He turned around quickly, but there was no hint of building or portal. Murray stood in the midst of a meadow of tall, waving grass. The field ran unbroken to the horizon, the light turquoise color of the grass making the scene more like a seascape than virgin prairie. To his left, on a small knoll, stood a house. Murray walked toward it, enjoying the odd smells of the plants and the moist red soil. The sun was low in the sky; whether it was rising or setting he could not immediately decide. The star around which Planet C traveled was of a more orange color than Earth's sun. And the sky had a magenta tint to it that startled Murray several times on the way to the house.

A note was tacked to the front gate. It said:

Congratulations, Murray S. Rose! Welcome to your new home! The crops in your fields are nearly ready to be harvested. These fruits and vegetables have been grown under the supervision of the Representatives, and are recommended for flavor and nutrition. Cooking instructions and menu suggestions will be found in the kitchen, along with helpful hints toward saving seeds, etc., for next year's crops. Though the plants may look bizarre and unsavory, you will soon learn to value their manifold benefits.

In the small outbuilding you will find a variety of native animals, psychotamed for your convenience. Some of them will augment your diet, others are merely work animals. Full descriptions of their roles, needs, and natural histories will be found in the barn.

All utilities are built into the house. No maintenance is necessary. The house is supplied with a Mark VII tect to replace the one you left on Earth, which has been reclaimed. Your tect here on Planet C will serve all functions to the best of its capabilities. It is linked directly to TECT, to provide you with uninterrupted service and advice in your new surroundings.

Finally, do not worry over your apparent isolation. Your life and happiness are still matters of concern to your Representative, who is proud of you and your achievements. Merely because you reside on a far-flung planet does not mean that the eyes of the Representative are not cast protectively on you. You will be married within two years. The usual delay of eight years for first-born offspring will be waived in your special case. All services and privileges due a citizen of North America will be fulfilled promptly and with special enthusiasm. Enjoy Planet C. Congratulations!

There are no locks on the doors.

Murray took the note and walked up the path to the house. It looked like a typical midwestern farmhouse, with picket fence, porch swing, curtained windows, and smoking chimney. The one error was the color. The house was painted a traditional farmhouse red, which looked terrible in the orange light, under a magenta sky. Murray made a mental note to do something about it. Inside, the house was lovely. It was furnished in an old-fashioned, comfortable style. The kitchen and the bathroom plumbing were efficient and attractive. Murray wandered through the rooms, climbed the stairs and explored more rooms, gazed through all the windows until he realized how silent it was. It was incredibly quiet.

He grew hungry. There was no food in the kitchen at all. There were the promised leaflets, though. One said, *Welcome to Planet C!* in huge Gothic script letters. It gave a short description of the various edible plants growing in Murray's fields, with photographs of the fruits or vegetables in ripe and unripe stages. Murray wanted something quick to munch on, before he got on with the job of settling in.

He riffled through the pamphlets until he came to a description of a semi-aware creature housed in the barn. The thing was actually a colony of dozens of football-sized, amoebalike creatures. These jellyballs could be found oozing along the ground during the summer, and frozen into solid white stones in the wintertime. In the soft stage, two or more could be tossed into a container, where they would coalesce into a single entity. When this happened, the creature would begin producing tough gray objects, about once a week. If more single jellyballs were added and assimilated, the gray lumps formed more frequently. These gray things, according to the booklet, settled down through the unsolid body of the aggregate creature; the lumps were a great deal more dense, and in the wild eventually were left behind in the path of the jellyball. The creature in the barn was housed in a wooden tub with a trapdoor on the bottom. Just inside, between the trapdoor and the creature, was a layer of wire netting with holes large enough for the gray lumps to pass through. Murray had merely to open the trapdoor to let the gray lumps fall out, and close it before the jellyanimal itself began to drip down. If more young jellyballs were found, they could always be tossed in to improve the stock. The gray lumps had to be boiled thoroughly; otherwise they were intensely poisonous. Afterward they were softer and quite palatable. According to the pamphlet.

Obviously, the gray lumps were supposed to become a staple of his diet. Murray felt a queasy feeling grow in his stomach. The other beasts with which the planet and the thoughtfulness of the

Representative provided him were equally as unsettling. But a living had to be made from them. Murray went outside to the barn, to inspect his cattle.

As the weeks passed, Murray adjusted quickly to the new environment. There was too much work to do to waste time in loneliness and petty regrets. Every day after dark, when he had made himself a strange-looking but nonetheless appetizing meal, Murray entertained himself with the tect. He had no lack of reading material, nor would he ever. The tect supplied him with movies, music, games, and almost everything else stored within TECT's immense subterranean memory banks. Yet sometimes Murray wondered if this were the sort of goal toward which Grandpa Zalman had urged him with his eccentric scholarship.

After a while Murray learned the planet's oddities. Days were twenty-six hours long. The year was nearly a month shorter than on Earth. Planet C had no moons. Seasonal weather patterns became familiar. The various instructions for the feeding of livestock and the care of the field crops were inaccurate or incomplete in places; practical experiments complemented the information supplied by TECT. Sometimes Murray was lonely, of course; after the arrival of winter, with the snow piled around the house so deeply that he despaired of getting into the barn to feed the animals, he had the first real opportunity to ponder and to experience an initial tinge of sorrow. He went for walks across the snow-deadened prairie, staring at the new constellations that glowed in the moonless sky like fiery eyes in a fading dream. He liked to stand and look back toward the house; the lights and the fireplace blazing through the front windows gave him a sense of belonging that he had never felt at home with his parents. This was *his* world. He could name those eerie constellations, and no one could dispute him. He could travel the face of the world and name continents, oceans, deserts, ranges of mountains. He could raise cities to rival the choking metropolises of Earth. . . .

When he began to think like that, he always laughed. Out in the snow, his breath blowing out in quick clouds, Murray admitted his loneliness but was content nonetheless. He was building, and it gave him satisfaction. Even if Planet C never did have sprawling cities, it made no difference. Murray was happy. He felt an unshakeable unity with the world, a sort of faith in himself and in God's eternal gifts; even here, circling Pasogh 1874, Grandpa Zalman's simple ideals seemed to apply. Wherever he went in his immense realm, Murray felt the presence of Grandpa Zalman. And, eventually, Murray informed TECT that from then on Planet C would be known as Zalman.

The winter passed slowly but enjoyably. Murray had followed the advice of TECT and stored food for himself and the livestock; there was no problem at all about running out of provisions. Fuel for the fire was not essential, as the house seemed to be receiving natural gas from some local supply. Murray had learned that the dried stalks of one of the food crops made excellent, slow-burning firewood, but he hadn't been able to store enough for frequent fires. Next year he'd know better, but now he had to ration the fuel. That was a shame, because there was nothing he enjoyed more than building a fire in the living room fireplace and listening to music.

Spring came, and with it an incredible amount of work. Alone, Murray had to prepare the fields for planting, seed the few acres, and maintain the young plants against the natural pests that lived in the high grass around the farm. Murray worked long days, glad of the extra hours of sunlight that Zalman's slower rotation allowed him. Perhaps because he was laboring for himself alone, the work was never frustrating or tedious. At night, exhausted and aching, he was nevertheless satisfied. He knew that he could never have achieved that degree of fulfillment on Earth.

In the middle of the summer Murray realized that he had been on Zalman for almost a year, and had thought very little about his parents. He wondered if somehow he could contact them. He asked the tect, and it suggested that Murray dictate a letter, which would be relayed to a public tect near Murray's old home, and from there by messenger to Murray's parents. He was glad to have the chance, but he was nervous, too. He wondered if his parents could understand how happy he was, how what had seemed like a strange and cruel punishment was really the reward the Representative had promised. He wondered if he could try to explain that without hurting their feelings. Finally, he addressed a short, noncommittal note to them; he never received a reply to it.

The summer and then the autumn passed. It was time again to begin the harvest. Murray's livestock had multiplied during the year, as well. He now had three large tubs of jellyanimals, each producing three or four gray lumps a day. He learned that the lumps could be stored unboiled for an indefinite length of time, and that after boiling they could be chopped and fed to the other animals; the livestock seemed to thrive with this addition to their diet. The draft animals, which Murray had named "stupes," were large bearlike creatures with shaggy white coats. They had intelligent expressions, but three of them had almost starved before Murray realized that they were too stupid to look for their food beyond its normal place. He had rearranged the inside of the barn and moved the feeding troughs; the stupes had nearly died before they adjusted. Now there were six adult stupes and four helpless cubs. The TECT booklet said that they might be slaughtered for food, but Murray tended to doubt that. He preferred to delay that experiment, at least another year. The other animals were doing just as well; there were a dozen creatures that looked like squirrels the size of large dogs, which supplied Murray with a thin blue "milk"; there were scores of tiny things which Murray called "mice," although they were more like lizards with fur, and which had an inscrutable but vital relationship with the stupes; there were several members of a trisexual species of flightless bird, which ate the unboiled gray lumps of the jellyanimals and regurgitated an ugly but nutritious porridge; and there were other animals, to all of which Murray had grown accustomed and even fond.

The second winter began, raged, and passed. A new spring woke the land, and with it came the first communication from Earth in

many months. Murray was astonished to see the red *Advise* light
flashing when he came in for the evening meal. He hurried to read
the message:

**ROSE, Murray S.   —ExtT— RepNA Dis9 Sec14 Loc58-NY-337
M154-62-485-39Maj

22:43:12 8Feb 469 YR RepGreet   ReplReq**

**ROSE, Murray S.:
Notification of Majority. Waiver of CAS term (Details
follow)**
**ROSE, Murray S.:
Congratulations! Today you are nineteen years
old, and an adult citizen under the protection of
the Representative of North America. We understand
that as a resident of the planet Zalman, you may feel
somewhat apart from the day-to-day affairs of your
fellow citizens; but be assured that you are never
long out of our thoughts. Now that you are officially
an adult citizen, we are even more concerned for you
and your future**
**ROSE, Murray S.:
Upon notification of the attainment of majority, a
citizen of North America is usually presented with
a list of alternative services under the CAS authority
which he may choose to fulfill his civic responsibility.
As this is physically impossible under the circumstances,
and as we are happy to waive this duty as a further
reward for your outstanding record, you are to consider
this aspect of your citizenship satisfactorily discharged**
**ROSE, Murray S.:
Other facets of adulthood, about which you may have
questions, will be discussed with you according to
proper standards, modified by your special situation
and the wishes of the Representative of North America**
**ROSE, Murray S.:
You are ordered to appear at the Hall of Adjustments

at 12:00:00 on 15March 469 YR to be married. A TECT
TELETRANS portal will be subceived for your convenience
one hour before this deadline. It will appear not
more than one hundred yards from your domicile, and
indicated by a semicircle of red flares. Failure
to comply will be considered Contempt of RepWish and
Wilfull Neglect of PropFunc**
**ROSE, Murray S.:
Understanding of above to be indicated**
**ROSE, Murray S.:
Affirm?**

"Yes," said Murray, mystified and somewhat upset. "Query," he said.

> ****ROSE, Murray S.:**
> ?**

"Whom am I marrying?" he asked.

> ****ROSE, Murray S.:**
> STONE, Sharon F.   RepNa Dis3 Sec5 Loc36-SD-848
> F293-49-272-63Maj**

"Oh," said Murray. Then he went into the kitchen to boil some gray lumps.

Like the periodic Tests in school, like the seemingly arbitrary way in which Murray had been settled on Zalman, the order to appear and be married reflected the total control possessed by the Representatives. Early in his life Murray had learned not to try to comprehend their sometimes baffling commands; now, he had the spring planting to worry about. He gave no further thought to the situation until the day of his return to Earth.

Murray knew that the subceiver would appear at eleven o'clock, RepNA time. He had to ask his tect what time that would be on Zalman; it was three o'clock in the morning. Murray sighed; he was glad the portal would be marked by flares. Still half asleep after the tect roused him according to his instructions, Murray hurried into his clothes and drank a quick cup of prairie grass tea. He wasn't excited at all, not about returning to Earth or getting married. He checked his animals carefully, giving them a double ration of fodder in case he had to be away longer than he planned. Then he went out into the chilly darkness and walked toward the flares and the faintly glowing portal.

He stepped through, into a long hallway of gray cinderblocks. There was a large green arrow fastened to the wall, and Murray followed it toward a green metal door at the end of the hall. He paused outside for a moment, then knocked. A voice from the other side called to him to enter.

There were a couple of dozen chairs inside, most of them occupied by young men and women with anxious expressions. There was also a long line of couples leading up to a battered brown desk. The man behind the desk looked up from a form he was filling out and glanced at Murray. "Name?" he asked.

"Murray. Murray Rose."

"Last name first, first name, middle initial," said the exasperated clerk.

"Oh. Rose, Murray S."

The clerk frowned. "All right. Let's see, you're with, uh, Stone, Sharon F. She's not here yet. Take a seat. When she comes in, you can both get in this line."

Murray sat down and waited, feeling at last some nervous symptoms. While he waited, he examined the other people in the room. They all seemed to be bright young men and women; who could tell what roles the Representative had chosen for them? Murray wondered if he looked any different than they, if his two years of hard work on Zalman showed in his face, his hands, his bearing. Soon he noticed his eyes burning; the air in the room was obnoxiously foul. The dense gray clouds of smog outside the Hall would excite no nostalgic thrills in Murray. Neither would the crowded streets and the filthy sidewalks. Murray was shocked by his own reaction. After all, here he was after a long absence, once more on the planet of his birth; all he felt was an impatience to get it all over with and go home—back to Zalman.

After about twenty minutes, the door opened and a young woman entered. The clerk shot his harried look at her and asked her name. "Stone," she said. Murray watched her with more interest. This was the girl whom the Representative and TECT had picked to be his wife.

"You're with Rose, over there," said the clerk. "The two of you get at the back of the line."

Murray stood and met her at the end of the line. He smiled hesitantly. "I'm Murray Rose," he said.

She sighed. "Hello," she said. There didn't seem to be anything else to say, so they waited in silence. The marriage routine was very short, being merely a few questions concerning data updates, new addresses, future plans, and so on, and then the bride and groom's presentation of positive identification.

When they had satisfied the clerk's impersonal curiosity, he waved them away. "Next," he said wearily.

"Is that all?" asked Murray later, as they searched for the way out of the building. "No official congratulations or anything?"

"What do you want?" asked Sharon. "A national yontif?"

"I don't know," said Murray. "I guess I'm more sentimental than I should be."

"So," said Sharon, "we're eppes married. How many kids do we want?" She laughed, and Murray looked at her, bewildered; then he laughed.

"It *is* a little strange. What do we do now? You want to tell me all about yourself?"

"No. We have years for that. Where do you live?"

Murray paused briefly. "Well, see, it's like this. I live on another planet."

Sharon stopped short. *"What?"* she cried.

"I did pretty well in school. After the Twelfth-year Test they gave me this planet. I have a small farm. It's a lot of work, but it's very nice. I think you'll like it."

"Nu! You're Jewish, right?"

Murray shrugged. "Sort of," he said. "Nobody in my family really practiced at it."

"Still," said Sharon bitterly. "That's the way the Representatives work it, you know. If they find a smart Jew, they figure some way of getting him out of circulation. They've bought you out. You won't make any trouble for them wherever it is you live."

"That's politics," said Murray. "I don't believe in politics. At least, not on my wedding day."

"Yes, but I *do,*" said Sharon. "Man, they really pulled a good one this time. They took care of the both of us in one shot."

They walked some more, at last finding the door out of the Hall of Adjustments. "Where to?" asked Murray.

"My folks live in San Diego," said Sharon. "I don't know anybody in this town."

"Maybe we could visit my parents. That would surprise them."

Murray's parents were surprised. "I thought you were off on some weird star or something," said his father.

"I was brought back. The Representative ordered me. I got married this afternoon."

"Married!" cried Murray's mother. "Is this her? Your wife, I mean?"

"Yes; this is Sharon. Sharon, these are my parents." The four of them talked for a while, and then Murray excused himself to go to sleep. As he left, his parents and Sharon were discussing plans for a wedding reception. Murray's mother was already on the phone, calling relatives.

It was evening when Murray awoke. Sharon and his parents were eating dinner. They greeted him when he came into the kitchen. "Sit down, son," said Murray's father. "I want to hear all about this place you live on."

"I sent you a letter a while ago," said Murray. "Didn't you ever get it?"

"No," said his mother. "But that's the post office for you."

"I named the planet after Grandpa Zalman."

There was a long pause. "Oh," said Murray's father. "What do you do for a living these days?"

Murray sighed. "I farm," he said. "I have some fields and some livestock. It's good, honest, hard work. I like it."

"What do you do the rest of the time?" asked his mother. "You don't go into town and fool around, do you? Sharon, you'll have to watch him, I know. He's at that age now. You'll see." The two women exchanged smiles, and Murray's father slapped his son's shoulder.

"There isn't any town," said Murray. "I'm the only one there."

"How far away are your neighbors, then?" asked his father.

"No neighbors. I'm the only one on the whole world."

Murray's mother frowned. "That's stupid, Murray," she said. Sharon said nothing, but carried her plate to the sink. There was another silence.

"There's going to be a party tomorrow, Murray," said Sharon at last. "Your mother called all your old friends, too."

"Great," he said. "I've been wondering what happened to them all."

The next afternoon Sharon, Murray, and his parents arrived at the Gutrune Kaemmer Jewish Community Center; the main hall was filling with Murray's relatives and friends. It had been hastily decorated; a photographer from the local newstape took pictures, for Murray's Test scores and his unique award had made him a celebrity in the neighborhood. Murray smiled and shook hands with everyone, and tried to introduce his new wife; he found to his dismay that he had trouble remembering the names of even some of the nearest relatives and closest friends. Finally, he was able to get away from the crowd with Billy Corman, his best friend from school, and Sharon.

"Things have really changed," said Corman.

"I see already," said Murray. "What happened to the big whatchamacallit—"

"Mogen David," said Sharon quietly.

"Yeah," said Murray. "They used to have it hanging on the wall there. A big, heavy old stainless steel thing."

"I don't know," said Corman. "Some building inspector was checking on the wiring in the new wing, and decided they needed some kind of connections. I think they had to take down some of the paneling, right where the Star was. When the workmen left, they forgot to put it back. I guess the Center just never got around to it."

"Very shrewd," said Sharon. "They must send those inspectors to special school to learn that kind of thing."

"Huh?" said Corman.

"I think my bride here is a radical," said Murray. "A paranoid radical."

Corman looked embarrassed. "Those are the worst kind," he said, straining to make a joke. No one acknowledged it.

Murray and Sharon said goodbye to the friends and relatives soon thereafter; they had to be back at the TELETRANS Substation by five o'clock that evening. Murray's parents wished them luck, and Murray's mother kissed Sharon and cried. Everyone shouted their farewells, and Murray escorted his wife from the Center; they got a cab almost immediately, went straight to the Substation, and soon had signed in at the TECT desk. The yawning attendant indicated the portal, and Murray stepped through. A few seconds later Sharon joined him in the gently waving grasses of Zalman. It was only a few hours after dawn on his planet.

"For a sky, that's a pretty strange color," said Sharon. She was pushing the tall grass away from her, but the turquoise stalks swept back and brushed her face. She frowned in annoyance.

"I guess you'll have to get used to it," said Murray. "I have. Come on; you can see the house. I want to check the livestock."

"What do you have?"

"They're not earth animals. You'll have to be prepared."

"Look, Murray, this isn't my idea. If I don't feel up to playing the courageous chalutz, I won't. Who knows? You may have gotten a real bad bargain. What if I go crazy?"

"It's really a good farm," said Murray. "And now there won't be as much work."

"There won't be as much for you, let me remind you. I get the feeling there's going to be a whole lot *more* for me."

"It's a good farm."

"It's how they bought your manhood, yekl," said Sharon. Murray didn't answer. "Wonderful, what a match that shadchen machine stuck me with," she muttered.

"Look," called Murray. "This is one of the animals that live around here." He held up a small jellyball. "You get a couple of them and they sort of mush together. They make gray things that you can eat."

"Feh!" said Sharon.

"*You* carry it," said Murray. "You have to get over your fear."

"It isn't fear," she said shrilly. "It's disgust."

The first few days were unpleasant. Sharon refused to have anything to do with the animals. Even the vegetables from the fields made her run from the table at mealtime. Soon her hunger grew to the point where she had to compromise. She ate a few vegetables, and some of the boiled gray lumps. She admitted that they were reasonably pleasant in taste; but her intellect betrayed her, and after she thought about the source of the food she hurried to the bathroom again. It wasn't as bad the next day, and then it wasn't long before she was eating well again. From then on she helped Murray in all the day's chores, although forever after she had a particular distaste for the jellyanimals.

Murray had come back to the house for a quick lunch one day. It was now near the end of summer, and the day's routines had none of the urgency of the spring planting or the fall harvest. Sharon had fixed a special meal for him, hamburgers made from ground stupe meat.

"You're incredible," said Murray.

"I figured you'd like it," said Sharon. "How long has it been since you had a good old greasy hamburger?"

"Too long. One of the things I was hoping to do when I went back to get married was fill up on things like that. You know, pizzas and cheap French fries."

"I know how you feel already. I'd give anything for some honest drive-in trayf. It wouldn't be so bad, except that this isn't *our* choice. If you never had the chance to decide, you never had the chance to make your own mistake. The Representatives have cheated you out of your own humanity. They've just forgotten about free will."

Murray sighed. "Don't start that again, Sharon, okay? This is my little Garden of Eden. You keep forgetting if you're Eve or the serpent. You're forever trying to make the Representatives sound like corruption personified. How many other people do you know who have a whole, clean, beautiful world all to themselves? You just can't make a gift like that out of evil intentions."

"For thousands of years we've swallowed that einredenish. They say, 'Go on. Make money. Gather possessions. But just don't get pushy.' And the nuchshleppers go right along with them. Every time we seem to be pulling our people together, somebody throws cold water on our smoldering desire, scatters the flame of our spirit. Being driven out of our own land into exile wasn't bad enough. But then for centuries, wherever small communities of Jews gathered, the machers in power devoted themselves to splitting up even those tiny groups."

"That's the racial paranoia my father yelled about all the time," said Murray. "It's stupid. What's the matter, you *need* to be persecuted? You can't have someone hand you a gift horse without looking it in the mouth?"

"Bubkes! I know some Trojans that would've been a lot better off if they had. Anyway, now the Representatives have found the real answer. This is a neat thing they've done. Nobody can accuse them of genocide. Even you can't see what they're doing."

"What *are* they doing?"

"You know what the Diaspora means?"

"No," said Murray.

"It used to mean the community of Jews living outside Israel. There used to be great numbers of Jews throughout the world. Now there isn't. Mostly, there are a couple of million Jews in Israel, living in sort of an amusement park for the Representatives. And some more scattered neighborhoods in the rest of the world. Now they're taking the best of our people and spreading them even further. A dispersion of the Dispersion. It's much more effective than killing them would be. No one is angered, no one is vengeful. I mean, you certainly looked happy enough when you visited your parents, nu?"

"All right," said Murray, rubbing his eyes with his rough fingers, "suppose you tell me why they bother?"

"Go to that damn machine of yours," said Sharon. Murray frowned, not understanding, but he went to the tect. "Now ask it a question," she said. "Ask it what a Jew is."

Murray did so. The answer was immediate:

> **ROSE, Murray S.:*
> *A Jew is a kind of person***

"That's why they bother," said Sharon. "It's all the reason they need."

Her ideas were as foreign to Murray as Grandpa Zalman's had been; but, after he had thought about them, he discovered that he couldn't find an easy reply. When he had made that admission, Murray decided that Sharon at least deserved the attention he had given to his grandfather's odd ways. The summer ended. Several weeks later, he went to the tect and asked a few more questions. "How many other individuals have been given their own planet?" he said.

> **ROSE, Murray S.:*
> *Seven thousand, four hundred and twelve***

"What percentage of those people are Jewish or of Jewish extraction?"

> **ROSE, Murray S.:*
> *Thirty-nine percent***

"And what percentage of the population of the Earth is Jewish or of Jewish extraction?"

> **ROSE, Murray S.:*
> *Less than one-half of one percent***

Those figures seemed to substantiate Sharon's angry charges. But, still, Murray didn't agree that giving virgin worlds away was a scheme to destroy the Jewish people. It may just be the result of a natural superiority among Jewish students, at least as far as what the Twelfth-year Test measured. But then Murray had a sudden thought. "How many known, habitable worlds are there in the universe, besides Earth?" he asked.

**ROSE, Murray S.:
*Six hundred and thirty-six***

There! "How many other people are living on the world known as Zalman, other than Murray and Sharon Rose?"

**ROSE, Murray S.:
*Twenty-two***

Murray took the information to Sharon. "I have to apologize," he said. "It looks like your view of things may be a little more accurate than mine. I'm either naïve or just stupid. If the Representatives will lie about meaningless things like this, who knows what else they've been lying about?"

Sharon smiled at him sadly. "Twenty-two other people, scattered around the face of a world. A regular little shtetl, if we could all get together. That's what Jews have been saying since Genesis."

"I guess it's too late, now."

"It may be too late for you and me," said Sharon. "We've sold the birthright. We've betrayed our ancestors. And for what? Some gray lumps."

Murray was still upset by his discoveries, and Sharon's words only irritated him. He grew defensive. "So what *should* I be doing?" he said loudly. "Fighting them by myself?"

"We should be conserving what little remains of our heritage," said Sharon softly. "You never cared much for that, did you?"

"You can't blame me for my environment," said Murray.

"I can, if you keep making its mistakes."

Murray slammed his hand down on the table. "You want me to

go back to Earth? Lead an uprising? Murray Maccabeus, for pity's sake?"

"Murray, that light on the machine is flashing," said Sharon. He turned around, startled. There was a message coming through.

"You think they've been listening?" asked Murray.

"Probably," said Sharon with a scowl. "What difference does it make?"

Murray hurried to the tect. The CRT screen displayed the news:

**ROSE, Murray S. —ExtT—   *RepNA Dis9 Sec14 Loc58-NY-337*
M154-62-485-39Maj

07:33:02 27May 469 YR   *DatAdvis***

**ROSE, Murray S.:
Notification of Propagation Assent (RoutProc follows)
(Specifications follow)**
**ROSE, Murray S.:
The office of the Representative of North America
extends its warmest greetings and congratulations.
It has been decided that, due to your unusual and
somewhat severe conditions, you and your wife,
MRS. SHARON F. S. ROSE, will be permitted to begin
your child. The Representative is certain you
will be as excited and pleased as he is**

**ROSE, Murray S.:
A package containing the pills and injections necessary
for the successful fabrication of your offspring
will be subceived twenty-four hours after this
message. The location of the package will be marked
by a red flare. Immediate implementation of the
contents of the package is necessary for the safety
of both MRS. SHARON F. S. ROSE and the offspring**

**ROSE, Murray S.:
Your offspring will be male; weight at birth seven

*pounds, six ounces; hair brown; eyes brown; estimated
height at maturity five feet, eleven inches; estimated
weight at maturity one hundred ninety-five pounds;
right-handed; allergies: none; pre-diabetic condition
at age twenty-two; hearing normal; eyesight normal;
Intelligence Level B+; sober disposition; taciturn;
strong; hard-working; not unhandsome by contemporary
standards. Congratulations!***

***ROSE, Murray S.:*
*Offspring will be born 18July, 470 YR, between
05:00 and 05:45***

***ROSE, Murray S.:*
*Failure to comply with the above will be considered
Contempt of RepWish and Wilfull Neglect of PropFunc***

"Congratulations," said Murray. "The Representative strikes
again."

"Have you noticed how when that gonif strikes, he always seems
to hit *me?*" said Sharon. Murray looked at her; she laughed, and
he felt relieved. "Having a baby has taken more than one good
revolutionary out of the action," she said. "But at least I can train
him to take care of those jellyanimals. That's the trouble with this
planet. No hired hands."

"That's a terrible thing to say," said Murray. "Our baby—"

"I was only kidding."

"I had this vision of you raising him to be an employee instead
of a son. I can never tell when you're serious."

"Wait until you get to know me," she said. *"Then* you can
worry."

"So tell me. How are you going to raise a kid without chicken
soup?"

Sharon laughed. "I was waiting for that. No, really, I figure we
can make a good enough broth out of stupe bones. Stupe soup.
Feh!"

"And then this champion we're raising can go back to Earth and bust heads for us," said Murray.

Sharon suddenly got serious. "You know, Murray," she said, "I don't want to believe we're the only ones who have discovered what the Representatives are doing. I mean, they've scattered our best minds, but those minds are still functioning. Our kid won't be any Messiah. Not by himself. But maybe around these planets, we're making a *generation* of Messiahs."

"That's a very heroic thought," said Murray. "I guess you *have* to tell yourself things like that, to keep yourself going." Now Sharon stared at her husband, until he laughed.

"I'm going to crown you one of these days, chachem, if you don't stop mocking me. Look, the Hebrews were wandering around leaderless, oppressed by all sorts of people and ideas. Then came Moses. Now *everybody's* oppressed and lost, not just our small tribe. So instead of one man, the world needs one strong family of men to stand up and fight back. What Moses is to the Jews, the Jews can be to all mankind."

"And before the Messiah comes, isn't the prophet Elijah supposed to return?" asked Murray with a smile. "I like that. It makes me Elijah. Mom would be proud."

"No," said Sharon, "it makes *us* Elijah. And the spirit of Elijah is with us. It's Succoth."

"What?"

"A feast. A harvest thanksgiving. There are traditions. We'll build a booth in the fields, and we'll eat our meals there. It will remind us of the temporary shelters of the Hebrews in their years of wandering. It can mean the temporary kind of dominance the Representatives have over us, if you want. We're supposed to have willow and myrtle and other branches, but I suppose we can substitute. It's the thought that counts, isn't it?"

Murray kissed Sharon lightly on the cheek. "You're very special," he said. "You're a little insane, but you're special."

"And you, luftmensh, you're just dumb."

"Let's hurry up and have that baby, so we can all get out of here," said Murray, sighing.

"Relax. We've waited this long, we can wait a little longer."

"What do I do in the meantime?" asked Murray.

"You can help me get the rest of those bluebeans in," she said. "And then we can start on the booth." Murray nodded and started to go back outside. "Nu," said Sharon. "I made this for you."

Murray looked at the little thing she had pulled from her pocket. "What is it?" he asked.

"It's a yarmulke. Take it."

He hesitated for a second. Then he took it from her and put it on. It was time they got to work.

ROBERT SHECKLEY

Street of Dreams, Feet of Clay

Ess, ess, mein kindt *(eat, eat, my child)—the cry of the Jewish mother as told by Borscht Belt comedians to sympathetic audiences. The Jewish mother becomes a modern Earth mother, another pop culture metaphor that is not strictly Jewish, but Jewish-American. She is the archetypical giver of security and chicken soup, the selfless soul who lives only for others, who is always clean, tidy, and hopeful, who nags, pleads, admonishes, serves, and suffers—all this out of lovelovelove. She is the instiller of Jewish guilt, the unwanted advisor and eternal consoler, the matriarch with the steel-reinforced apron strings, and her obedient son's one true love. And should he not be obedient, she will suffer and accept the responsibility of shame.*

But the "Jewish-mother-shtik" has been done to death in Mainstream fiction; it's an old routine for the new comics, although one that's guaranteed to get a few laughs. Like the Western and the vampire story, it has been worked and reworked into stylized parody. It is a cue—there's no mystery or excitement, only familiarity, easy identification, and, of course, a few well-worn belly laughs.

New ideas are sorely needed. The following story by Robert Sheckley represents a new comedy based on the tenets, not the materials of the old—it is an infusion of originality and excitement into a fallow theme, a new fertilization. Science fiction provides new grist for the mill. Take Bellwether, a nice city that talks in your sleep, a perfect place to be for your own good, a tempting, taunting representation of something lost in the past, only to be found in the future.

J. D.

*

CARMODY HAD NEVER REALLY PLANNED to leave New York. Why he did so is inexplicable. A born urbanite, he had grown accustomed to the minor inconveniences of metropolitan life. His snug apartment on the 290th floor of Levitfrack Towers on West Ninety-ninth Street was nicely equipped in the current "Spaceship" motif. The windows were double-sealed in tinted lifetime plexiglass, and the air ducts worked through a blind baffle filtration system which sealed automatically when the Combined Atmosphere Pollution Index reached 999.8 on the Con Ed scale. True, his oxygen-nitrogen air recirculation system was old, but it was reliable. His water purification cells were obsolete and ineffective; but then, nobody drank water anyhow.

Noise was a continual annoyance, unstoppable and inescapable. But Carmody knew that there was no cure for this, since the ancient art of soundproofing had been lost. It was urban man's lot to listen, a captive audience, to the arguments, music and watery gurglings of his adjacent neighbors. Even this torture could be alleviated, however, by producing similar sounds of one's own.

Going to work each day entailed certain dangers; but these were more apparent than real. Disadvantaged snipers continued to make their ineffectual protests from rooftops and occasionally succeeded in potting an unwary out-of-towner. But as a rule, their aim was abominable. Additionally, the general acceptance of lightweight personal armor had taken away most of their sting, and the sternly administered state law forbidding the personal possession of surplus cannon had rendered them ineffectual.

Thus, no single factor can be adduced for Carmody's sudden

decision to leave what was generally considered the world's most exciting megapolitan agglomeration. Blame it on a vagrant impulse, a pastoral fantasy, or on sheer perversity. The simple, irreducible fact is, one day Carmody opened his copy of the *Daily Times-News* and saw an advertisement for a model city in New Jersey.

"Come live in Bellwether, the city that cares," the advertisement proclaimed. There followed a list of utopian claims which need not be reproduced here.

"Huh," said Carmody, and read on.

Bellwether was within easy commuting distance. One simply drove through the Ulysses S. Grant Tunnel at 43rd Street, took the Hoboken Shunt Subroad to the Palisades Interstate Crossover, followed that for 3.2 miles on the Blue-Charlie Sorter Loop that led onto U.S. 5 (The Hague Memorial Tollway), proceeded along that a distance of 6.1 miles to the Garden State Supplementary Access Service Road (Provisional), upon which one tended west to Exit 1731A, which was King's Highbridge Gate Road, and then continued along that for a distance of 1.6 miles. And there you were.

"By jingo," said Carmody, "I'll do it."

And he did.

II

King's Highbridge Gate Road ended on a neatly trimmed plain. Carmody got out of his car and looked around. Half a mile ahead of him he saw a small city. A single modest signpost identified it as Bellwether.

This city was not constructed in the traditional manner of American cities, with outliers of gas stations, tentacles of hot-dog stands, fringes of motels and a protective carapace of junkyards; but rather, as some Italian hill towns are fashioned, it rose abruptly, without physical preamble, the main body of the town presenting itself at once and without amelioration.

Carmody found this appealing. He advanced into the city itself.

Bellwether had a warm and open look. Its streets were laid out generously, and there was a frankness about the wide bay windows of its store-fronts. As he penetrated deeper, Carmody found other delights. Just within the city he entered a piazza, like a Roman piazza, only smaller; and in the center of the piazza there was a fountain, and standing in the fountain was a marble representation of a boy with a dolphin, and from the dolphin's mouth a stream of clear water issued.

"I do hope you like it," a voice said from behind Carmody's left shoulder.

"It's nice," Carmody said.

"I constructed it and put it there myself," the voice told him. "It seemed to me that a fountain, despite the antiquity of its concept, is aesthetically functional. And this piazza, with its benches and shady chestnut trees, is copied from a Bolognese model. Again, I did not inhibit myself with the fear of seeming old-fashioned. The true artist uses what is necessary, be it a thousand years old or one second new."

"I applaud your sentiment," Carmody said. "Permit me to introduce myself. I am Edward Carmody." He turned, smiling.

But there was no one behind his left shoulder, or behind his right shoulder, either. There was no one in the piazza, nobody at all in sight.

"Forgive me," the voice said. "I didn't mean to startle you. I thought you knew."

"Knew what?" Carmody asked.

"Knew about me."

"Well, I don't," Carmody said. "Who are you and where are you speaking from?"

"I am the voice of the city," the voice said. "Or to put it another way, I am the city itself, Bellwether, the actual and veritable city, speaking to you."

"Is that a fact?" Carmody said sardonically. "Yes," he answered himself, "I suppose it is a fact. So all right, you're a city. Big deal!"

He turned away from the fountain and strolled across the piazza like a man who conversed with cities every day of his life, and who was slightly bored with the whole thing. He walked down various streets and up certain avenues. He glanced into store windows and noted houses. He paused in front of statuary, but only briefly.

"Well?" the city of Bellwether asked after a while.

"Well what?" Carmody answered at once.

"What do you think of me?"

"You're okay," Carmody said.

"Only okay? Is that all?"

"Look," Carmody said, "a city is a city. When you've seen one, you've pretty much seen them all."

"That's untrue!" the city said, with some show of pique. "I am distinctly different from other cities. I am unique."

"Are you indeed?" Carmody said scornfully. "To me you look like a conglomeration of badly assembled parts. You've got an Italian piazza, a couple of Greek-type buildings, a row of Tudor houses, an old-style New York tenement, a California hot-dog stand shaped like a tugboat and God knows what else. What's so unique about that?"

"The combination of those forms into a meaningful entity is unique," the city said. "These older forms are not anachronisms, you understand. They are representative styles of living, and as such are appropriate in a well-wrought machine for living. Would you care for some coffee and perhaps a sandwich or some fresh fruit?"

"Coffee sounds good," Carmody said. He allowed Bellwether to guide him around the corner to an open-air cafe. The cafe was called "O You Kid" and was a replica of a Gay Nineties' saloon, right down to the Tiffany lamps and the cut-glass chandelier and the player piano. Like everything else that Carmody had seen in the city, it was spotlessly clean, but without people.

"Nice atmosphere, don't you think?" Bellwether asked.

"Campy," Carmody pronounced. "Okay if you like that sort of thing."

A foaming mug of cappuccino was lowered to his table on a stainless steel tray. Carmody sipped.

"Good?" Bellwether asked.

"Yes, very good."

"I rather pride myself on my coffee," the city said quietly. "And on my cooking. Wouldn't you care for a little something? An omelette, perhaps, or a soufflé?"

"Nothing," Carmody said firmly. He leaned back in his chair and said, "So you're a model city, huh?"

"Yes, that is what I have the honor to be," Bellwether said. "I am the most recent of all model cities; and, I believe, the most satisfactory. I was conceived by a joint study group from Yale and the University of Chicago, who were working on a Rockefeller fellowship. Most of my practical details were devised by M.I.T., although some special sections of me came from Princeton and from the RAND Corporation. My actual construction was a General Electric project, and the money was procured by grants from the Ford and Carnegie Foundations, as well as several other institutions I am not at liberty to mention."

"Interesting sort of history," Carmody said, with hateful nonchalance. "That's a Gothic cathedral across the street, isn't it?"

"Modified Romanesque," the city said. "Also interdenominational and open to all faiths, with a designed seating capacity for three hundred people."

"That doesn't seem like many for a building of that size."

"It's not, of course. Designedly. My idea was to combine awesomeness with coziness."

"Where are the inhabitants of this town, by the way?" Carmody asked.

"They have left," Bellwether said mournfully. "They have all departed."

"Why?"

The city was silent for a while, then said, "There was a breakdown in city-community relations. A misunderstanding, really. Or perhaps I should say, an unfortunate series of misunderstandings. I suspect that rabble-rousers played their part."

"But what *happened*, precisely?"

"I don't know," the city said. "I really don't know. One day they simply all left. Just like that! But I'm sure they'll be back."

"I wonder," Carmody said.

"I am convinced of it," the city said. "But putting that aside: why don't *you* stay here, Mr. Carmody?"

"I haven't really had time to consider it," Carmody said.

"How could you help but like it?" Bellwether said. "Just think —you would have the most modern up-to-date city in the world at your beck and call."

"That does sound interesting," Carmody said.

"So give it a try, how could it hurt you?" the city asked.

"All right, I think I will," Carmody said.

He was intrigued by the city of Bellwether. But he was also apprehensive. He wished he knew exactly why the city's previous occupants had left.

At Bellwether's insistence, Carmody slept that night in the sumptuous bridal suite of the King George V Hotel. Bellwether served him breakfast on the terrace and played a brisk Haydn quartet while Carmody ate. The morning air was delicious. If Bellwether hadn't told him, Carmody would never have guessed it was reconstituted.

When he was finished, Carmody leaned back and enjoyed the view of Bellwether's western quarter—a pleasing jumble of Chinese pagodas, Venetian footbridges, Japanese canals, a green Burmese hill, a Corinthian temple, a California parking lot, a Norman tower and much else besides.

"You have a splendid view," he told the city.

"I'm so glad you appreciate it," Bellwether replied. "The problem of style was argued from the day of my inception. One group held for consistency: a harmonious group of shapes blending into a harmonious whole. But quite a few model cities are like that. They are uniformly dull, artificial entities created by one man or one committee, unlike real cities."

"You're sort of artificial yourself, aren't you?" Carmody asked.

"Of course! But I do not pretend to be anything else. I am not a fake 'city of the future' or a mock-Florentine bastard. I am a true agglutinated congeries. I am supposed to be interesting and stimulating in addition to being functional and practical."

"Bellwether, you look okay to me," Carmody said, in a sudden rush of expansiveness. "Do all model cities talk like you?"

"Certainly not. Most cities up to now, model or otherwise, never said a word. But their inhabitants didn't like that. It made the city seem too huge, too masterful, too soulless, too impersonal. That is why I was created with a voice and an artificial consciousness to guide it."

"I see," Carmody said.

"The point is, my artificial consciousness personalizes me, which is very important in an age of depersonalization. It enables me to be truly responsive. It permits me to be creative in meeting the demands of my occupants. We can reason with each other, my people and I. By carrying on a continual and meaningful dialogue, we can help each other to establish a dynamic, flexible and truly viable urban environment. We can modify each other without any significant loss of individuality."

"It sounds fine," Carmody said. "Except, of course, that you don't have anyone here to carry on a dialogue with."

"That is the only flaw in the scheme," the city admitted. "But for the present, I have you."

"Yes, you have me," Carmody said, and wondered why the words rang unpleasantly on his ear.

"And, naturally, you have me," the city said. "It is a reciprocal relationship, which is the only kind worth having. But now, my dear Carmody, suppose I show you around myself. Then we can get you settled in and regularized."

"Get me what?"

"I didn't mean that the way it sounded," the city said. "It simply is an unfortunate scientific expression. But you understand, I'm sure, that a reciprocal relationship necessitates obligations on the part of both involved parties. It couldn't very well be otherwise, could it?"

"Not unless it was a *laissez-faire* relationship."

"We're trying to get away from all that," Bellwether said. *"Laissez-faire* becomes a doctrine of the emotions, you know, and leads non-stop to *anomie*. If you will just come this way. . . ."

III

Carmody went where he was asked and beheld the excellencies of Bellwether. He toured the power plant, the water filtration center, the industrial park and the light industries section. He saw the children's park and the Odd Fellow's Hall. He walked through a museum and an art gallery, a concert hall and a theater, a bowling alley, a billiards parlor, a Go-Kart track and a movie theater. He became tired and wanted to stop. But the city wanted to show itself off, and Carmody had to look at the five-story American Express building, the Portuguese synagogue, the statue of Buckminster Fuller, the Greyhound Bus Station and several other attractions.

At last it was over. Carmody concluded that beauty was in the eye of the beholder, except for a small part of it that was in the beholder's feet.

"A little lunch now?" the city asked.

"Fine," Carmody said.

He was guided to the fashionable Rochambeau Cafe, where he began with *potage au petit pois* and ended with *petits fours*.

"What about a nice Brie to finish off?" the city asked.

"No, thanks," Carmody said. "I'm full. Too full, as a matter of fact."

"But cheese isn't filling. A bit of first-rate Camembert?"

"I couldn't possibly."

"Perhaps a few assorted fruits. *Very* refreshing to the palate."

"It's not my palate that needs refreshing," Carmody said.

"At least an apple, a pear and a couple of grapes?"

"Thanks, no."

"A couple of cherries?"

"No, no, no!"

"A meal isn't complete without a little fruit," the city said.

"My meal is," Carmody said.

"There are important vitamins only found in fresh fruit."

"I'll just have to struggle along without them."

"Perhaps half an orange, which I will peel for you? Citrus fruits have no bulk at all."

"I couldn't possibly."

"Not even one quarter of an orange? If I take out all the pits?"

"Most decidedly not."

"It would make me feel better," the city said. "I have a completion compulsion, you know, and no meal is complete without a piece of fruit."

"No! No! No!"

"All right, don't get so excited," the city said. "If you don't like the sort of food I serve, that's up to you."

"But I do like it!"

"Then if you like it so much, why won't you eat some fruit?"

"Enough," Carmody said. "Give me a couple of grapes."

"I wouldn't want to force anything on you."

"You're not forcing. Give me, please."

"You're quite sure?"

"Gimme!" Carmody shouted.

"So take," the city said and produced a magnificent bunch of muscatel grapes. Carmody ate them all. They were very good.

"Excuse me," the city said. "What are you doing?" Carmody sat upright and opened his eyes. "I was taking a little nap," he said. "Is there anything wrong with that?"

"What should be wrong with a perfectly natural thing like that?" the city said.

"Thank you," Carmody said, and closed his eyes again.

"But why nap in a chair?" the city asked.

"Because I'm *in* a chair, and I'm already half asleep."

"You'll get a crick in your back," the city warned him.

"Don't care," Carmody mumbled, his eyes still closed.

"Why not take a proper nap? Over here, on the couch?"

"I'm already napping comfortably right here."

"You're not really comfortable," the city pointed out. "The human anatomy is not constructed for sleeping sitting up."

"At the moment, mine is," Carmody said.

"It's not. Why not try the couch?"

"The chair is fine."

"But the couch is finer. Just try it, please, Carmody. Carmody?"

"Eh? What's that?" Carmody said, waking up.

"The couch. I really think you should rest on the couch."

"All right!" Carmody said, struggling to his feet. "Where is this couch?"

He was guided out of the restaurant, down the street, around the corner, and into a building marked "The Snoozerie." There were a dozen couches. Carmody went to the nearest.

"Not that one," the city said. "It's got a bad spring."

"It doesn't matter," Carmody said. "I'll sleep around it."

"That will result in a cramped posture."

"Christ!" Carmody said, getting to his feet. "Which couch would you recommend?"

"This one right back here," the city said. "It's a king-size, the best in the place. The yield-point of the mattress has been scientifically determined. The pillows—"

"Right, fine, good," Carmody said, lying down on the indicated couch.

"Shall I play you some soothing music?"

"Don't bother."

"Just as you wish. I'll put out the lights, then."

"Fine."

"Would you like a blanket? I control the temperature here, of course, but sleepers often get a subjective impression of chilliness."

"It doesn't matter! Leave me alone!"

"All right!" the city said. "I'm not doing this for myself, you know. Personally, I never sleep."

"Okay, sorry," Carmody said.

"That's perfectly all right."

There was a long silence. Then Carmody sat up.

"What's the matter?" the city asked.

"Now I can't sleep," Carmody said.

"Try closing your eyes and consciously relaxing every muscle in your body, starting with the big toe and working upward to—"

"I can't sleep!" Carmody shouted.

"Maybe you weren't very sleepy to begin with," the city suggested. "But at least you could close your eyes and try to get a little rest. Won't you do that for me?"

"No!" Carmody said. "I'm not sleepy and I don't need a rest."

"Stubborn!" the city said. "Do what you like. I've tried my best."

"Yeah!" Carmody said, getting to his feet and walking out of the Snoozerie.

IV

Carmody stood on a little curved bridge and looked over a blue lagoon.

"This is a copy of the Rialto bridge in Venice," the city said. "Scaled down, of course."

"I know," Carmody said. "I read the sign."

"It's rather enchanting, isn't it?"

"Sure, it's fine," Carmody said, lighting a cigarette.

"You're doing a lot of smoking," the city pointed out.

"I know. I feel like smoking."

"As your medical advisor, I must point out that the link between smoking and lung cancer is conclusive."

"I know."

"If you switched to a pipe your chances would be improved."

"I don't like pipes."

"What about a cigar, then?"

"I don't like cigars." He lit another cigarette.

"That's your third cigarette in five minutes," the city said.

"Goddamn it, I'll smoke as much and as often as I please!" Carmody shouted.

"Well, of course you will!" the city said. "I was merely trying to advise you for your own good. Would you want me to simply stand by and not say a word while you destroyed yourself?"

"Yes," Carmody said.

"I can't believe that you mean that. There is an ethical imperative involved here. Man can act against his best interests; but a machine is not allowed that degree of perversity."

"Get off my back," Carmody said sullenly. "Quit pushing me around."

"Pushing you around? My dear Carmody, have I coerced you in any way? Have I done any more than advise you?"

"Maybe not. But you talk too much."

"Perhaps I don't talk enough," the city said. "To judge from the response I get."

"You talk too much," Carmody repeated and lit a cigarette.

"That is your fourth cigarette in five minutes."

Carmody opened his mouth to bellow an insult. Then he changed his mind and walked away.

"What's this?" Carmody asked.

"It's a candy machine," the city told him.

"It doesn't look like one."

"Still, it is one. This design is a modification of a design by Saarionmen for a silo. I have miniaturized it, of course, and—"

"It still doesn't look like a candy machine. How do you work it?"

"It's very simple. Push the red button. Now wait. Press down one of those levers on Row A; now press the green button. There!"

A Baby Ruth bar slid into Carmody's hand.

"Huh," Carmody said. He stripped off the paper and bit into the bar. "Is this a real Baby Ruth bar or a copy of one?" he asked.

"It's a real one. I had to subcontract the candy concession because of the pressure of work."

"Huh," Carmody said, letting the candy wrapper slip from his fingers.

"That," the city said, "is an example of the kind of thoughtlessness I always encounter."

"It's just a piece of paper," Carmody said, turning and looking at the candy wrapper lying on the spotless street.

"Of course it's just a piece of paper," the city said. "But multiply it by a hundred thousand inhabitants and what do you have?"

"A hundred thousand Baby Ruth wrappers," Carmody answered at once.

"I don't consider that funny," the city said. "You wouldn't want to *live* in the midst of all that paper, I can assure you. You'd be the first to complain if this street were strewn with garbage. But do you do your share? Do you even clean up after yourself? Of course not! You leave it to me, even though I have to run all of the other functions of the city, night and day, without even Sundays off."

Carmody bent down to pick up the candy wrapper. But just before his fingers could close on it, a pincer arm shot out of the nearest sewer, snatched the paper away and vanished from sight.

"It's all right," the city said. "I'm used to cleaning up after people. I do it all the time."

"Yuh," said Carmody.

"Nor do I expect any gratitude."

"I'm grateful, I'm grateful!" Carmody said.

"No, you're not," Bellwether said.

"So okay maybe I'm not. What do you want me to say?"

"I don't want you to say anything," the city said. "Let us consider the incident closed."

"Had enough?" the city said, after dinner.

"Plenty," Carmody said.

"You didn't eat much."

"I ate all I wanted. It was very good."

"If it was so good, why didn't you eat more?"

"Because I couldn't hold any more."

"If you hadn't spoiled your appetite with that candy bar . . ."

"Goddamn it, the candy bar didn't spoil my appetite! I just—"

"You're lighting a cigarette," the city said.

"Yeah," Carmody said.

"Couldn't you wait a little longer?"

"Now look," Carmody said. "Just what in hell do you—"

"But we have something more important to talk about," the city said quickly. "Have you thought about what you're going to do for a living?"

"I haven't really had much time to think about it."

"Well, I have been thinking about it. It would be nice if you became a doctor."

"Me? I'd have to take special college courses, then get into medical school, and so forth."

"I can arrange all that," the city said.

"Not interested."

"Well . . . What about law?"

"Never."

"Engineering is an excellent line."

"Not for me."

"What about accounting?"

"Not on your life."

"What do you want to be?"

"A jet pilot," Carmody said impulsively.

"Oh, come now!"

"I'm quite serious."

"I don't even have an air field here."

"Then I'll pilot somewhere else."

"You're only saying that to spite me!"

"Not at all," Carmody said. "I want to be a pilot, I really do. I've *always* wanted to be a pilot! Honest I have!"

There was a long silence. Then the city said, "The choice is entirely up to you." This was said in a voice like death.

"Where are you going now?"

"Out for a walk," Carmody said.

"At nine-thirty in the evening?"

"Sure. Why not?"

"I thought you were tired."

"That was quite some time ago."

"I see. And I also thought that you could sit here and we could have a nice chat."

"How about if we talk after I get back?" Carmody asked.

"No, it doesn't matter," the city said.

"The walk doesn't matter," Carmody said, sitting down. "Come on, we'll talk."

"I no longer care to talk," the city said. "Please go for your walk."

V

"Well, good night," Carmody said.

"I beg your pardon?"

"I said, 'good night.' "

"You're going to sleep?"

"Sure. It's late, I'm tired."

"You're going to sleep now?"

"Well, why not?"

"No reason at all," the city said, "except that you have forgotten to wash."

"Oh. . . . I guess I did forget. I'll wash in the morning."

"How long is it since you've had a bath?"

"Too long. I'll take one in the morning."

"Wouldn't you feel better if you took one right now?"

"No."

"Even if I drew the bath for you?"

"No! Goddamn it, no! I'm going to sleep!"

"Do exactly as you please," the city said. "Don't wash, don't study, don't eat a balanced diet. But also, don't blame me."

"Blame you? For what?"

"For anything," the city said.

"Yes. But what did you have in mind, specifically?"

"It isn't important."

"Then why did you bring it up in the first place?"

"I was only thinking of you," the city said.

"I realize that."

"You must know that it can't benefit *me* if you wash or not."

"I'm aware of that."

"When one cares," the city went on, "when one feels one's responsibilities, it is not nice to hear oneself sworn at."

"I didn't swear at you."

"Not this time. But earlier today you did."

"Well . . . I was nervous."

"That's because of the smoking."

"Don't start that again!"

"I won't," the city said. "Smoke like a furnace. What does it matter to me?"

"Damned right," Carmody said, lighting a cigarette.

"But my failure," the city said.

"No, no," Carmody said. "Don't say it, please don't!"

"Forget I said it," the city said.

"All right."

"Sometimes I get overzealous."

"Sure."

"And it's especially difficult because I'm right. I am right, you know."

"I know," Carmody said. "You're right, you're right, you're always right. Right right right right right—"

"Don't overexcite yourself bedtime," the city said. "Would you care for a glass of milk?"

"No."

"You're sure?"

Carmody put his hands over his eyes. He felt very strange. He also felt extremely guilty, fragile, dirty, unhealthy and sloppy. He felt generally and irrevocably bad, and it would always be this way unless he changed, adjusted, adapted. . . .

But instead of attempting anything of the sort he rose to his feet, squared his shoulders, and marched away past the Roman piazza and the Venetian bridge.

"Where are you going?" the city asked. "What's the matter?"

Silent, tight-lipped, Carmody continued past the children's park and the American Express building.

"What did I do wrong?" the city cried. "What, just tell me what?"

Carmody made no reply but strode past the Rochambeau Cafe and the Portuguese synagogue, coming at last to the pleasant green plain that surrounded Bellwether.

"Ingrate!" the city screamed after him. "You're just like all the others. All of you humans are disagreeable animals, and you're never really satisfied with anything."

Carmody got into his car and started the engine.

"But of course," the city said, in a more thoughtful voice, "you're never really *dissatisfied* with anything either. The moral, I suppose, is that a city must learn patience."

Carmody turned the car onto King's Highbridge Gate Road and started east, toward New York.

"Have a nice trip!" Bellwether called after him. "Don't worry about me, I'll be waiting up for you."

Carmody stepped down hard on the accelerator. He really wished he hadn't heard that last remark.

ISAAC BASHEVIS SINGER

Jachid and Jechidah

*Hell's bells tinkle in urban glades where love is an infirm-
ity leading to death, where green fields and blue skies are the
manifold blessings of corruption and the vulgarity of death is
nothing but a short episode in the eternity of life. Isaac Bashevis
Singer, a recognized master of Jewish fiction, pours black paint
over modern man's favorite philosophical toys with a cheerful
vengeance. With the blind, mocking eyes of an omniscient skeptic
he examines acceptable reality, throws stones at it, and pushes
past its cardboard parameters. The result is a happy exercise in
Jewish iconoclasm.*

J. D.

*

IN A PRISON where souls bound for Sheol—Earth they call it there
—await destruction, there hovered the female soul Jechidah. Souls
forget their origin. Purah, the Angel of Forgetfulness, he who
dissipates God's light and conceals His face, holds dominion everywhere beyond the Godhead. Jechidah, unmindful of her descent
from the Throne of Glory, had sinned. Her jealousy had caused
much trouble in the world where she dwelled. She had suspected
all female angels of having affairs with her lover Jachid, had not
only blasphemed God but even denied him. Souls, she said, were
not created but had evolved out of nothing: they had neither
mission nor purpose. Although the authorities were extremely
patient and forgiving, Jechidah was finally sentenced to death.
The judge fixed the moment of her descent to that cemetery
called Earth.

The attorney for Jechidah appealed to the Superior Court of
Heaven, even presented a petition to Metatron, the Lord of the
Face. But Jechidah was so filled with sin and so impenitent that no
power could save her. The attendants seized her, tore her from
Jachid, clipped her wings, cut her hair, and clothed her in a long
white shroud. She was no longer allowed to hear the music of the
spheres, to smell the perfumes of Paradise and to meditate on the
secrets of the Torah, which sustain the soul. She could no longer
bathe in the wells of balsam oil. In the prison cell, the darkness of
the nether world already surrounded her. But her greatest torment was her longing for Jachid. She could no longer reach him
telepathically. Nor could she send a message to him, all of her
servants having been taken away. Only the fear of death was left
to Jechidah.

Death was no rare occurrence where Jechidah lived but it befell only vulgar, exhausted spirits. Exactly what happened to the dead, Jechidah did not know. She was convinced that when a soul descended to Earth it was to extinction, even though the pious maintained that a spark of life remained. A dead soul immediately began to rot and was soon covered with a slimy stuff called semen. Then a grave digger put it into a womb where it turned into some sort of fungus and was henceforth known as a child. Later on, began the tortures of Gehenna: birth, growth, toil. For according to the morality books, death was not the final stage. Purified, the soul returned to its source. But what evidence was there for such beliefs? So far as Jechidah knew, no one had ever returned from Earth. The enlightened Jechidah believed that the soul rots for a short time and then disintegrates into a darkness of no return.

Now the moment had come when Jechidah must die, must sink to Earth. Soon, the Angel of Death would appear with his fiery sword and thousand eyes.

At first Jechidah had wept incessantly, but then her tears had ceased. Awake or asleep she never stopped thinking of Jachid. Where was he? What was he doing? Whom was he with? Jechidah was well aware he would not mourn for her for ever. He was surrounded by beautiful females, sacred beasts, angels, seraphim, cherubs, ayralim, each one with powers of seduction. How long could someone like Jachid curb his desires? He, like she, was an unbeliever. It was he who had taught her that spirits were not created, but were products of evolution. Jachid did not acknowledge free will, nor believe in ultimate good and evil. What would restrain him? Most certainly he already lay in the lap of some other divinity, telling those stories about himself he had already told Jechidah.

But what could she do? In this dungeon all contact with the mansions ceased. All doors were closed: neither mercy, nor beauty entered here. The one way from this prison led down to Earth, and to the horrors called flesh, blood, marrow, nerves, and breath. The God-fearing angels promised resurrection. They preached that the soul did not linger forever on Earth, but that after it had endured its punishment, it returned to the Higher Sphere. But Jechidah, being a modernist, regarded all of this as superstition. How would a soul free itself from the corruption of the body? It was scientifically impossible. Resurrection was a dream, a silly comfort of primitive and frightened souls.

One night as Jechidah lay in a corner brooding about Jachid and the pleasures she had received from him, his kisses, his caresses, the secrets whispered in her ear, the many positions and games into which she had been initiated, Dumah, the thousand-eyed Angel of Death, looking just as the Sacred Books described him, entered bearing a fiery sword.

"Your time has come, little sister," he said.

"No further appeal is possible?"

"Those who are in this wing always go to Earth."

Jechidah shuddered. "Well, I am ready."

"Jechidah, repentance helps even now. Recite your confession."

"How can it help? My only regret is that I did not transgress more," said Jechidah rebelliously.

Both were silent. Finally Dumah said, "Jechidah, I know you are angry with me. But is it my fault, sister? Did I want to be the Angel of Death? I too am a sinner, exiled from a higher realm, my punishment to be the executioner of souls. Jechidah, I have not willed your death, but be comforted. Death is not as dreadful as you imagine. True, the first moments are not easy. But once you have been planted in the womb, the nine months that follow are not painful. You will forget all that you have learned here. Coming out of the womb will be a shock; but childhood is often pleasant. You will begin to study the lore of death, clothed in a fresh, pliant body, and soon will dread the end of your exile."

Jechidah interrupted him. "Kill me if you must, Dumah, but spare me your lies."

"I am telling you the truth, Jechidah. You will be absent no more than a hundred years, for even the wickedest do not suffer longer than that. Death is only the preparation for a new existence."

"Dumah, please. I don't want to listen."

"But it is important for you to know that good and evil exist there too and that the will remains free."

"What will? Why do you talk such nonsense?"

"Jechidah, listen carefully. Even among the dead there are laws and regulations. The way you act in death will determine what happens to you next. Death is a laboratory for the rehabilitation of souls."

"Make an end of me, I beseech you."

"Be patient, you still have a few more minutes to live and must receive your instructions. Know, then, that one may act well or evilly on Earth and that the most pernicious sin of all is to return a soul to life."

This idea was so ridiculous that Jechidah laughed despite her anguish.

"How can one corpse give life to another?"

"It's not as difficult as you think. The body is composed of such weak material that a mere blow can make it disintegrate. Death is no stronger than a cobweb; a breeze blows and it disappears. But it is a great offense to destroy either another's death or one's own. Not only that, but you must not act or speak or even think in such a way as to threaten death. Here one's object is to preserve life, but there it is death that is succoured."

"Nursery tales. The fantasies of an executioner."

"It is the truth, Jechidah. The Torah that applies to Earth is based on a single principle: Another man's death must be as dear to one as one's own. Remember my words. When you descend to Sheol, they will be of value to you."

"No, no, I won't listen to any more lies." And Jechidah covered her ears.

Years passed. Everyone in the higher realm had forgotten Jechidah except her mother who still continued to light memorial candles for her daughter. On Earth Jechidah had a new mother as well as a father, several brothers and sisters, all dead. After attend-

ing a high school, she had begun to take courses at the university.
She lived in a large necropolis where corpses are prepared for all
kinds of mortuary functions.

It was spring, and Earth's corruption grew leprous with blos-
soms. From the graves with their memorial trees and cleansing
waters arose a dreadful stench. Millions of creatures, forced to
descend into the domains of death, were becoming flies, butterflies, worms, toads, frogs. They buzzed, croaked, screeched, rat-
tled, already involved in the death struggle. But since Jechidah
was totally inured to the habits of Earth, all this seemed to her part
of life. She sat on a park bench staring up at the moon, which from
the darkness of the nether world is sometimes recognized as a
memorial candle set in a skull. Like all female corpses, Jechidah
yearned to perpetuate death, to have her womb become a grave
for the newly dead. But she couldn't do that without the help of
a male with whom she would have to copulate in the hatred which
corpses call love.

As Jechidah sat staring into the sockets of the skull above her,
a white-shrouded corpse came and sat beside her. For a while the
two corpses gazed at each other, thinking they could see, although
all corpses are actually blind. Finally the male corpse spoke:

"Pardon, Miss, could you tell me what time it is?"

Since deep within themselves all corpses long for the termina-
tion of their punishment, they are perpetually concerned with
time.

"The time?" Jechidah answered. "Just a second." Strapped to
her wrist was an instrument to measure time but the divisions
were so minute and the symbols so tiny that she could not easily
read the dial. The male corpse moved nearer to her.

"May I take a look? I have good eyes."

"If you wish."

Corpses never act straightforwardly but are always sly and devi-
ous. The male corpse took Jechidah's hand and bent his head
toward the instrument. This was not the first time a male corpse
had touched Jechidah but contact with this one made her limbs

tremble. He stared intently but could not decide immediately. Then he said: "I think it's ten minutes after ten."

"Is it really so late?"

"Permit me to introduce myself. My name is Jachid."

"Jachid? Mine is Jechidah."

"What an odd coincidence."

Both hearing death race in their blood were silent for a long while. Then Jachid said: "How beautiful the night is!"

"Yes, beautiful!"

"There's something about spring that cannot be expressed in words."

"Words can express nothing," answered Jechidah.

As she made this remark, both knew they were destined to lie together and to prepare a grave for a new corpse. The fact is, no matter how dead the dead are there remains some life in them, a trace of contact with that knowledge which fills the universe. Death only masks the truth. The sages speak of it as a soap bubble that bursts at the touch of a straw. The dead, ashamed of death, try to conceal their condition through cunning. The more moribund a corpse the more voluble it is.

"May I ask where you live?" asked Jachid.

Where have I seen him before? How is it his voice sounds so familiar to me? Jechidah wondered. *And how does it happen that he's called Jachid? Such a rare name.*

"Not far from here," she answered.

"Would you object to my walking you home?"

"Thank you. You don't have to. But if you want. . . . It is still too early to go to bed."

When Jachid rose, Jechidah did, too. Is this the one I have been searching for? Jechidah asked herself, the one destined for me? But what do I mean by destiny? According to my professor, only atoms and motion exist. A carriage approached them and Jechidah heard Jachid say:

"Would you like to take a ride?"

"Where to?"

"Oh, just around the park."

Instead of reproving him as she intended to, Jechidah said: "It
would be nice. But I don't think you should spend the money."

"What's money? You only live once."

The carriage stopped and they both got in. Jechidah knew that
no self-respecting girl would go riding with a strange young man.
What did Jachid think of her? Did he believe she would go riding
with anyone who asked her? She wanted to explain that she was
shy by nature, but she knew she could not wipe out the impression
she had already made. She sat in silence, astonished at her behav-
ior. She felt nearer to this stranger than she ever had to anyone.
She could almost read his mind. She wished the night would continue for ever. Was this love? Could one really fall in love so
quickly? And am I happy? she asked herself. But no answer came
from within her. For the dead are always melancholy, even in the
midst of gaiety. After a while Jechidah said: "I have a strange
feeling I have experienced all this before."

"*Déjà vu*—that's what psychology calls it."

"But maybe there's some truth to it. . . ."

"What do you mean?"

"Maybe we've known each other in some other world."

Jachid burst out laughing. "In what world? There is only one,
ours, the earth."

"But maybe souls do exist."

"Impossible. What you call the soul is nothing but vibrations of
matter, the product of the nervous system. I should know, I'm a
medical student." Suddenly he put his arm around her waist. And
although Jechidah had never permitted any male to take such
liberties before, she did not reprove him. She sat there perplexed
by her acquiescence, fearful of the regrets that would be hers
tomorrow. I'm completely without character, she chided herself.
But he is right about one thing. If there is no soul and life is nothing
but a short episode in an eternity of death, then why shouldn't one
enjoy oneself without restraint? If there is no soul, there is no God,
free will is meaningless. Morality, as my professor says, is nothing

but a part of the ideological superstructure.

Jechidah closed her eyes and leaned back against the upholstery. The horse trotted slowly. In the dark all the corpses, men and beasts, lamented their death—howling, laughing, buzzing, chirping, sighing. Some of the corpses staggered, having drunk to forget for a while the tortures of hell. Jechidah had retreated into herself. She dozed off, then awoke again with a start. When the dead sleep they once more connect themselves with the source of life. The illusion of time and space, cause and effect, number and relation ceases. In her dream Jechidah had ascended again into the world of her origin. There she saw her real mother, her friends, her teachers. Jachid was there, too. The two greeted each other, embraced, laughed and wept with joy. At that moment, they both recognized the truth, that death on Earth is temporary and illusory, a trial and a means of purification. They traveled together past heavenly mansions, gardens, oases for convalescent souls, forests for divine beasts, islands for heavenly birds. No, our meeting was not an accident, Jechidah murmured to herself. There is a God. There is a purpose in creation. Copulation, free will, fate— all are part of His plan. Jachid and Jechidah passed by a prison and gazed into its window. They saw a soul condemned to sink down to Earth. Jechidah knew that this soul would become her daughter. Just before she woke up, Jechidah heard a voice:

"The grave and the grave digger have met. The burial will take place tonight."

TRANSLATED BY the Author and Elizabeth Pollet

HARLAN ELLISON

I'm Looking for Kadak

Can the heroic figure be, at the same time, a Ulysses, a mensch, a meshugge, and a comedian with a heart of gold? Perhaps only if he's Jewish. So here is a tall tale, a myth about a Jewish Ulysses with caterpillar feet and blue skin. It's a tummel, a joyful shouting in the face of sorrow, an uplifting. It's a fairy tale with Jewish words—and that presents a problem.

To quote Harlan Ellison, "There are three ways to write a story using words in a foreign tongue. The first is to explain every single word as it is used, by restating its meaning in English, or by hoping its use in context will clarify for the reader. The second is to attempt by syntactical manipulation an approximation of the dialect and tongue, eschewing the use of any foreign words. The third is to provide a glossary."

Therefore, "Ellison's Grammatical Guide and Glossary for Goyim" has been appended to the end of the story to aid the reader and provide a few belly-laughs. And since a fairy tale should have a picture, award-winning artist Tim Kirk has drawn the hero, Evsise, the Zsouchmoid.

J. D.

EDITOR'S NOTE: *This is an original story written expressly for this volume.*

*

YOU'LL PARDON ME but my name is Evsise and I'm standing here in the middle of sand, talking to a butterfly, and if I sound like I'm talking to myself, again you'll pardon but what can I tell you? A grown person standing talking to a butterfly. In sand.

So *nu?* What else can you expect? There are times you got to make adjustments, you got to let be a little. Just to get along. I'm not all that happy about this, if you want the specific truth. I've learned, God knows I've learned. I'm a Jew, and if there is a thing Jews have learned in over six thousand years, it's that you got to compromise if you want to make it to seven thousand. So, let be. I'll talk to this butterfly, hey you butterfly, and I'll pray for the best.

You don't understand. You got that look.

Listen: I read once in a book that they found a tribe of Jewish Indians, somewhere deep in the heart of South America. That was on the Earth. The Earth, *shtumie!* It's been in all the papers.

So. Jewish Indians. What a thing! And everyone wondered and yelled and made such a *mishegoss* that they had to send historians and sociologists and anthropologists and all manner of very learned types to establish if this was a true thing or maybe somebody was just lying.

And what they found was that maybe what had happened was that some *galus* from Spain, fleeing the Inquisition, got on board with Cortez and came to The New World, *kayn-ahora,* and when no one was looking, he ran away. So then he got *farblondjet* and wound up in some little place full of very suggestive native types, and being something of a *tummeler* he started teaching them about being Jewish—just to keep busy, you know what I mean?

because Jews have never been missionaries, none of that "converting" crap; *other*, I shouldn't name names, religions need to keep going, unlike Judaism which does very cute thank you on its own —and by the time all the smart-alecks found the tribe, they were keeping kosher, and having *brises* when the sons were born, and observing the High Holy Days, and not doing any fishing on the *Shabbes*, and it was a very nice thing altogether.

So it shouldn't surprise anyone that there are Jews here on Zsouchmuhn. Zoochhhhhh-moooohn. With a *chhhhh*, not a *kuh*. You got a no-accent like a Litvak.

It shouldn't even surprise that I'm a Jew and I'm blue and I have eleven arms thereby defying the Law of Bilateral Symmetry and I am squat and round and move very close to the ground by a series of caterpillar feet set around the rim of ball joints and sockets on either side of my *tuchis* which *obeys* the Law of Bilateral Symmetry and when I've wound the feet tight I have to jump off the ground so they can unwind and then I move forward again which makes my movement very peculiar I'm told by tourists without very much class.

In the Universal Ephemeris I am referred to as a native of Theta 996:VI, Cluster Messier 3 in Canes Venatici. The VI is Zsouchmuhn. A baedeker from some publisher in the Crab came here a few turns ago and wrote a travel pamphlet on Zsouchmuhn; he kept calling me a Zsouchmoid; he should grow in the ground, headfirst like a turnip. I am a Jew.

I don't know what a turnip is.

Now I'm raving. What it'll do to you, talking to a butterfly. I have a mission, and it's making me crazy, giving me *shpilkess*, you could die from a mission like this. I'm looking for Kadak.

Hey you butterfly! A blink, a flutter, a movement it wouldn't hurt, you should make an indication you can hear me, I shouldn't stand like a *schlemiel* telling you all this.

Nothing. You wouldn't give me a break.

Listen: if it wasn't for that *oysvorf*, that bum, Snodle, I wouldn't be here. I would be with my family and my lust-nest concubines on Theta 996:III, what the Ephemeris calls Bromios, what we Jews call Kasrilevka. There is historical precedent for our naming Bromios another name, Kasrilevka. You'll read Sholom Aleichem, you'll understand. A planet for *schlimazels*. I don't want to discuss it. That's where they're moving us. Everyone went. A few crazy ones stayed, there are always a few. But mostly, everyone went: who would want to stay? They're moving Zsouchmuhn. God knows where. Every time you look around they're dragging a place off and putting it somewhere else. I don't want to go into that. Terrible people, they got no hearts in them.

So we were sitting in the *yeshiva*, the last ten of us, a proper *minyan*, getting ready to sit *shivah* for the whole planet, for the last days we would be here, when that *oysvorf* Snodle had a seizure and up and died. Oh, a look: a question, maybe? Why were we sitting *shivah* in the rabbinical college when everybody else was running like a thief to get off the planet before those *gonifs* from the Relocation Center came with their skyhooks, a *glitch* if ever I saw one, shady, disreputable, to give a yank and drag a place out of orbit and give a shove and jam in big *meshiginah* magnets to float around where a nice, cute world was, just to keep the Cluster running smooth, when they pull out a world everything shouldn't go bump together . . . ? Why, you ask me. So, I'll tell you why.

Because, Mr. I-Won't-Talk-Or-Even-Flap-My-Wings Butterfly, *shivah* is the holiest of the holies. Because the Talmud says when you mourn the dead you get ten Jewish men who come to the home of the deceased, not eight or seven or four, but *ten* men, and you sit and you pray, and you hold services, and you light the *yorzeit* candles, and you recite the *kaddish* which as every intelligent life-form in the Cluster except maybe a nut butterfly knows is the prayer for the dead, in honor and praise of God and the deceased.

And why do we want to sit *shivah* for a world that was such a good home for us for so many turns? Because, and it strikes me foolishness to expect a *farchachdah* butterfly to grasp what I'm trying to say here, because God has been good to us here, and we've property (which now is gone) and we've got families (which now are gone) and we've got our health (which, if I continue talking to you, I'll be losing shortly) and God's name can be hallowed by word of mouth only in the presence of others—the community of worshippers—the congregation—the *minyan* of ten, and *that's* why.

You know, even for a butterfly, you don't *look* Jewish.

So *nu*, now you understand a little maybe? Zsouchmuhn was the *goldeneh medina* for us, the golden country; it was good here, we were happy here, now we have to move to Kasrilevka, a world for *schlimazels*. Not even a Red Sea to be parted, it isn't slavery, it's just a world that's not enough, you know what I mean? So we wanted to pay last respects. It's not so crazy. And everyone went, and only the ten of us left to sit the seven turns till we went away and Zsouchmuhn was *goniffed* out of the sky to go God-knows-where. It would have been fine, except for that Snodle, that crazy. Who seized up and died on us.

So where would we get a tenth man for the *minyan?*

There were only nine Jews on the whole planet.

Then Snodle said, "There's always Kadak."

"Shut up, you're dead," Reb Jeshaia said, but it didn't do any good. Snodle kept suggesting Kadak.

You should understand, one of the drawbacks of my species, which maybe a butterfly wouldn't know, is that when we die, and pass on, there's still talking. *Nuhdzhing.* Oh. You want to know how that can be. How a dead Jew can talk, through the veil, from the other side. What am I, a science authority, I should know how that works? I wouldn't lie on you: I don't know. Always it's been the same. One of us seizes up and dies, and the body squats there and doesn't decay the way the tourists' do when they get *shikker* in a blind pig bar in downtown Houmitz and stagger out in the gutter and get knocked over by a tumbrel on the way to the casinos.

But the voice starts up. *Nuhdzhing!*

It probably has something to do with the soul, but I wouldn't put a bet on that; all I can say is thank God we don't worship ancestors here on Zsouchmuhn, because we'd have such a sky full of *nuhdzhing* old farts telling us how to run our lives, it wouldn't be worth it to keep on this side of the veil. Bless the name of Abraham, after a while they shut up and go off somewhere.

Probably to *nuhdz* each other, they should rest in peace already and stop talking.

But Snodle wasn't going away. He died, and now he was demanding we not only sit *shivah* out of courtesy for having lived here so prosperously, but we should also, you shouldn't take it as an imposition, sit *shivah* for *him!* An *oysvorf,* that Snodle.

"There's always Kadak," he said. His voice came from a no-where spot in the air about a foot above his body, which was dumped upside-down on a table in the *yeshiva.*

"Snodle, if you don't mind," said Shmuel with the one good antenna, "would you kindly shut your face and let us handle this?" Then seeing, I suppose for the first time, that Snodle was upside-down, he added, but softly he shouldn't speak ill of the dead, "I always said he talked through his *tuchis.* "

"I'll turn him over," said Chaim with the defective unwind in his hop.

"Let be," said Shmuel. "I like this end better than the other."

"This is getting us nowhere," said Yitzchak. "The *gonifs* come in a little while to take away the planet, we can't stay, we can't go, and I have lust-nest concubines lubricating and lactating on Bromios this very minute."

"Kasrilevka," said Avram.

"Kasrilevka," Yitzchak agreed, his prop-arm, the one in the back, curling an ungrammatical apology.

"A planet of ten million Snodles," said Yankel.

"There's always Kadak," said Snodle.

"Who is this Kadak the *oysvorf*'s babbling about?" asked Meyer Kahaha. The rest of us rolled our eyes at the remark. Ninety-six *tsuris*-filled eyes rolled. Meyer Kahaha was always the town *schlemiel;* if there was a bigger *oysvorf* than Snodle, it was Meyer Kahaha.

Yankel stuck the tip of his pointing arm in Meyer Kahaha's ninth eye, the one with the cataract. "Quiet!"

We sat and stared at each other. Finally, Moishe said, "He's right. It's another tragedy we can mourn on *Tisha Ba'b* (if they have enough turns on Kasrilevka for *Tisha Ba'b* to fall in the right month), but the *oysvorf* and the *schlemiel* are right. Our only hope is Kadak, lightning shouldn't strike me for saying it."

"Someone will have to go find him," said Avram.

"Not me," said Yankel. "A mission for a fool."

Then Reb Jeshaia, who was the wisest of all the blue Jews on Zsouchmuhn, even *before* the great exodus, one or two of them it wouldn't have hurt if they'd stayed behind to give a little help so we shouldn't find out too late we were in this miserable state of things because Snodle seized up and died, Reb Jeshaia nodded that it was a mission for a fool and he said, "We'll send Evsise."

"Thanks a lot for that," I said.

He looked at me with the six eyes on the front, and he said, "Evsise. Should we send Shmuel with one good antenna? Should we send Chaim with a defective hop? Should we send Yitzchak who is so crippled with lust he gets cramps? Maybe we should send Yankel who is older than even Snodle and would die from the journey then we'd have to find *two* Jews? Moishe? Moishe argues with everyone. Some cooperation *he'd* get."

"What about Avram?" I asked. Avram looked away.

"You want I should talk about Avram's problem here in front of an open Talmud, here in front of the dead, right here in front of God and everyone?" Reb Jeshaia looked stern.

"Forget it. I'm sorry I mentioned," I said.

"Maybe I should go myself, the Rabbi should go? Or maybe you'd prefer we sent Meyer Kahaha?"

"You made your point," I said. "I'll go. I'm far from a happy person about this, you should know it before I go. But I'll do it.

You'll never see me again, I'll die out there looking for that Kadak, but I'll go."

I started for the burrow exit of the *yeshiva*. I passed Yitzchak, who looked sheepish. "Cramps," I muttered. "It should only wither up and fall off like a dead leaf."

Then I rolled, hopped and unwound my way up the tunnel to the street, and went looking for Kadak.

The last time I saw Kadak was seventeen turns ago. He was squatting in the synagogue during Purim, and suddenly he rolled into the aisle, tore off his *yarmulkah*, his *tallis* and his *t'fillin*, all at once with his top three arms on each side, threw them into the aisle, yelled he had had it with Judaism, and was converting to the Church of the Apostates.

That was the last any of us saw of him. Good riddance to bad rubbish, you ask me. Kadak, to begin with, was never my favorite person, if you want the truth. He snuffled.

Oh, that isn't such an *averah*, I can see you think I'm making a big something out of a big nothing. Listen, Mr. Terrific-I-Flap-My-Wings-And-You-Should-Notice-Me, I'm a person who says what's on his mind, I don't make no moofky-foofky with anyone. You want someone who beats around the bushes you should talk to that Avram. Me, I'll tell you I couldn't stand that Kadak's snuffling, all the time snuffling. You sit in the *shoul* and right in the middle of the *Shema*, right in the direct absolute center of "Hear O Israel, the Lord, Our God, the Lord is One," comes a snuffle that sounds like a double-snouted peggalomer in a mud-wallow.

He had a snuffle made you want to go take a bath.

A terrible snuffle, if you'll listen to me for a minute. He was the kind, that Kadak, he wouldn't care *when* he'd snuffle. When you were sleeping, eating, *shtupping*, making a ka-ka, he didn't care . . . would come a blast, a snort, a rotten snuffle could make you want to get rid of your last three or four meals. And forget talking to him: how can you talk to a person who punctuates with a snuffle?

So when he went off to convert to the Apostates, sure there was a scandal . . . there weren't that many Jews on Zsouchmuhn . . . *any*thing was a scandal . . . but to be absolutely frank with you, I'll speak my mind no matter what, we were very relieved. To be free of that snuffle was already a *naches*, like getting one free. Or seven for five.

So now I had to go all over there and back, looking for that terrible snuffle. It was an ugliness I could live without, you should pardon my frankness.

But I went through downtown Houmitz and went over to the Holy Cathedral of the Church of the Apostates. The city was in a very bad way. When everyone had gone to Kasrilevka, they took everything that wasn't bolted down. They also took everything that *was* bolted down. They also took the bolts. Not to mention a lot of the soil it was all bolted down into. Big holes, everywhere. Zsouchmuhn was not, at this point in time I'm telling you about, such a cute little world anymore. It looked like an old man with a *krenk*. Like a *pisher* with acne. Very unpleasant, it wasn't a trip I care to talk about.

But there was a little left of that crazy *farchachdah* Cathedral still standing. Why shouldn't they let it stand: how much does it cost to make a new one? String. The dummies, they make a holy place from string and spit and bits of dried crap off the streets and their bodies, I don't even want to think about what a sacrilege.

I rolled inside. The smell, you could die from the smell. On Zsouchmuhn here, we got a groundworm, this filthy little segmented thing everyone calls a pincercrusher. *Lumbricus rubellus Venaticus* my Uncle Beppo, the lunatic zoologist, calls it. It isn't at all peculiar why I remember a foreign name like that—Latin is what it is, I'm a *bissel* scholar, too, you know, not such a dummy as you might think, and it's no wonder Reb Jeshaia sent me on this it-could-kill-a-lesser-Jew mission to find Kadak. I remember because once I had one of them bite me in the *tuchis* when I went swimming, and you learn these things, believe you me, you learn them. This rotten little worm it's got pinching things in the front

and on the sides, and it lies in wait for a juicy *tuchis* and when
you're just ready to relax in a swim, or maybe to take a nap on a
picnic, *chomp!*, it goes right for the *tuchis*. And it hangs on with
those triple-damned the entire species should go straight to
Gehenna pinch-things, and it makes me sick to remember, but it
sucks the blood right out of you, right through your *tuchis*. And
you couldn't get one off, medical science as hootsy-tootsy as it is,
you could *varf* from the size of a doctor's bill, even the hootsy-
tootsies can't get one off you. The only thing that does it, is you get
a musician and he bangs together a pair of cymbals, and it falls off.
All bloated up with your blood, leaving a bunch of little pinch-
marks on your *tuchis* you're ashamed to let your lust-mates see it.
And don't ask why the doctors don't carry cymbals with them for
such occasions. You wouldn't be *lieve* the union problems here on
Zsouchmuhn, which includes musicians and doctors both, so you'd
better be near a band and not a hospital when a pincercrusher
bites you in the *tuchis*, otherwise forget it. And when the terrible
thing falls off, it goes *pop!* and it bursts, and all the awful crap it
had in it makes a stink you shouldn't even think about it, the eyes,
all twelve of them could roll up in your head, with the smell of all
that *feh!* and blood and crap.

Inside the Cathedral of the Church of the Apostates, the smell.
Like a million popped pincercrushers. I almost went over on my
face from that smell.

It took three hands to hold all of my nose, a little whiff shouldn't
slip through.

I started reeling around, hitting the strings they called walls.
Fortunately, I rolled around near the entrance, and I stretched my
nose a couple of feet outside, and I took a *very* deep breath, and
snapped my nose back, and held it, and looked around.

There were still half a dozen of them who hadn't run off to
Kasrilevka, all down on their stomachs, their feet winding up and
unwinding, very fast, their faces down in the mud and crap in
front of the altar, doing what I suppose they call praying. To that
idol of theirs, Seymour, or Simon, or Shtumie, whatever they call

it. I should know the name of a heathen idol, you bet your life never, better I should know the Latin name of a miserable worm that stinks first, let me tell you.

So there they were, and let me assure you it pained me in several more than a couple of ways to have to go over to them, but . . . I'm looking for Kadak.

"Hey," I said to one of them. A terrific look at his *tuchis* I got. Such a perfect *tuchis*, if ever there was one, for a pincercrusher to come and *chomp!*

Nothing. "Hey!" I yelled it a second time. No attention. Crazy with their faces down in the crap. "Listen, hey!" I yelled at the top of my voice, which isn't such a soft niceness when I'm suffocating holding my nose with three hands and I want to get out of that place already.

So I gave him a *zetz* in the *tuchis*. I wound up every foot on the left side, and I let it unwind right where a pincercrusher would have brunch.

Then the dummy looked up.

A sight you could become very ill with. A nose covered with crap from the floor, a bunch of eyes filled with blue jelly, a mouth from out of which could only come heathen hosannahs to a dummy idol called Shaygets or something.

"You kicked me," he said.

"All by yourself you figured that out, eh?"

He looked at me with six, and blinked, and started to fall over on his *punim* again, and I started to wind up I'd give him such a *zetz* I'd kick him into a better life.

"We don't accept violence," he said.

"That's a terrific saying," I told him. "Meanwhile, I don't accept an unobstructed view up your *tuchis*. So if you want I should go away and stop kicking you, so you can go root around in the *dreck* some more, what you'd better do is come up here a minute and talk to me."

He kept looking. I wound up tighter. You could hear my sockets creaking. I'm not such a young one anymore. He got up.

"What do you want? I'm worshipping to Seymool."

Seymool. That's a name for a God. I wouldn't even *hire* something called a Seymool.

"You'll worship later. That *buhbie* isn't going anywhere."

"But Zsouchmuhn *is.*"

"Very correct. Which is the same reason I got to talk to you now. Time is a thing I got very little of, if you catch my meaning here."

"Well, what is it you want, precisely?"

Oy, a Talmudic scholar, no less. *Precisely.* "Well, Mr. Precisely, I'll tell you what it is *precisely* I want. You know where it is I can find a no-good snuffler called Kadak?"

He stared at me with six, then blinked rapidly, in sequence—two and four, three and five, one and six—then went back in reverse order. "You have a nauseating sense of humor. May Seymool forgive you."

Then he fell back on his face, his legs up winding and unwinding, his nose deep in *dreck.* "I say Kadak, he says Seymool. I'll give you a Seymool!"

I started to wind up for a kick would put that *momzer* in the next time-zone, when a voice stopped me. From over the side of that stinking Cathedral—and you can bet I was turning yellow from not breathing—a woman said, "Come outside. I'll tell you about your friend Kadak."

I turned to look, and there was this *shikseh,* all dolled up in such a pile of colored *shmatehs* and baubles and bangles and crap from the floor, I thought to myself, *Gevalt! this turn I should never have crawled out of the burrow.*

So anyhow I followed her outside, thank God, and let my nose extend to its full length and breathed such a deep one my cheeksacs puffed up like I had a pair of *bialies* stuffed in. So now this *bummerkeh,* this floozie, this painted hussy says to me, "What do you want with Kadak?"

"Wait a minute," I said, "I'll get upwind from you, meaning no offense, lady, but you smell like your Church." I rolled around her and got a little away, and when it was possible to breathe like a person, I said, "What I *want* is to go join my lust-mates on Kas—, on Bromios, but what I *got* to do, is I *got* to find Kadak. We need him for a very sacred religious service, you'll excuse me for saying this, dear lady, but you being Gentile, you wouldn't understand what it is."

She batted four eyelids and flapped phony eyelashes on three of them. Oy, a *nafkeh*, a lady of easy virtue, a courtesan of the byways, a *bummerkeh*. "Would you contribute to a worthy charity to find this Kadak?"

I knew it. I knew somewhere on that damned looking for Kadak it would cost me a little something out of pocket. She was looking directly at my pouch. "You'll take a couple of coins, is that right?"

"It isn't exactly what I was thinking of," she said, still looking at my pouch, and I suddenly realized with what I'll tell you honestly was a chill, that she was cross-eyed in four of her front six. She was staring at my *pupik*. What? I'm trying to tell you, butterfly, that she wasn't staring at my pouch which was hanging to the left side of my stomach. She was staring with that cockeye four at my cute little *pupik*. What? You'll forgive me, Mr. Silent Butterfly With the Very Dumb Expression, I should know that butterflies don't have *pupiks*? A navel. A belly-button. Now you understand what it is a *pupik*? What? Maybe I should get gross and explain to a butterfly that *shtups* flowers, that we have sex through our *pupiks*. The female puts her long middle finger of the bottom arm on the right side, straight into the *pupik* and goes moofky-foofky, and that's how we *shtup*. You needed that, is that right? You needed to know how we do it. A filth you are, butterfly; a very dirty mind.

But not as dirty as that *nafkeh*, that saucy baggage, that whore of Babylon. "Listen," I said, "meaning no offense, lady, but I'm not that kind of a person. I'm saving myself for my lust-mates. I'm sure you'll understand. Besides, meaning no offense, I don't *shtup* with strangers. It wouldn't be such a good thing for you, either, believe me. *Every*body says Evsise is a rotten *shtup*. I got very little feeling in my *pupik*, you wouldn't like it, not even a little. Why don't I give you a few nice coins, you could use them on Kasri—

on Bromios. You could maybe set yourself up in business there, a pretty lady such as yourself." God shouldn't strike me down with a bolt of lightning in the *tuchis* for telling this filthy-mind cockeye heathen *nafkeh* what a cutie she is.

"You want to find this Kadak?" she asked, staring straight at two things at the same time.

"Please, lady," I said. My nose started running.

"Don't cry," she said. "Seymool is my God, I trust in Seymool."

"What the hell has that got to do with anything?"

"We are the last of the Faithful of the Church. We plan to stay on Zsouchmuhn when they Relocate it. Seymool has decreed it. I have no hope of living through it. I understand cataclysms are commonplace when they pull a planet out of orbit."

"So run," I said. "What kind of dummies are you?"

"We are the Faithful."

It gave me pause. Even Gentiles, even nut cases like these worshippers of Shmoe-ool, whoever, even *they* got to believe. It was nice. In a very dumb way.

"So what has all that got to do in even the slightest way with me, lady?"

"I'm horny."

"Well, why not go in your Cathedral there and *shtup* one of your playmates?"

"They're worshipping."

"To that statue that looks like a big bug picking its nose, with the *dreck* and crap and mud all over it?"

"Don't speak disrespectfully of Seymool."

"I'll cut out my tongue."

"That isn't necessary, just stick out your navel."

"Lady, you got a dirty mouth."

"You want to know where Kadak is?"

I won't tell what nasty indignities came next. It makes me very ashamed to even think about it. She had a dirty fingernail.

So I'll tell you only that when she was done ravaging my *pupik* and left me lying there against a mud-wall of a building, the pink *schmootz* running down my stomach, I knew that Kadak had been as lousy an Apostate as he had been a Jew. One afternoon, just like in the synagogue years before, he ran amuck and started biting the statue of that bug-God they got. Before they could pry him off, he had bitten off the kneecap of Shmoogle. So they threw him out of the Church. This *nafkeh* knew what had happened to him, because he had used her services, you could *brechh* from such a thought, and he still owed her some coins. So she'd followed him around, trying to get him to pay, and she'd seen he'd bounced from religion to religion until they accepted him as a Slave of the Rock.

So I got up and went to a fountain and washed myself the best way I could, and said a couple of quick prayers that I wouldn't get knocked up from that dirty finger, and I went looking for the Slaves of the Rock, still looking for that damned Kadak. I walked with an uneven roll, hop, unwind. You would, too, if you'd been ravished, butterfly.

Just a second you'd think on it, how would *you* feel if a flower grabbed you by the *tuchis* and stuck a pistil and stamen in *your pupik?* What? Oh, terrific. Butterflies don't have *pupiks.*

Talking to you, standing here in sand, is not necessarily the most sensational thing I've ever done, you want to know.

The Slaves of the Rock were all gathered in a valley just outside the city limits of Houmitz. The Governors wouldn't let them inside the city. Who can blame them. If you think those Apostates were pukers, you should only see the Rocks. Such cuties. It is to *varf!*

Big rocks they turned themselves into. With tongues like string, six or seven feet long, all rolled up inside. And when a krendl or a znigh or a buck-fly goes whizzing past, *slurp!* out comes that ugly tongue like a shot and snags it and wraps around and comes whipping back and smashes the bug all over the rock, and then the rock gets soft and spongy like a piece rotten fruit and absorbs all the *dreck* and crap and awfulness squished there. Oh, such terrifics, those Rocks. Just the kind of thing I would expect a Kadak to be when he couldn't stand being himself no more. Thank you oh so very greatly, Reb Jeshaia for this looking mission.

So I found the head Rock and I stood there in that valley, all surrounded by Rocks going *slurp!* and *squish!* and sucking up bug food. This was not the best part of my life I'm telling you about.

"How do you do?"

I figured it was the most polite way to talk to a rock.

"How did you know I was the chief Slave?" the Rock said.

"You had the longest tongue."

Slurp! A znigh on the wing, cruising by humming a tune, minding its own business, got it right in the *punim,* a tongue like a wet noodle, splat right in the *punim,* and a quick overhead twist and *squish!* all over the Rock. It splattered on me, gooey and altogether puke-making. Definitely not the kind of individual to have a terrific dinner out with. The *guderim* was all over me.

"Excuse the mess," said the chief Slave. He really sounded sorry.

"Think nothing," I said. "That was a very cute little overhand twist you gave it there at the last minute."

He seemed flattered. "You noticed that, did you?"

"How could I help? Such a class move."

"You know, you're the first one who's ever noticed that. There have been lots of studies made, by all kinds of foreigners, from other worlds, other galaxies, even, but never once did one of them notice that move. What did you say your name was?"

The bug ooze was dripping down my stomach. "My name is Evsise, and I'm looking for a person who used to be a person named Kadak. I was given to understand that he'd become a Rock a few years ago. I have a great need to find this Kadak rock, he should drop dead already such a rotten time he's been making for me."

"Listen," said the chief Slave (as the remains of the znigh oozed down through the spongy surface), "I like you. Have you ever thought of converting?"

"Forget it."

"No, really, I'm serious. To Worship the Rock is such an enriching experience, it really isn't smart to dismiss it without giving it a try. What do you say?"

I figured I had to be a little smartsy then, just a little. "Say, I wish I could. You got no *idea* what a nice proposition that is you're making to me. And in a quick second I'd take you up on it, but I got this one *bissel* tot of a problem."

"Would you like to talk about it?"

A psychiatrist rock, yet. I really needed this.

"I'm afraid from bugs," I said.

He didn't say anything for a moment. Then, "I see your point. Bugs are a very big part of our religion."

"I can see that."

"Ah, well. I'm sorry for you. But let's see if I can help you. What did you say his name was?"

"Kadak."

"Oh yeah, I remember now. What a creep."

"That's him."

"Let me see now," said the Rock. "If I recall correctly, we threw him out of the order for being a disruptive influence, oh, it must have been fifteen years ago. He used to make the ugliest noises I've ever heard out of a Rock."

"Snuffling."

"I beg your pardon?"

"Snuffling is what he did. A terrible snort noise, all wet and cloggy, it could make you sick to be near it."

"Yes, that was it."

"So what happened to him, I'm afraid to ask."

"He reconstituted his atoms and became just like you again."

"Not like me, please."

"Well, I mean the same species."

"And he went off?"

"Yes. He said he was going to try the Fleshists."

"I wish you hadn't told me that."

"I'm sorry."

I sat down. Settled my *tuchis* right down between my rims, drew up my legs, and dropped my head into a half dozen of my hands. I was very glum.

"Would you like to sit on me?" the Rock asked.

It was a nice offer. "Thanks," I said politely, looking at the last slimy ooze of the znigh on the Rock, "but I'm too miserable to be comfortable."

"What do you need him for?" he asked.

So I explained the best I could—this was, after all, to a rock, a piece of stone, even if it *could* talk—about the *minyan* of ten. The chief Slave asked me why ten.

So I said, "On the Earth, a long time ago . . . you know about the Earth, right? Right. Well, on the Earth, a long time ago, God was going to give a terrific *zetz* to a place called Sodom. What it was, this Sodom, was a whole city *full* of Fleshists. Not a nice place."

"I can't conceive of an entire *city* of Fleshists," the rock Rock said. "That's rather an ugly thought."

"That's the way God looked at it."

We were both quiet for a while, thinking about that.

"So, anyhow," I said, "Abraham, blessed be his name, who was this very holy Jew even if he wasn't blue, you shouldn't hold that against him—"

"I won't."

"—uh. Yes. Right. Well, Abraham pleaded with God to save Sodom."

"Why did he do that . . . a city *full* of Fleshists. Yechh."

"How do *I* know? He was holy, that's all. So God must have thought that was a little *meshugge* . . . a little crazy . . . also, you know God is no dummy . . . and he told Abraham he'd spare Sodom if Abraham could find fifty righteous men living there—"

"Just men? What about women?"

"There isn't scripture on that one."

"Sounds like your God is a sexist."

"At least, you'll pardon my frankness now, but at least he isn't a thing that lies in a valley for birds to make ka-ka on."

"That's rather rude of you."

"I'm terribly sorry, but it isn't nice to call the one true God a rotten name."

"I was only asking."

"Well, it isn't too classy for a rock to ask them kinds questions. Now do you want to hear this or don't you?"

"Yes, sure. But—"

"But *what!?*"

"Why did this God haggle with this Abraham? Why didn't he just tell him he was going to do it, and then do it?"

I was getting pretty upset, you know what I mean? "It was because Abraham was a *mensch*, a real terrific person, *that's* why, okay?"

The rock didn't answer. I guess he was sulking. So okay, let him sulk. "Then Abraham said, okay, what if I can only find *forty* righteous men? And God said, okay, let be forty. So Abraham said what if only thirty, and God said, *nu*, let be *thirty* already, and then Abraham said what if only twenty, and God started yelling all right stop *nuhdzhing* me, let be *twenty* . . ."

"Let me guess," the rock said, "Abraham said ten, and your God got really mad and said ten was it, and no further, and that's how you came up with ten men for the congregation."

"You've heard it," I said.

The rock was silent again.

Finally, he said, "Listen, I like your idea of religion. I'm not altogether happy being a Slave of the Rock, even if I am the *chief* Rock. How about if I converted and came back with you, and made the tenth for the *minyan?*"

I thought about that for a while. "Well," I said slowly, "the Talmud *does* say, 'Nine free men and a slave may be reckoned together for a quorum,' but against that is quoted that Rabbi Eliezer went into a Synagogue and didn't find ten there, so he freed his slave and with him completed the number, but if there had only been seven and he had freed *two* slaves, it wouldn't have been *kosher*. But with one freed slave and the Rabbi it made ten. So, clearly, as all agree, eight freemen and two slaves would *not* answer the purpose. But, if you just put yourself in my place for a moment, you're not, even remotely speaking, *my* slave. You're the Slave of the Rock. And besides, it takes a long time to convert. Can you speak Hebrew? Even a little?"

"What's Hebrew?"

"Forget it. How about keeping *kosher*?"

"What are they? I'll keep them if it's part of the program. After all, when you've been a Rock, eating bugs all your life, keeping some kind of pet doesn't sound too difficult."

It was hopeless. For a minute there I gave it a maybe, you know what I mean. But the more I thought about it, even if I could summon up the *chutzpah* to go back to Reb Jeshaia with a rock, not with a Kadak, it wouldn't work. This Rock was a nice enough fellow, you know what I mean, but even as I sat there pondering, he shot out that ick tongue of his, and snared a buck-fly and whipped it in that move he thought was such a sensational thing, and splatted it all over the place, and started eating it. And clearly, very clearly, Genesis 9:4 forbade animal blood to all the seed of Noah, so how could I bring a Rock back and say, here, I freed this Slave of the Rock, and he'll be the tenth man, and then right in the middle of *Adonai*, out would come that crummy tongue and eat a bug off the wall. Forget it.

"Listen," I said, as gentle as I could, I didn't want to hurt his feelings, "it's a strictly great offer you've made, and under other circumstances I'd take you up on that, you know what I'm saying? But right now I'm really pressed for time and it would take too long for you to learn Hebrew, so let's let it sit for a while. I'll get back to you."

He wasn't happy about that, I could tell. But he was a real *mensch*. He told me he understood, and he wished me good luck with the Fleshists, and he let me run away fast. I could see his point, though, and I was very sorry about his not being a possible. I mean, how would *you* like it to sit all day baking in the sun, with birds making pish in your face, and the best you got to look forward to is a juicy bug.

And if I'd known what I had coming, what *tsuris*, I'd have gladly only, happily yet, you can believe it, taken that Rock back with me, bug *dreck* and all. Believe me, there are worse things than a rock that eats bugs.

I'll make a long story short. I followed the trail of that *putz* Kadak from the pit of the Fleshists (where I lost the use of my *pupik*, all my coin, the sight of one eye in the back, the second arm on the left side, and my *yarmulkah*), to the embarkation dock at the spaceport where the sect called the Denigrators were getting on board ships for that Bromios (where I got beat up so bad I crawled away), to the lava beds where the True Believers of Suffering were doing their last rites before leaving (where I suffered first degree miserable and such a pain you wouldn't ac*cept* over half my poor body), to the Tabernacle of the Mouth (where some big deal prophet that was all teeth bit off the tip of one antenna, God knows why, maybe out of pique at being left behind), to the Caucus Race of the Malforms (where I fit right in, as crapped up and bloody as I was), to the Lair of the Blessed Profundity of the Unspeakable Trihll (which I could not, even if I had *several* mouths, pronounce . . . but they punched and kicked me anyhow, really sensational people), to the Archdruid of Nothingness, always following that miserable creep Kadak from religion to religion—and let me tell you, *no one* had a good word for that *schmuck*, not even the worst of those heathens—and it was there, *kayn-ahora*, that the Archdruid told me the last he'd seen of Kadak was ten years earlier, when he had changed him into a butterfly, and sent him out into the desert to hopefully drop dead in the heat.

Which is why, finally, I'm standing here talking to you, dumb creep butterfly. So now I've told it all, and you see what a puke condition I'm in, don't for a minute think that Avram or those others will respect me for what I did, they'll only *nuhdz* me about how long it took, and that's why you got to come back with me.

Not a word. Not a sound through all this. Not a flap or a flitter or a how are you Evsise. Nothing.

Look. I'm not going to *tummel* with you, Mr. I-Can't-Make-Up-My-Mind-What-Kind-of-Religion-I-Want-To-Be butterfly.

You think I stood here all this time, sinking in up to my rims in sand, just to tell you a cute story? I *know* you're Kadak! And how do I know?

Go ahead, snuffle like that again and ask me how I know!

Come on. You'll come either by yourself or I'll drag you by your wings, you know for a butterfly you're not even a nice-*looking* butterfly? You're an ugly, is what you are. And as for being a Jew, only that by birth, such a disgrace to the entire blue Jews on Zsouchmuhn.

As you can see, I'm getting angry. You've gotten me raped, crapped on, burned, maimed, crippled, blinded, insulted, run around, exposed to heathens, robbed, sunburned, covered with bug *shmootz*, altogether miserable and unhappy, and I'll tell you, very frankly, you'll come with me, Mr. Kadak, or I'll choke you dead right here in this *farblondjet* desert!

Now what do you say?

I thought that's what you'd say.

"Here he is."

Yankel didn't believe it. Chaim laughed. Shmuel started to cry, his nose running green. Snodle coughed. And Reb Jeshaia hung his head. "I should have sent Avram," he said.

Avram looked away. Like a dead leaf it should fall off.

"Here he is, is what I said, and here he is, is what it is," I said. "This is your Kadak, may he rot in his cocoon."

Then I told them the whole story.

At least they had the grace to be amazed.

"*This* is what makes the *minyan?*" Moishe said. "This?"

"Make him change back, and that's him," I said. "I wash my hands of it." I went over in a corner of the *shoul* and settled down. It was their problem now.

For hours they went at him. They tried everything. They threatened him, they begged him, they implored him, they intimidated him, they cajoled him, they *shmacheled* him, they insulted him, they slugged him, they chased his *tuchis* all over the *shoul. . . .*

Sure. Of course. Wouldn't you know. That rotten Kadak wouldn't change back. At last, he found a thing he wanted to be. A dumb creep butterfly.

With a snuffle. Still with a rotten snuffle. Did you ever know how much *worse* a butterfly snuffles than a person?

You could *plotz* from it.

And finally, when they couldn't get him to change back—and if you want to know the truth, I don't think he *could* change back after that weirdnik *buhbie* Archdruid changed him—they held him down and Reb Jeshaia made the rabbinical decision that his *presence* was enough, in this great emergency. So Meyer Kahaha sat on him, and we started to sit *shivah*, finally, for Zsouchmuhn and for Snodle.

And then Reb Jeshaia got a terrible look on his face and he said, "Oh my God!"

"What!? What what!?" I yelled. "What now, what?"

Very softly, Reb Jeshaia asked me, "Evsise, how long ago did the Archdruid say he changed Kadak into this thing?"

"Ten years ago," I said, "but what—"

And I stopped. And I sat down again. And knew we had lost, and we would still be there when the *gonifs* came to rip the planet out of orbit, and we would die, along with the crazies in the Apostate Cathedral and the *nafkeh*, and the Rock and the Archdruid and everyone else who was too nuts to get safely away the way they were supposed to.

"What's the matter?" asked Meyer Kahaha, the *oysvorf.* "What's wrong? Why does it matter he's been a butterfly for ten years?"

"*Only* ten years," said Shmuel.

"Not thirteen, *schmuck*, only ten," said Yankel, sticking his pointing arm in Meyer Kahaha's ninth eye.

We looked at Meyer Kahaha till the light dawned, even for him.

"Oh my God," he said, and rolled over on his side. The butterfly, that miserable Kadak, fluttered up and flew around the *shoul*. No one paid any attention to him. It had all been in vain.

Scripture says, very clearly there should be no mistake, that all ten of the participants of a *minyan* have to be over thirteen years old. At thirteen, for a Jew, a boy becomes a man. "Today I am a man," it's an old gag. Ha ha. Very funny. It's the reason for the bar mitzvah. Thirteen. Not ten.

Kadak wasn't old enough.

Still dead, still lying on his face, Snodle began weeping.

Reb Jeshaia and the other seven, the last blue Jews on Zsouch-muhn, now doomed to die without ever again gumming their lust-nest concubines, they all slumped into seats and waited for destruction.

I felt worse than them. I hurt in more places.

Then I looked up, and began to smile. I smiled so wide and so loud, everyone turned to look at me.

"He's gone crazy," said Chaim.

"It's better that way," said Shmuel. "He won't feel the pain."

"Poor Evsise," said Yitzchak.

"Dummies!" I shouted, leaping up and rolling and hopping and unwinding like a *tummeler*. "Dummies! Dummies! Even you, Reb Jeshaia, you're a dummy, we're *all* dummies!"

"Is that a way to talk to a Rabbi?" said Reb Jeshaia.

"Sure it is," I yowled, reeling and rocking, "sure it is, sure it is, sure it is, sure it is . . ."

Meyer Kahaha came and sat on me.

"Get off me, you *schlemiel!* I know how to save us, it's been here all the time, we *never* needed that creep snuffle butterfly Kadak!"

So he got off me, and I looked at them with great pleasure because I was about to demonstrate that I was a *folks-mensch* of the first water, and I said, "Under a ruling in Tractate *Berakhot*, nine Jews and the holy ark of the law containing the Torah may, *together*, hey *nu, nu,* do you get what I'm saying, may *together* be considered for congregational worship!"

And Reb Jeshaia kissed me.

"Evsise, Evsise, how did you remember such a thing? You're not a Talmudic scholar, how did you remember such a wonderful thing?" Reb Jeshaia hugged and kissed and babbled in my face at me.

"*I* didn't," I said, "Kadak did."

And they all looked up, as I'd looked up, and there was that not-such-an-altogether-worthless-after-all Kadak, sitting up on top of the Holy Ark, the *Aronha-Kodesh*, the sacred cabinet holding the sacred scrolls of the Lord. Sitting up there, a butterfly, always to remain a butterfly, sitting and beating his wings frantically, trying to let someone know what *he* knew, something even a Rabbi had forgotten.

And when he came down to perch on Reb Jeshaia's shoulder, we all sat down and rested for a minute, and then Reb Jeshaia said, "Now we will sit *shivah*. Nine men, the Holy Ark and one butterfly make a *minyan*."

And for the last time on Zsouchmuhn, which means look for me, we said the holy words, this last time for the home we had had, the home we would leave. And all through the prayers, there sat Kadak, flapping his dumb wings.

And you want to know a thing? Even *that* was a *mechaieh*, which means a terrific pleasure.

Ellison's Grammatical Guide
and Glossary for Goyim

Adonai—The sacred title of God. Pronounced *ah-doe*-NOY.

averah—Loosely, an unethical or undesirable act.

bar mitzvah—The ceremony, as in many cultures, of the beginning of puberty; held in a temple, it is the ceremony in which a thirteen-year-old Jewish boy reaches the status and assumes the duties of a "man."

bialy(ies)—A flat breakfast roll, shaped like a round wading pool, sometimes sprinkled with onion.

bissel—A little bit.

brechh—A sound you make when *varf*ing.

bris(es)—The circumcision ceremony.

buhbie—Usually an affectionate term of endearment, although occasionally it is used sardonically.

bummerkeh—A female bum, a loose lady. A *nafkeh*.

chutzpah—Gall, brazen nerve, audacity, presumption-plus-arrogance such as no other word, and no other language, can do justice to.

dreck—Shit, dung, garbage, trash, excrement, crap.

Evsise—A native of Theta 996:VI, Cluster Messier 3 in Canes Venatici. (See illustration.)

farblondjet—Lost (but *really* lost), mixed-up, wandering around with no idea where you are.

farchachdah—Dizzy, confused, dopey, punchy.

feh!—An exclamatory expression of disgust.

folks-mensh—This has many meanings. In the story it is intended to convey the meaning of a person who is interested in Jewish life, values, experience, and wants to carry on the tradition.

galus—An exile.

Gentile—The goyim. Non-Jews.

gevalt!—A cry of fear, astonishment, amazement.

glitch—A shady, not *kosher* or reputable affair.

goldeneh medina—Literally, "golden country"; originally, it meant America to Jews fleeing the European pogroms; a land of freedom, justice, and rare opportunity. Well, two out of three ain't bad.

gonif(s)—A thief, a crook; sometimes said with affection

goniffed—to mean a clever person; a dishonest businessman; the act of stealing, as in swiping Zsouchmuhn out of its orbit.

guderim—My mother used to say, "That kid is eating out my *guderim* from aggravation," which leads me to believe the word means, literally, heart, guts, liver-and-lights, stomach, everything in the middle of your body. Pronounced: *guh*-DARE-*im*.

Kaddish—A prayer glorifying God's name. The most solemn and one of the most ancient of all Jewish prayers; the mourner's prayer.

kayn-ahora—The phrase uttered to show that one's praises are genuine and not contaminated by envy.

kike—A word you won't find in this story.

kosher—As a Hebrew-Yiddish word it means only one thing: fit to eat, because ritually clean according to the dietary laws. As American slang it means authentic, the real McCoy, trustworthy, reliable, on the up-and-up, legal.

krenk—An illness. Also used to mean "nothing" in a sentence like, "He asked me for a loan of fifty bucks; a *krenk* I'll give him!"

mechaieh—Pleasure, great enjoyment, a real joy. Pronounced: *m'*-KHY-*eh*, if you roll the *kh* like a Scotsman.

mensch—Someone of consequence, someone to emulate and admire; a terrific human being; I always pictured a *mensch* as someone who knew *exactly* how much to tip.

meshiginah, meshugge, mishegoss—Crazy, nuts, wildly extravagant, absurd. There are spellings for male and female, but I've written it the way it sounded when my mother called me it. *Meshugge* is to be a *meshiginah* and *mishegoss* is the crazy stuff a *meshiginah* is doing.

minyan—Quorum. The ten male Jews required for a religious service. Solitary prayer is laudable, but a *minyan* possesses special merit, for God's Presence is said to dwell among them.

momzer—A bastard, an untrustworthy person; a stubborn, difficult person; a detestable, impudent person.

naches—Proud pleasure, special joy, pride-plus-pleasure.

nafkeh—Also *nafka*. A prostitute.

nu(?)(!)—A remarkably versatile interjection, interrogation, expletive; like, "So?"

nuhdz, nuhdzhing—To bore, to pester, to nag, to be bugged to eat your asparagus, to wake up and take her home, etc.

oysvorf—A scoundrel, a bum, an outcast, an ingrate.

pisher—A young, inexperienced person, a "young squirt," an inconsequential person, a "nobody."

plotz—To split, to burst, to explode; to be outraged; to be aggravated beyond bearing.

punim—Face.

pupik—Navel. Belly-button.

putz—Literally, vulgar slang for "penis" but in usage a term of contempt for an ass, a jerk, a fool, a simpleton or yokel. It is *much* stronger than *schmuck* and shouldn't be used unless you know some crippling Oriental martial art-form.

Reb—Rabbi.

schlemiel—A foolish person, a simpleton; a consistently unlucky or unfortunate person; a clumsy, gauche, butterfingered person; a social misfit; this term is more pitying than *schlimazel* and more affectionate by far than *schmuck*.

schlimazel—Same as above, but different in tone. A *schlimazel* believes in luck, but never has any. The terms are often interchangeable, by people who don't perceive the subtle differences.

schmuck—Literally, a penis, but in common usage, a dope, a jerk, a boob; or, a son of a bitch.

Shabbes—The Sabbath.

Shema—The first word of the most common of Hebrew prayers: "Shema Yisrael," Hear O Israel: The Lord our God, the Lord is One!

shikker—A drunk or, as an adjective, drunkenness.

shikseh—A non-Jewish woman, especially a young one.

shivah—The seven solemn days of mourning for the dead.

shmachel—To flatter, to fawn, to butter up, usually to outfox someone to get them to do what you want.

shmatehs—A rag, literally. But in common usage to mean a cheap, shoddy, junky dress.

shmootz—Dirt.

shoul—Synagogue.

shpilkess—As my mother used it, to mean aggravation, an unsettlement of self, jumping stomach. But I've been advised it really means "ants in the pants."

shtumie—Another word like *schlemiel*, but more offhand, less significant; the word you use to bat away a gnat.

shtup—To have sexual intercourse.

shtupping—See *shtup*.

tallis—Prayer shawl, used by males at prayer at religious services.

Talmud—A massive and monumental compendium of sixty-three books: the learned debates, dialogues, conclusions, commentaries, etc., of the scholars who, for over a thousand years, interpreted the *Torah*, the first five books in the Bible, also known as the Five Books of Moses. The *Talmud* is not the Bible, it is not the Old Testament. It is not meant to be read, but to be studied.

t'fillin—Phylacteries worn during morning prayers by Orthodox males past the age of bar mitzvah.

Tisha B'ab—"The blackest day in the Jewish calendar." Usually falls during August, climaxing nine days of mourning during which meat is not eaten and marriages are not performed. Commemorates both the First (586 B.C.) and Second (A.D. 70) destruction of the Temple in Jerusalem. A deadly day of sorrow.

tsuris—Troubles.

tuchis—The backside, the buttocks, your ass.

tummel—Noise, commotion, noisy disorder.

tummeler—One who creates a lot of noise but accomplishes little; a fun-maker, a live wire, a clown, the "life of the party." You know when Jerry Lewis does a talk show and he starts eating the draperies and screaming and running so much you change the channel? He's *tummeling*.

varf—To puke. Brechh.

yarmulkah—The skullcap worn by observing Jewish males.

yeshiva—A rabbinical college or seminary.

yorzeit—The anniversary of someone's death, on which candles are lit and an annual prayer is said.

zetz—A strong blow or punch.

Zsouchmoid—A native of Theta 996:VI, Cluster Messier 3 in Canes Venatici, like Evsise. (See illustration.)

(NOTE: The author wishes to give credit where due. The Yiddish words are mine, they come out of my childhood and my heritage, but the definitions were compiled with the aid of Leo Rosten's marvelous and utterly indispensable sourcebook, *The Joys of Yiddish*, published by McGraw-Hill, which I urge you to rush out and buy, simply as good reading.)

About Jewish Lights

People of all faiths and backgrounds yearn for books that attract, engage, educate, and spiritually inspire.

Our principal goal is to stimulate thought and help all people learn about who the Jewish People are, where they come from, and what the future can be made to hold. While people of our diverse Jewish heritage are the primary audience, our books speak to people in the Christian world as well and will broaden their understanding of Judaism and the roots of their own faith.

We bring to you authors who are at the forefront of spiritual thought and experience. While each has something different to say, they all say it in a voice that you can hear.

Our books are designed to welcome you and then to engage, stimulate, and inspire. We judge our success not only by whether or not our books are beautiful and commercially successful, but by whether or not they make a difference in your life.

For your information and convenience, at the back of this book we have provided a list of other Jewish Lights books you might find interesting and useful. They cover all the categories of your life:

Bar/Bat Mitzvah	Life Cycle
Bible Study / Midrash	Meditation
Children's Books	Parenting
Congregation Resources	Prayer
Current Events / History	Ritual / Sacred Practice
Ecology / Environment	Spirituality
Fiction: Mystery, Science Fiction	Theology / Philosophy
Grief / Healing	Travel
Holidays / Holy Days	12-Step
Inspiration	Women's Interest
Kabbalah / Mysticism / Enneagram	

 **Jack Dann** has written or edited over sixty books, including *More Wandering Stars: An Anthology of Outstanding Stories of Jewish Fantasy and Science Fiction* (Jewish Lights) and the international bestselling novel about Leonardo da Vinci, *The Memory Cathedral*. Already translated into ten languages, this novel won Australia's Aurealis Award and a selection won the coveted Nebula Award. Dann's work has been compared to Jorge Luis Borges, Roald Dahl, Lewis Carroll, Carlos Castaneda, J. G. Ballard, Philip K. Dick, and Mark Twain. He lives in Australia on a farm overlooking the sea and "commutes" back and forth to Los Angeles and New York. Visit his website at eidolon.net/jack_dann.

"Heaven sent. . . . Brilliant."
—Stanley Elkin

"I recommend the book to anyone who appreciates Jewish literature, or science fiction, or who, like me, enjoys both."
—Carl Rosenberg, *Outlook* magazine

"A delightful book of stories by well-known authors....
A diverse and mostly humorous lot."
—*Ottawa Jewish Bulletin*

"The stories in Dann's collection provide a combination and a contrast of the old, the modern and the future."
—*Jewish State*

For People of All Faiths, All Backgrounds

JEWISH LIGHTS Publishing
www.jewishlights.com

Printed in the USA
CPSIA information can be obtained
at www.ICGtesting.com
JSHW012023140824
68134JS00033B/2851